SPIRITED

13 haunting tales

Edited by Kat O'Shea

Leap Books, LLC
Powell, WY
www.leapbks.com
First Edition March 2012

Publisher's Cataloging-in-Publication Data
Snyder, Maria V.
Spirited authors / Maria V. Snyder, Candace Havens, et al; editor : Kat O'Shea.—
1st ed.
p. cm.
Summary: Thirteen ghostly tales from steampunk to cyberpunk. Supernatural stories of ancient Egypt, Salem witch hunts, Viking treasure, contemporary romance, space travel, and the underworld. Includes augmented reality.

ISBN 978-1-61603-020-9

[1. Supernatural—Fiction. 2. Fantasy—Fiction. 3. Science fiction. 4. Fantasy. 5. Young adult fiction. 6. Short stories.] I. Havens, Candace, 1963– II. O'Shea, Kat. III. Title.

PZ5 .S75348 2012   [Fic]   2011941415

Printed in the United States of America

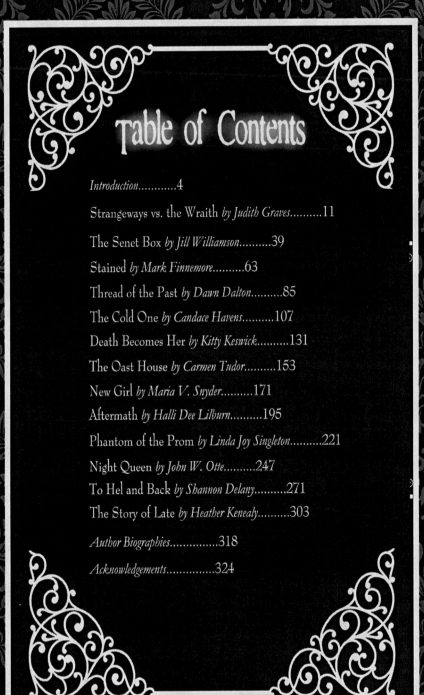

Table of Contents

Introduction............4

The Strangeways vs. the Wraith *by Judith Graves*..........11

The Senet Box *by Jill Williamson*..........39

Stained *by Mark Finnemore*..........63

Thread of the Past *by Dawn Dalton*..........85

The Cold One *by Candace Havens*..........107

Death Becomes Her *by Kitty Keswick*..........131

The Oast House *by Carmen Tudor*..........153

New Girl *by Maria V. Snyder*..........171

Aftermath *by Halli Dee Lilburn*..........195

Phantom of the Prom *by Linda Joy Singleton*..........221

Night Queen *by John W. Otte*..........247

To Hel and Back *by Shannon Delany*..........271

The Story of Late *by Heather Kenealy*..........303

Author Biographies...............318

Acknowledgements...............324

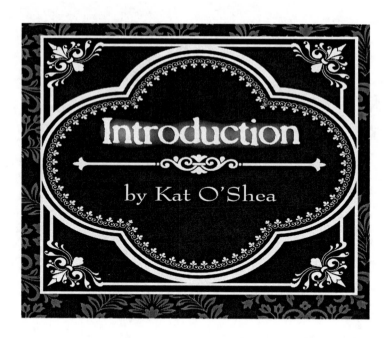

Introduction

by Kat O'Shea

At midnight, curtains flutter in the breeze creating ghostly shadows in the corners of your room. Do you clutch the covers to your chin and peer over them in terror? Or do you hop out of bed to investigate?

Me? I'm a cover-clutcher, so I haven't slept with the lights off since I started editing this collection. Not so much because the tales themselves are overtly frightening, but because they stimulate my imagination and make me wonder: What if I were trapped forever in small claustrophobic dark space? What if an angry spirit were pursuing me? What if the line between reality and fantasy blurred, and I remained trapped between the two?

Even more terrifying, what if seeing specters is a sign of insanity? If it is, I'm in trouble, because most of the characters are so well fleshed out that they've stepped off the pages and into my world. Some have taken on a life of their own and are certain to appear in future novels.

If you're brave enough to open the covers, rather than hiding under them, inside you'll confront both friendly and malevolent spirits. You'll also encounter jealousy, rivalry, and touches of romance along with a variety of genres. The tales range from steampunk to cyberpunk, historical to dystopian, contemporary to sci-fi. And if you prefer your apparitions 3-D rather than 2-D, slide the icons in "To Hel and Back" under your webcam to see the augmented reality leap off the page.

Many of our *Spirited* authors will be hauntingly familiar to fans of the paranormal. Others are talented newcomers. But all of them were willing to donate their time to benefit charity, because they believe there's nothing scarier than illiteracy. So when you read these spooktacular tales, you, too, will be erasing the specter of illiteracy, because all proceeds from *Spirited* will be donated to 826 National, a nonprofit organization dedicated to assisting students, ages 6–18, to improve their writing skills. The 826 mission is based on the understanding that great leaps in learning can happen with one-on-one attention and that strong writing skills are fundamental to future success.

826 National

If you've visited the Leap Books website, you know we lean toward the eccentric and snarky. So when we found an organization that's a little off-the-wall and dovetails with our goals—reading and writing—we couldn't resist.

Kids ages 6 to 18 are enticed in by storefronts, which caught our eye (our third eye, too). Here are a few of the offbeat stores:

> • Museum of Unnatural History (Washington, DC) specializing in saber tooth dental floss and unicorn burps;
>
> • pirate store (San Francisco) selling glass eyes and peg legs (be sure to check the sizing chart to properly fit yours);
>
> • space travel supply company (Seattle) sporting rocket fuel to ray guns;
>
> • superhero outlet (Brooklyn) furnishing capes and grappling hooks;

- spy store (Chicago) dealing in periscopes and night-vision goggles;
- time travel mart (Echo Park, CA) stocking dino eggs and dodo chow;
- robot repair shop (Ann Arbor, MI) marketing robot emotion upgrades and positronic brains;
- Bigfoot Research Institute (Boston) offering Yeti hairballs and sea serpent secretions.

What kid wouldn't be lured in?

If that weren't enough to intrigue, once the kids walk through the doors, the center provides free tutoring by professional volunteers and a variety of writing programs to increase literacy skills, so it seemed like a natural—or should I say, supernatural—match for us.

PAST

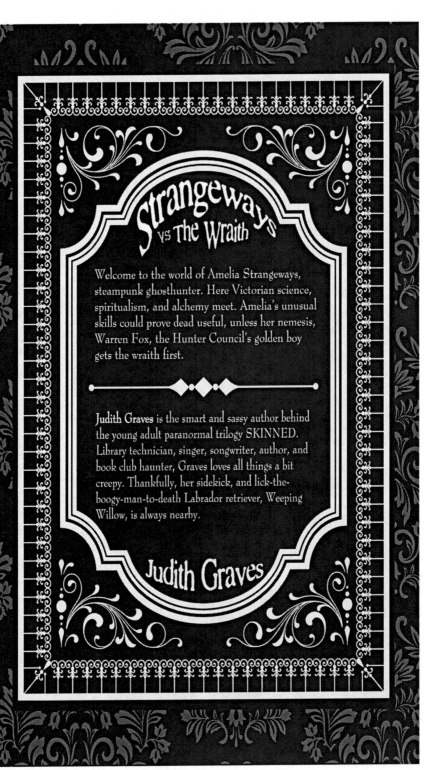

Strangeways
vs The Wraith

Welcome to the world of Amelia Strangeways, steampunk ghosthunter. Here Victorian science, spiritualism, and alchemy meet. Amelia's unusual skills could prove dead useful, unless her nemesis, Warren Fox, the Hunter Council's golden boy gets the wraith first.

Judith Graves is the smart and sassy author behind the young adult paranormal trilogy SKINNED. Library technician, singer, songwriter, author, and book club haunter, Graves loves all things a bit creepy. Thankfully, her sidekick, and lick-the-boogy-man-to-death Labrador retriever, Weeping Willow, is always nearby.

Judith Graves

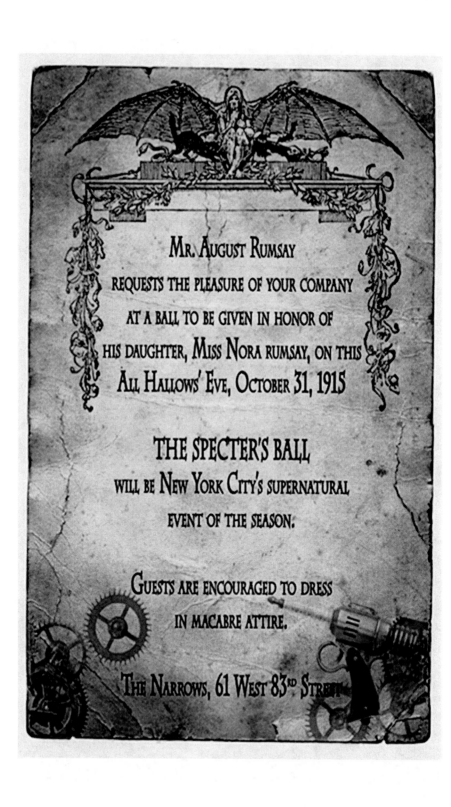

Mr. August Rumsay

requests the pleasure of your company

at a ball to be given in honor of

his daughter, Miss Nora rumsay, on this

All Hallows' Eve, October 31, 1915

THE SPECTER'S BALL

will be New York City's supernatural

event of the season:

Guests are encouraged to dress

in macabre attire.

The Narrows, 61 West 83rd Street

This would not do.

I crouched over the slim form of Nora Rumsay and administered smelling salts to my unconscious companion, who, but seconds before, had fainted in a dead heap at the top of The Narrows grand staircase.

Another eerie wail, an exact replica of the one that had sent Nora off, rumbled from the lower level, reverberating underfoot as the very floorboards absorbed the sound. The howl of a crazed beast. A demon seeking a soul.

And annoying as hell.

Seeing Nora begin to stir, I tucked the vial of salts into a hidden pocket sewn within the folds of my skirt. It clanked against the Hylo derringer also encased within. These days it sticketh closer than a sister.

I gathered my skirts and swept to my feet.

"Jefferson Rumsay," I roared, "play that infernal gramophone disk once more, and I'll flay the flesh from your bones. I won't stop there, no sir. I'll stretch your skin over the disk and see what pretty songs your rotting hide sings beneath the needle."

From below, a flash of dark hair, spindly limbs trapped in a day suit, and then Nora's younger brother appeared, saying,

"Someone's testy."

And someone was lucky to be alive.

"You don't think I have cause? Of course not, because you don't *think*. Ever. I almost had your sister feeling quite confident at the prospect of descending twenty-seven stairs while in full debut ball finery. Almost had her able to hold her chin high and face the scrutiny of the lowest echelon of New York society known as the upper class." I gestured to Nora. "Now look at her."

"Oh, that didn't sound flattering, now did it?" Nora said as she struggled to her feet against yards of petticoat.

I shot her a reassuring smile and a low, "Of course you look lovely as always, my dear."

I scowled down at the brat who stood at the base of the stairs, leaning a nonchalant arm on the intricate handrail.

I placed my hands on my hips. "We can't have the debutante fainting every two seconds because her father insists on this ridiculous Specter's Ball theme, despite knowing she's scared witless of anything supernatural." I smiled at Nora, all reassurance. "Not that I think you're witless. Of course I don't."

Mr. Rumsay, however, was a different matter. The recent widower, and founding member of the New York branch of the Ghost Club, had no idea how terrified his daughter was of his occult dabbling since her mother's death the year before. His obsession to prove contact with the other side was impossible had marked him as one of society's most vociferous debunkers of spiritualism. To Rumsay, the inventor of numerous mechanical gadgets and the smallest steam-driven engines in the world, every supposed supernatural occurrence had a scientific explanation.

Yet the man also mourned his wife with a tenaciousness that was not healthy. If a way existed to contact her dead spirit, he'd discover it. By any means. Even if it meant embracing the possibilities of the magical world.

The fool.

Neither Nora nor her father were aware that I, Miss Amelia Strangeways, had proof Rumsay had done more than debunk the dark arts. He'd begun practicing them.

If the man hadn't been about to call on the powers of hell, I'd have been impressed. Not many attempted the ritual known as the Widow's Curse, mainly due to the sheer amount of time it took to see results. Those seduced by the power of the dark arts were prone to impatience—often the trait that got them killed by the very magic they sought to wield.

The Widow's Curse required the soul of the initial sacrifice to burn in hell for a year and a day before the culmination took hold. The same amount of time as an old-world handfasting.

And the dead would walk once more.

Rumsay had the audacity to bring New York's elite to witness his efforts and then planned to gut them like feted sheep.

On the eve of Nora's debut.

A series of imposing chimes drummed through the house, announcing the arrival of the first of the two hundred and fifty-seven illustrious guests.

All soon to be pawns in the supernatural gamble of a madman.

No, I thought as I assisted Nora to her feet and hurried her back to her expansive rooms.

Maggie was a screamer. He'd told her he liked that in a prostitute. It was the main reason she'd been hired for this bizarre occasion. That and her ability to hold an entire dance hall transfixed by her gyrations.

Maggie knew where her talents lay.

Still, there was no call for this kind of treatment. She was a professional.

"Watch where you put those hands or I'll slit your face." Suspended two feet from the stone floor, Maggie slapped Jones, a cloddish buffoon, sharply across the face.

"Hanson," Jones growled, tightening the rigging around her waist. "Control this one, or you'll soon have to find another."

Maggie tilted her head back and laughed. "You'll never find a stand-in this late in the game, two hours before show time." Nor one willing to pretend to be a dead girl.

Hanson, Rumsay House's overseer, cleared his throat, reminding Maggie that he observed the preparations with narrowed eyes. Her back burned, recalling the sting of the switch he now tapped against his thigh.

"Indeed. But I have every confidence that our Maggie will give the performance of a lifetime," Hanson said, the steel in his tone bringing Maggie to cooperation where the buffoon's pinching and groping had failed. "Rumsay has requested we make it look real," he continued. "If she gives you any more trouble, feel free to add a few flesh wounds for the sake of believability."

Maggie's fingers clenched into fists, though she didn't fight any longer. What choice did she have? She had bairns to feed. Debts to settle.

Hanson strode across the room. Stood before her and took her pointed chin in his hand. "Your safety is assured. The ropes are harnessed to a stable structure. When you fall, you might earn a bruise or two." His dark gaze slid down to the expanse of breast revealed by her tattered gown. "No more than the average night's work, I'm sure."

She didn't return his patronizing leer and refused to flinch as Jones tightened the rope around her neck, though the coarse threads made her skin pucker and itch.

"Remember," Hanson coached, "all you have to do is scream as if you're terrified for your very soul."

Maggie had a feeling that wouldn't be a problem.

"Do lift the material if you're going to keep pacing like a resident of Blackwell's Island," I admonished as Nora stumbled over the length of her skirt. Truly, I'd spent most of my life hiding what I was, what I was capable of, for fear of being sent to one of Blackwell's institutions. Once you went Black, you never came back. "You're going to fray your hems."

"That's not all that's frayed. I'm coming unhinged."

"Stuff and nonsense. You're perfectly assembled. You're beautiful. You'll have them eating from your delicate palms. There's nothing to fear."

"Easy for you to say, you're not the one about to be paraded before every eligible bachelor of suitable means, expected to look serene, yet dazzling. And all the while ghosts and ghouls are flitting about your head."

True. That fate would never be mine. As the passably attractive daughter of a reclusive publisher of spiritualism texts, a debut would not be required. I was of the working class, barely tolerated by society as it was. If they knew the true nature of my family's work, we'd all be sent to Blackwell's. Not that I'd ever wish that fate upon myself—a debut and all the related trappings, I mean.

Marriage was a cage of expectation and obligation. I had duties beyond fulfilling the needs of one man.

Such as saving the souls of many.

Some might perceive my inheritance as a curse. I considered it a calling. And tonight I heard my mission in the sharp and piercing laughter that drifted from the lower level. Protect the pretentious creatures now stuffing their faces in the ballroom below from whatever demons Rumsay conjured and, more importantly, ensure Nora's debut would be the stuff of societal legend.

It was the least I could do for the only girl to befriend me at the preparatory school my parents had insisted I attend—putting their hard-earned money to good use as usual.

The Hylo derringer in my skirts warmed, heating the material at my hip, reacting to the increase of electromagnetic energy in the air and setting the tiny boiler to life.

A specter was near.

I shot to my feet. "I must leave you," I said to a pale-faced Nora, who seemed barely capable of understanding my words. "Won't be long." I paused. "If I miss your entrance, remember, don't hold the handrail as you descend the stairs. Bad form."

"Amelia, you can't be serious…"

I shut the imposing walnut door behind me, drowning out Nora's words. She wouldn't follow. Nora wouldn't leave the room until she was called down to make her grand entrance. For all her explanations that it was the ghoulish theme of the night she feared, Nora was more scared of the devils her father had invited into their home.

The ton of New York society. The gossipmongers and those who would woo her for her father's wealth.

But there were worse things to strike terror in a human heart.

I held my breath. Listening. Blocking out the muffled laughter and clink of glasses from below, where the guests awaited Nora's entrance and the supernatural spectacle that Rumsay had promised.

Gusts of wind whistled down the dim, gas-lit hall. Wooden floor beams creaked and shifted as if an invisible form stepped down on them. I withdrew my weapon, such as it was, and held it high.

I took a few cautious steps forward, scanning the shadows for movement. Hand-carved molding, heavy and gothic, hung over me like claws descending from the ceiling. With each step, hollow-eyed faces in gilded frames seemed to track my movements. I suspected the paintings lining the walls were not family portraits and that Rumsay had only purchased them for their unsettling effects on one's nerves.

A whirring sound and the steady pulse of a metronome had me frozen in place.

Ack, not now.

I concealed my derringer in the folds of my skirt and spun to face one of Rumsay's clockwork creations. The blithe smile on my lips wavered as the six-foot-tall automaton approached, the mockery of a bewigged footman in a Louis XIV embroidered coat with a ruffle at its neck.

"Miss Strangeways," the guard spoke in a stringent voice, its mechanical mouth opening and closing just shy of the correct timing to phrase my name. "Do you require assistance? The needs of every guest must be met."

"No, I do not require your aid." I enunciated each word with the precision of a marksman. The creature would hover if I didn't make my meaning clear on the first go. "However, Miss Rumsay seeks a tumbler of raspberry cordial before joining the party."

The guard slid backward on ball bearings. "Miss Rumsay will be nourished. Needs must be met." It darted down one of the servant corridors apparently to procure a drink.

I let out a relieved sigh.

How Nora could stand to live amongst such creatures, I'd never know. I stared down at my derringer, now cool to the touch. The specter had moved on.

Surely my cup of missed opportunities runneth over.

I shook the miniature weapon. Hard. This was my issue with such confounded gadgetry. Specters had to be too close for comfort for the thing to function. Adjustments would be required when my father returned from his own hunt.

So focused was I on my griping that the hand that settled upon my shoulder pulled a startled screech from my throat and a reflexive jerk on my trigger finger. In seconds I'd spun and blasted a very shocked young man in the face with lukewarm, silver-infused holy water.

Oh, for suffering cats.

"Your presence is… refreshing as always, Miss Strangeways," he said, calm despite the liquid dripping down his sculpted cheek. Warren Fox was brilliant in his beauty, robbing me of what little breath I had in my confining corset. His suit was of the most impeccable standards, cut to the breadth of his broad shoulders. His angular features framed dazzling gray eyes. Some would find him blinding, but then, if the good book was to be believed, even Satan disguised himself as an angel of light.

"Where the devil did you come from?" I sputtered, tucking my weapon away with shaking hands.

A dark brow arched. "If you must know, I started the evening off at the Knick, endured a dismal game of bridge, and then dutifully made my way to the *supernatural event of the season*." His lips twisted as he repeated the phrase engraved upon the Specter's Ball invitations. "Upon my arrival at this, the Rumsay's mansion, I thought I'd have a chat with young Jonathan. The boy owes me substantial funds."

Though just nineteen, Warren prefaced the name of every acquaintance of a lesser age with "the young." A habit I found particularly off-putting, as I myself was one year his junior.

Warren paused a moment to dry his face with his handkerchief and return it to his suit coat pocket. "Instead, I encountered you and your water pistol. Fortuitous, wouldn't you agree?"

I blinked. "Hardly. Now, if you'll excuse me." I proceeded down the hall, intent on escape.

The blighter followed.

"What, no apologies for the drenching? No explanation as to why you're stalking Rumsay's halls without young Nora at your side?" His long strides shortened to match mine. "I'm intrigued."

"And I'm busy."

"So I gathered. What is it this time, a table-rapping poltergeist? Another doppelganger?"

I shot him a dark look. "We both know Rumsay's opening a Pandora's Box tonight. Still, your presence here could be misconstrued. Are you here as a control measure? Or is the Hunter Council openly endorsing the dark arts now?"

"Never."

Warren's jaw clenched, bringing a smile to my lips. Served him right if my jibes were getting under his skin. Warren's father, Mr. Fox Sr., had rejected each and every application I'd made to serve the council as an official hunter, though my father had trained me to take his place. Father retained a unique role within the council, one I would soon be qualified to fill, if the council could accept a young woman among their ranks.

"You shouldn't be hunting on your own," Warren said. "Perhaps I can be of assistance."

I whirled, my skirts wrapping around Warren's leg as if intending a lengthy stay. Traitorous taffeta. I pulled at the material with a harsh jerk. "For the last time, I don't need the help of any man. Warm-blooded or mechanical."

"Warm-blooded?" Warren grinned, took a step closer, where the space for such a step did not exist, pressing my back to the wall. "Am I overheating the little progressive? How dreadfully bold."

I dipped my head, sucked in a breath, but made no move to push him away. It was true—each encounter between us was more combustible than the last. But I couldn't let my confounded emotions make me stray from my intent. My handsome nemesis placed a palm on the wall, crowding me, adding fuel to the fire.

My heart thrummed in response.

"Amelia?"

Had Warren groaned my name, or had I imagined it?

A demon's wail echoed through the hall. For an instant I feared it came from my own throat. What Warren Fox did to my self-composure was a sin. Then I remembered the wailing beast was the signal for Nora's descent.

I ducked under Warren's arm. He clasped a quick hand around my wrist with a disbelieving laugh.

"Where are you going?"

I tugged from his grip. "I can't miss Nora's entrance."

He eyed the distance to the staircase and then started for the servant's corridor the guard had taken.

"This way," he said, disappearing into the darkness.

I followed him down the narrow ramp, and we descended into another world. The ballroom had become the embodiment of Rumsay's interpretation of the underworld. It held too many gothic tapestries, replicas of tombstones, ornate arrangements of blood-red roses, and too little silver for my liking. Guests wore elaborate costumes, having taken the invitation to dress macabre quite to heart. Angels, devils, witches, and more, all clad in feathers, headdresses, beads, and painted papier-mâché masks.

I secretly relished the ease with which we navigated the crowd thanks to Warren's commanding presence as he cut a swath through the crowd. Soon we stood at the frontline watching Nora step gracefully down the marble staircase. Nary a hand on the railing, despite her pallor.

That's my girl. I beamed proudly when I caught Nora's eye. Her own sparkled with repressed excitement and nerves. Swept up in the moment, I clutched Warren's hand and pressed it to my heart.

"If getting you to the front of the crowd is all it took to get this kind of reaction, you should have informed me sooner," Warren drawled in my ear.

Heat rushed to my cheeks. I dropped his hand as if I'd discovered I held a dead rat. I opened my mouth to give him yet another dressing down, when a haunting scream echoed through the mansion, drawing a collective gasp from all present.

In unison, everyone looked upward. A young woman, painfully thin, wearing a white cotton dressing gown, plummeted feet first over the railing at the top of the staircase as if she'd climbed atop the rails and simply stepped off. The noose around her neck stopped her fall with a tremendous jerk. Her neck broke with an audible snap. The room was silent save for the creaking of the rope as her gaunt form swayed a few feet from the floor. Each soul in attendance seemed fixed in place as if the very devil prowled around like a roaring lion, seeking someone to devour.

Nora reached the last step and touched the solid ground of the ballroom's marble flooring. My dear friend's gaze fixed on that of the dead girl, then she staggered and fell backward.

Mr. Rumsay caught his daughter before she could plummet to the floor and gave a hearty laugh. He announced in a booming voice, "What a performance, but there's plenty more to come. Let the Specter's Ball begin."

Instantly, relieved gasps and snorts of laughter rang through the crowd. Guests congratulated my friend on her dramatic entrance. She put a dazed hand to her forehead and did her best to smile. I lost sight of her as everyone glided toward the refreshment tables and away from the stairs. The quartet in the far corner began to play Baroque arrangements, enticing couples to dance.

Yet neither Warren nor I had moved. I doubted we even breathed as we, the only audience that remained, watched the girl sway.

"That was no performance," Warren said finally. "We just witnessed a murder. Either that or Rumsay did some recent grave robbing or purchased a cadaver for the occasion."

I shuddered. "There's but one way to be sure." I took a step forward.

"Amelia, do be careful." Warren looked over his shoulder and then came up behind me, blocking my actions from any who might glance our way. Such as the automaton guards hovering in the entranceway.

Damned if I didn't find strength in Warren's proximity.

I reached out, my fingers hovering over the woman's fine-boned wrist. A faint warmth radiated from her flesh, though she was definitely dead.

Until I touched her hand.

Then she jerked and gasped. Her clouded eyes blinked.

"They killed me, didn't they? Well, doesn't that just jar your gizzard," she said, her voice a whisper, blood sliding over her lips to drip down her chin.

"Who killed you? Do tell." I risked a glance at Warren. His grimace of disgust could have been for a number of reasons—that

the woman had been murdered for a bit of society entertainment, that the show of blood turned his stomach, or that the girl he'd just tried to kiss could bring the dead to life.

"My bairns will need feeding. You'll see to Maggie MacInnis's daughters." The dead woman's hand now grasped mine, nearly crushing my bones. "Get them out of Five Points, promise me that."

A low groan escaped me. Five Points? How on earth was I to find two children in the worst Irish slum in New York City? Still, a pact with the dead must be kept, or my soul would blacken beyond redemption.

"I swear I will," I said.

"Let her go," Warren snapped.

To me or the dead girl, I couldn't quite tell. I could barely breathe.

Intense pain did that to a person.

The whirring sound of a guard in motion reached my ears. Both Warren and I scraped at the rigid digits locked around my wrist.

"Rumsay's man promised me a good wage." Her nails elongated, digging into my flesh.

I tried to pry her fingers loose. Warren cursed, increasing his efforts.

"See that they both hang." With that she released my hand and returned to whence she came, her flesh cooling, her blood clotting at the corner of her mouth.

"Do you require assistance?" a guard asked in that sharp voice I so despised.

"No," Warren said. "But I do thank you for asking." He spun me around and guided me into a darkened corner.

The whirring faded as the guard drifted back to the crowd.

25

"I really don't like those things," I said on a near sob.

"They're harmless. Toys for the man who has everything. Here, let's see the damage." He lifted my arm for a better view of the semi-circular grooves carved into my wrist, the bruising that had already begun to show.

"She had such strength," I said, sucking in a breath, resting my free hand over my pounding ribcage.

"Of course, she was newly deceased and freshly awakened." Warren ran his thumb gently over my wounds. "I should call your father out for this. He declared you trained. Said you were fit for duty should the council get their heads out of their..." He trailed off as his eyes met mine.

If I could have shot flames from my eye sockets, I would have.

I twisted from his grip. "I am trained." I put my hands upon my waist. "Didn't you see what I did? I raised the dead."

Warren's gaze hardened. "A necromancer is no use to the council if she is wounded the second she raises a raving corpse. We hired your father not just to raise the dead, but also to command them, to gain information only those on the other side can provide. Why do you think your father has been preparing you to be his replacement? His age is a factor. He's weak. It takes great strength not to succumb to the dead. Their will is strong." Warren touched my cheek. "Yours must be stronger."

I jerked out of his reach.

"Believe me, my will is iron." I stalked toward the dancing, laughing throng, calling over my shoulder, "Now stay out of my way."

"Not a chance, Amelia." Warren's words struck me as if hurled at my back. "Once this night is behind us, we'll see if you hunt again."

My steps faltered as my ire rose. What did Warren know of

my training? How my father had risked everything to see that I had some modicum of control over my abilities? How hunting gave me purpose, focused my skills, and that, without it, Blackwell's would be the only place for me?

Warren and his ilk sought only to debunk and rid the world of magicks. My father and I had higher aims, a belief, a hope that the natural and preternatural worlds could co-exist. But Rumsay did have to be stopped. On that we were agreed.

And I vowed I would be the hunter to do it.

All because I had a locket of the late Mrs. Rumsay's pale blonde hair.

Thank goodness for death masks.

Hanson hunched over a stereopticon, watching as visual data streamed from the modified optics of Rumsay's guards. Mr. Fox and Miss Strangeways had lingered far too long around dear Maggie, and the XI unit had been too slow to respond to the command to investigate, so he hadn't had a clear view of the happenings. Still, something had occurred, of that he was certain.

Pressing a glowing amber button on the console, Hanson communicated with another guard, VII, closer to their master.

"Tell Rumsay it's now or never. The hunters are about to make their move."

He released the button and straightened, groaning at the ache in his lower back. He rubbed away the pain. Through the thick material of his suit coat, he massaged around the metal nubs fused to his spinal cord, making him a hybrid—part man, part machine.

He'd been remiss of late. Another procedure would be required. Soon. Thank the gears, he no longer had to rely on Rumsay for routine maintenance.

He wondered at what point the creation had begun to outshine his maker.

"Amelia, wherever did you get to?" Nora's tone was light, but her teeth chattered as she spoke, betraying her tension.

"Oh, just ensuring you have your moment to shine, but I'll join you now, if I may." I took her arm in a show of support.

The relieved smile she gave me went unnoticed by the gaggle of guests fawning around her, never meeting her eyes, seemingly bedazzled by the jewels around her neck, dangling from her delicate ears.

And they thought *me* uncouth.

"Mr. Clark has a fascinating theory of how my father was able to ensure that poor young woman's fake death looked quite the thing," Nora said, a hint of a waver in her voice.

"If you'll allow the speculations of skeptic, then I'll continue," Mr. Clark said with a superior smile. He did not give anyone enough time to voice an objection. "As I was saying, the girl is, of course, one of Rumsay's clockwork creations, built to scale, lifelike indeed, but nothing more than another of our host's servants." He glanced around and, upon spying one of the automaton guards, called it over with a sharp gesture.

"Do you require assistance?" the guard asked.

"Yes, I do, point of fact, and yours specifically. That girl who was hung, she was like you, correct?"

"How can I provide assistance?"

Mr. Clark rolled his eyes, and the milling group of guests laughed. "You do so, my thick friend, by answering the question. Who made the girl who hangs over there? You see? The one who looks dead."

The guard bucked on its wheels, causing a gasp to ring out. Then it stilled and in its usual harsh tone said, "Who made the girl is unknown. Our master oversees all discontinuations."

A titter of nervous laughter rang out as the guard glided to meet the needs of another guest.

Nora paled.

I held my breath.

Mr. Clark seemed unfazed, "There, you see," he said, "she was one of them and merely discontinued."

As if to punctuate Mr. Clark's ignorance, Rumsay addressed the crowd. He stood in the middle of the ballroom as guests formed a circle around the perimeter.

"Friends, it is time to further entertain you with the artwork of Ben Knightly and a shadow play technique known as phantasmagoria. The images you will see are the result of light and shadow, not specters and magic. No hard feelings, eh, Knightly?" Rumsay called out to a gentleman in a threadbare tuxedo.

Mr. Knightly gave a brief bow.

My heart pounded. Rumsay was up to something. I scanned the faces of those in attendance, skimming over the mouths open with anticipation until I saw a familiar jaw clenched in concern. Warren met my gaze. He raised an eyebrow.

I glanced at Nora.

Warren nodded.

Once I had Nora out of danger, we'd work together to see the fools safe, despite our mutual antagonism.

"Many among us tonight seek out the supernatural and profess to understand its inner workings," Rumsay continued. "I speak of my fellow members of the Ghost Club. For seven years I have attended their meetings and visited the sites of hauntings, attended séances, what have you. In all our dealings I have come to the conclusion that spiritualism is a hoax. Those who pursue it are blind to the scientific explanations readily available, if one is educated to look for them. Tonight I will prove it."

He waved again to Mr. Knightly. "On with the show."

At once the already dim gaslights died in a blackout. Faint cries of the startled guests echoed through the high-ceilinged ballroom. Whirring surrounded us and, when Mr. Knightly's machine sparked to life, giving enough light for movement, Rumsay's guards blocked each exit.

The phantasmagoria machine stood six feet high, four feet wide, and two feet deep. Constructed from solid oak and sporting intricately carved double doors, it was as unassuming as any French wardrobe, until Mr. Knightly dramatically swung the heavy doors open and steady gusts of fog trailed into the ballroom. Mysterious multicolored lights flickered from within the machine. A malevolent tune, haunting and dissonant, churned out of its depths from a gramophone, cranking all by itself.

Nora whimpered. She clutched at my gloved hand while the crowd around us gasped and stared in wonder.

Mr. Knightly took up position to work his macabre machine. He sat upon a wooden-backed Empire chair, mounted to the main platform. From our side view I could make out the terminal of buttons. Their soft green glow illuminated his pale, gaunt features as he flicked and pressed them with efficient fingers. No need for a mask to add an air of the supernatural to his visage, the man and his machine were both eerie and ominous.

"Time for a trip to the powder room, I think," I whispered in Nora's ear, pulling my friend behind me and making for the exit at the rear of the ballroom. I felt Warren's eyes on us, but refused to meet his gaze. I'd be back to help him once I had Nora safely tucked back in her rooms, or perhaps in the wine cellar. Yes, the cellar might provide more safety.

Specters despised the cold, lacking the warmth of life. When on our plane they sought heat. They'd be attracted to Mr. Knightly's machine with its red-hot lights.

At the edge of the crowd, one of Rumsay's footmen greeted us with a stern, "Guests are requested to remain in this location for the duration of the performance."

Nora retreated a step. "Let's try another way."

"There is no other way," I said. "Can't you see they have all the exits covered?" I turned my attention to the guard. "In case your mechanical eyes fail you, this is Miss Rumsay, your master's daughter. She is no guest. Now let us pass."

"Guests are requested—"

"I beg of you, a nourishing beverage of some sort," I changed tactics, trying my hand at appearing delicate and weak. Hard to do when one was twenty stone heavier than was fashionable. "I fear I may expire from the stifling heat." I put a hand to my throat. "Though atmospheric, the suffocating fog that Mr. Knightly has graced us with is clogging my airways. I have a sensitive constitution. My physician would be most displeased."

The footman whirred in place, shifting on its base, but despite my theatrics, the blasted thing remained unmoved.

"Get going, you blathering clockwork dandy, before I tell my father of your insolence!" Nora gave the guard a swift kick with her pointed lace-up boot.

The guard sputtered and then whirled off to do her bidding. Terror had made Nora intimidating.

"I was handling that," I muttered as she dragged me toward an archway leading to the main hall.

"Not from where I stood," a squeaky voice countered as Jefferson slipped out from behind a marble column. "No wonder my sister remains unattached if she's taking advice from you."

I put my hands on my hips, wondering how long the rotter had been skulking around the ballroom when he'd been strictly told to remain in his chamber. "You're lucky I have little time to devote to you, Jefferson, or I'd challenge you to a duel." I scowled at Nora's brother.

"Exactly what I meant," Jefferson said. "Girls don't go around challenging boys to duels, Amelia. It's just not done."

"Isn't it? How sad." I ushered my charges through the first floor parlor and stopped at a closed door. "All right, down you go." I pushed the door open. "Jefferson, your sister's had about all she can take of your father's nonsense. I need you to keep her down below until I come back for you."

"In the wine cellar?" Jefferson's eyes brightened with interest. "But I'm not allowed to go there."

"You are now."

Needing no other invitation, Jefferson grabbed his sister's arm and descended a step.

Nora balked. "Amelia, do be careful." She bit her lower lip. "Whatever he's done, Father hasn't been himself since mother died."

I gave my friend a reassuring smile. "I know. I'll make this right, don't you fret."

Nora hung on my every word. Her expression cleared only after I promised to keep her father safe, even from himself if necessary.

As I closed the door behind them, screams pierced the air from the ballroom. My Hylo derringer sparked to life, burning my side, making the promises I'd made weigh heavy on my heart.

The tongue might be a small part of the body, but it makes great boasts.

32

I returned to the ballroom, moving with stealth thanks to the cloying fog. I weaved undetected through the line of automaton guards, and it was as if I'd entered the gates of hell.

A heavy fog swirled, drifting between the lavishly costumed guests with purposeful, demonic energy. The undulating mist held New York's finest fixed with terror, knotting the air, making it difficult to breathe. Above diamond-studded, feathered coiffeurs, whitewashed specters dove and swooped at the crowd, revealing features best left in the grave. Gaping jaws, empty eye sockets, blackened teeth, bones, and rotting flesh.

"Rumsay, you go too far."

"Knightly, turn that blasted machine off."

Cries of terror rang out from the crowd. Rumsay paid little heed, his lips moving as he recited a silent chant.

A sudden heat, unrelated to the warmth of my derringer settled along my spine. I shot a glance over my shoulder to find Warren standing protectively at my back.

"Nora and Jefferson safely ensconced?" His breath thrilled along my nape.

"Just in time, I see," I said, withdrawing my Hylo and holding it high. I traced the movements of the dancing spirits, but refused to fire.

I had only one shot, and then the derringer would have to recharge, a necessity that took at least several minutes. Once I launched an attack, I hadn't a single second to squander.

"Knightly is dead," Warren said, dodging a screeching, clawing shape. "His heart appears to have stopped, though there is foam at his lips. He might have been poisoned."

Biting down a curse, I spotted the phantasmagoria operator

slumped over glowing dials. Knightly might have passed, but his machine continued to project its specters, blending false threats with the real.

"I can tackle Rumsay, break his concentration." Warren took a step toward the would-be sorcerer.

I blocked his advance. "No. We have to wait until his bride appears. I have a lock of her hair. It must be incinerated to negate the spell."

Warren held out his hand. "Give it to me, I'll set it burning. You keep Rumsay distracted."

I quirked a brow. "Leaving a woman to take on the enemy? Whatever would your father say?"

"I don't give a damn what my father says." Warren's eyes were steady on mine. "Besides, you're the one who's armed." He wiggled his fingers. "However, you are wasting precious time."

I sighed and handed over the tight coil of blonde hair.

Warren slipped through the crowd toward the overheated lights of the phantasmagoria machine. My eyes narrowed with appreciation as he pried off one of the protective metal screens, exposing the direct source of light—glowing coils. He held the lock of hair as he met my gaze. He'd wait until my signal.

I cut through the mob.

Rumsay's attention remained fixed upon a symbol painted on the marble floor in the center of the ballroom. I sucked in a breath, frantic to see the thing in full, yet knowing what I was likely to find. The Seal of Bune. The evocation of Bune, a spirit once entrapped by King Solomon himself, was necessary to complete the Widow's Curse. Legend had it Bune could exchange a living soul with that of the dead. Sure enough, the seal lay at Rumsay's feet. Drawn in blood.

Burning the hair wouldn't be enough. I'd have to break the

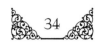

seal as well.

"Rumsay," I called out, derringer trained on the center of his forehead. "I don't think this is what Nora had in mind when she agreed to this fiasco."

Rumsay lifted his chin. Stared me down.

I swallowed hard. The silver-infused holy water brewing in my Hylo wouldn't kill Nora's father, but it would deal his growing power a heavy blow. Hopefully giving Warren enough time to set the lock of hair on fire. If Rumsay didn't attack me first.

"Amelia, I knew you'd make a timely appearance." Rumsay's smile was wrought with evil. "Come closer, my dear. I won't harm you. You're too valuable to me. Don't you see?"

Loud as thunder Rumsay's guards whirled into action, closing in on me before I could take my next breath. Herding me to Rumsay's side.

"I won't insult your intelligence with pretense. We both know what I've set in motion. "

I shook my head. "This won't bring your wife back. She won't be the same woman you buried. "

Rumsay laughed. "Of course not. Why would I wish that defective body on my beloved? No, she won't be the same. She'll be healthy. Strong. No more murmurs in her heart. Bune will see to that. Once he exchanges your soul for my long lost bride's."

I shuddered. Oh, the workings of this man's mind were far more twisted than I feared. I put a hand to my stomach, sickened at the thought of losing my soul, my body to this monster. In the center of the seal, a dense fog swirled and took shape. The haunted eyes of Nora's mother met mine. Her lips formed words. *Stop this.*

And so I would.

"Your guests are right, sir," I said. "You go too far."

Rumsay smiled. "On the contrary, my dear. I doubt I will

ever go far enough where you are concerned." His gaze softened as if he were imagining some crazed future where I housed the soul of his departed wife.

My stomach lurched. "Now, Warren!" I screamed, jerking my arm downward. I squeezed the trigger and fired the Hylo. A blast of steam shot from the barrel, made contact with the bloodlines on the marble floor, obscuring the seal. Destroying its power.

Rumsay roared and charged at me. His guards clasped my arms in a punishing grip. The slam of the back of his hand against my cheek caused me to stagger, but his guards kept me upright. My lip had split from the impact of the blow. A rush of copper filled my mouth.

A wail rose from the wraith, Nora's mother, as she slipped back from whence she had come.

"Why?" Her voice whipped the air. "Why did you do this?"

Rumsay fell to his knees. "Because I love you, wife."

"You never loved me. Power is your mistress, and you shall have it no more."

A blast of lightning. The crack of thunder.

The room went black.

When the gaslights sputtered to life, the mist crept back into the shadows. The spirits, both real and those generated by the phantasmagoria machine, faded to nothingness.

Warren reached my side. We watched, hard-eyed as Rumsay threw himself over the barren, bloody seal, sobbing into his hands.

"Damn them to hell!" Hanson shoved away from the stereopticon, unable to bear witness to his master's defeat any longer.

His hands moved in a blur as he flicked switches and twisted

dials, shutting down the observation site. He grabbed a black satchel and thrust a mélange of tools inside. He paused at the secret entrance to the laboratory, taking a last look at the site of his birth. The smell of formaldehyde, the tick and chink of exposed gears.

He would create a new home.

One where he was master.

And they would tremble in fear.

The ballroom sat in the bruised heart of The Narrows, empty of guests.

"I can't thank you enough, Warren," Nora said, her eyes damp with tears. She clutched Warren's hand to her breast. "Your quick thinking has saved us all."

"Well, not everyone." My lips slanted in a grimace as an officer draped a coat over Knightly's corpse. I resisted the urge to place my necromancer's touch on the man's hand to determine his exact cause of death.

Curiosity killed the cat, now didn't it?

Nora continued, "How clever of you to establish the cause of my father's bizarre behavior as a malfunction of the phantasmagoria machine. That toxic gas spewing forth affected his mind and corrupted the mechanics of his clockwork guards."

Warren pulled his hand from Nora's death grip. "I'm sure your father will be recovered all too soon." He transferred Nora's pale hand to her brother's.

"Jefferson, why don't you see your sister to her rooms? Surely a rest would serve her well."

Silence descended between us after the brother and sister departed.

"Each of the guards has been disengaged." Warren said finally, scanning my face with a dark expression on his own features. "They won't be able to harm anyone again."

His words reminded me of my injury, a pain that had settled to a dull ache in my jaw. I flicked out my tongue, testing for blood.

His eyes flickered.

"What will you tell your father?" I asked, bracing myself for his response.

"The truth."

I raised a brow.

Warren smiled. "That Amelia Strangeways is a necromancer to be reckoned with. That I request your name be officially submitted as a replacement for your father and be given the consideration of any other candidate. Sex notwithstanding."

I flushed at his bold choice of words.

He stepped back and gave me a deep bow. "It has been a pleasure hunting with you, Strangeways. I do believe I'll make my recommendation on one condition—that I am to be your only partner. Wouldn't want to saddle any other man with your temper."

I gasped. My hand shot out, but my intended blow to his cheek caught only air. Warren had already turned and jaunted away. I observed his fine form as he exited the ballroom. My heart leapt in my chest.

Warren would recommend me to the council. We'd hunt.

Together.

I pressed a hand to my heart, struggling to control its wild-horse pace.

Oh, this would not do. No, it would not do at all.

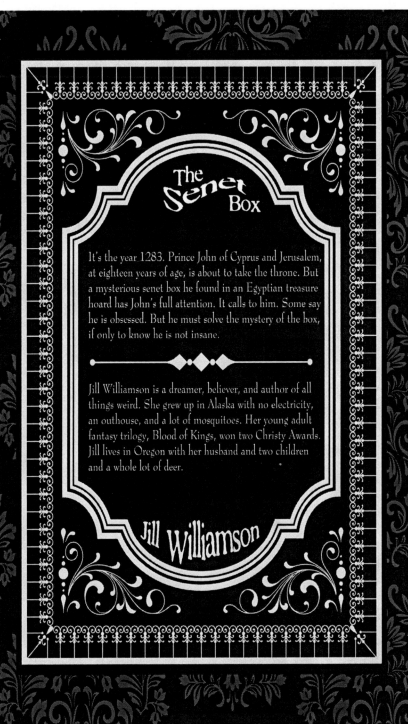

The Senet Box

It's the year 1283. Prince John of Cyprus and Jerusalem, at eighteen years of age, is about to take the throne. But a mysterious senet box he found in an Egyptian treasure hoard has John's full attention. It calls to him. Some say he is obsessed. But he must solve the mystery of the box, if only to know he is not insane.

Jill Williamson is a dreamer, believer, and author of all things weird. She grew up in Alaska with no electricity, an outhouse, and a lot of mosquitoes. Her young adult fantasy trilogy, Blood of Kings, won two Christy Awards. Jill lives in Oregon with her husband and two children and a whole lot of deer.

Jill Williamson

Amunet.

The name is Ancient Egyptian. It means *the hidden one*.

That she was, indeed. That she still is.

Hidden forever from me.

I first saw her in Nicosia, in the year of our Lord, 1283, after having celebrated my sixteenth birthday. I had just returned from Jerusalem with my father, Hugh de Lusignan III, King of Cyprus and Jerusalem—also called *the Great*—after an attempt to sort through the many factions vying for the throne of the ancient city. A visit had been necessary to restore order, but Father had little patience for insubordination and finally left Jerusalem in the hands of his bailiff.

From Jerusalem, we traveled to Oltremare, the main port of the eastern Mediterranean Sea in the city of *Saint-Jean d'Acre*. There we made our way down into the hold of a ship called *la Petite Baleine* that would carry us home to Cyprus. A great treasure had been seized in a battle against Mamluks in Egypt. Father wanted to see it before we set sail.

My father loved treasure.

The Senet Box

I ducked my head to follow my father and Captain Auveré down the narrow stairs to the lower deck, the captain's lantern the only source of light. I had never been so far below ship before. The smallness of everything surprised me. And the smell—mildew, rot, and something briny—worsened with each step that took us closer to the hold. I wrinkled my nose.

"It smells quite fresh today, Your Highness," Captain Auveré said, pinning me with an amused smile.

Fresh? I raised an eyebrow. "Does it?"

He chuckled. "You should smell her when she's full of livestock and men who haven't bathed for three weeks."

"A pleasure I am happy to forgo," I said.

I struck my forehead twice upon low beams in the passageways between stairwells. I don't know why father couldn't have waited until we got home to look at his new treasure. I certainly could have.

But then we reached the end of the stairs, passed the men standing guard at a thick wooden door, and entered a room in the hold. The light from Captain Auveré's lantern reflected off countless riches—gold, silver, bronze, jewels in every color, polished wood, ornate tapestries, shiny weapons.

The treasure's glow warmed my cheeks.

Crates and barrels held much of the hoard, yet many of these containers were opened, their contents spilling out, calling me to take a closer look. Masks, crowns, coins, jewelry, cups, platters, daggers, swords, spears, canopic jars, scepters, amulets, chunks of precious rocks, and lengths of unwrought metals. Some items were too big to put in any box: statues, vases, candelabrum, and tombs.

I gazed about, transfixed by such glory and wealth. No wonder my father could not wait to see such priceless plunder, this... *trésor recherché*.

"Choose, John," my father said to me. "Something for

yourself."

Choose. I walked among the piles of wealth, studying everything with a careful eye. As a prince—and the eldest of my brothers—I had plenty of crowns and buckles with which to adorn myself. I had no use for golden goblets or swords. And I wanted no part of tombs or jars holding bits of dead Egyptians. I shuddered at the very idea.

I strolled past the mounds of treasure, wondering how many the Crusaders had killed in the name of Our Lord to claim such wealth. I did not oppose the Crusades outright, but I somehow doubted that the Lord our God would be pleased by some of the methods used to claim this holy land. When my time came to rule Cyprus and Jerusalem, would I do the same to keep it? My brother Henry certainly would.

A whisper pulled my gaze to a carved, wooden box about a foot long, six inches wide, and four inches deep. Egyptian hieroglyphics were carved on all sides but the bottom, the images stained white.

An old senet game.

I had played senet with my brothers many times. I was not particularly good at the game, and this one was worn and cracked along one side. Why was something so shabby in with such riches?

I moved on and stopped to examine a golden crown. In the center, carved of copper, a scarab clutched a crescent moon. Two vipers, tails coiled, heads raised to strike, perched on either side of the beetle. Lapis and turquoise beads dangled around the bottom edge. I liked the sinister look of the creatures, but the beads would likely chafe my forehead.

"There are some fine rings in this box, John," my father said.

I owned dozens of rings already.

John.

I turned around, looking for the source of that whisper.

The Senet Box

My gaze fell to the senet box. My nerves tingled as if the box had whispered my name. Impossible. "Did you say something, Father?"

He looked at me with raised brows. "I did not." His lips curved into a smile. "Perhaps the voices of Egyptian ghosts are calling to you?"

"Doubtful."

In search of something unique, I passed over what many would claim. A turquoise amulet, a dagger with a carved ivory grip, a vase painted in black and gold checks, a scepter carved from dark wood, a Crusader shield from England, a matching sword.

I glanced at my father. "Some of this is English."

"The Nubian prince has a fondness for foreign things. As do I." Father peered through a death mask that had belonged to some ancient pharaoh, his eyes a glimmer edged in gold. The sight chilled me, for when my father died, I would be king.

I had yet to decide if I should crave or abhor such a destiny.

I turned back to the hoard and found myself standing before the senet game. I looked behind me. Hadn't the box been nearer the door?

I ran one finger along the worn cedar, and a tingle ran up my arm. I jerked away. But the feeling had not pained me, so I lifted the box into my hands. The tingle returned, a subtle pleasure.

John, it said to me.

Though it made no sense, I clutched the box to my chest, and the game pieces rattled inside. "I want this."

My father looked past a pair of gold vases to where I stood, his eyes narrowed. "That's it, John? A toy?"

I couldn't explain why I needed it. If I told my father how the feel of the wood on my skin made me tremble… that I felt a pull to the box like hair on wool… that I could hear it speaking to me… he would think me mad.

44

Come to think of it, I felt slightly mad.

I merely said, "*J'aime ça.*" I like it.

Father shrugged. "Have it if you must, but chose something of value as well."

Eager to take the box to my cabin, I grabbed the scarab crown and held it up.

Father smiled. "Interesting choice. It's a bit… angry, isn't it?"

"*J'aime ça,*" I said again. "May I return to my cabin?"

He turned his back and stepped past an intricately painted anthropoid sarcophagus. "I've barely had a look. Remain with me. Sit and play with your *toy* if you must."

I didn't like his tone, but I was not about to argue with *the Great.* I found a carved footstool, set the scarab crown on the floor by my feet, and held the senet box in my lap. I ran my index finger along each carving. A small thrill tingled through me as if I were petting a satisfied cat. How very odd.

I continued to stroke the box, delighted with my find.

Back home in Nicosia, my delight turned to frustration. Something was wrong with the box. No matter where I pushed or pulled, I couldn't open the drawers. The pieces rattled around inside, so there must be a way. I took the box along to dinner, puzzling over its mystery.

"What are you doing?" my brother Henry asked me.

"I can't open it."

"It looks ancient. Where did you get it?"

"*La Petite Baleine,*" I said.

"*That* is your treasure?" Henry scowled at me as if I were some Mamluk intruder. "Seriously, brother. I cannot understand why the Good Lord allowed you to be born before me. You are most bizarre. I shudder to think of how you will rule us someday. Will you demand all your subjects carry antique senet games wherever they go?"

"I simply want to open it," I said, knowing that it was a waste of time to provide any answer, that Henry would use it to make me look more the fool. Humiliating me was his method of diverting people's attention from his falling sickness.

As predicted, Henry delivered his slander straightaway. "If you continue to bring toys to the dinner table, John, perhaps we should call back our old nursemaid. Clearly you need someone to look after you."

Everyone chuckled. Henry's victory. I laid the senet game in my lap where it would be hidden and ate my dinner in silence.

Henry began talking with Father about politics, hinting that the pope should execute Charles Anjou and give Cyprus its own Crusader army.

"No more violence, Henry," Father said. "I'm tired of fighting the same battle."

"But if you would only listen, you'd see that one last, large battle could end this conflict for good. Traitors must be eliminated—before they can create more traitors. If we were to establish a *Curtia Regis*, a court of the King, administer a national law as Henry II did in England, court officials under your authority could judge local disputes, reduce the workload on royal courts, and deliver justice with greater efficiency. It's quite simple, really. I think it would strengthen our hold on Jerusalem."

Father snorted. "What hold? Jerusalem is a fish in my hands. Every time I manage to grasp her, she slips away."

"A court of the King would…" Henry went silent, his face ashen, his eyes staring off past Father's left ear. For at least a full ten seconds, Henry was lost to his illness. Then he came back, blinked a few times, and continued talking as if nothing had happened. "It would give you an iron grip that would hold any fish, Father."

Father pierced Henry with a barbed glare. "I'll have no more talk of this."

I wondered if Father's declaration was due to Henry's opinions on politics or his becoming stupefied at the dinner table. Henry's fits were the cause of much gossip in Cyprus. Some believed him to be possessed by demons. Henry himself had started the rumor that he was a prophet of God, and that when the Lord spoke to him, the power of God paralyzed his senses.

I didn't think either of those speculations were the full truth.

After dinner, I carried the box back to my room and spent the next few hours fiddling with it. It was no regular senet game; I saw that now. Some of the panels could be shifted, like a puzzle. I slid them around in an attempt to open the drawer.

It was no use.

Frustrated, I shoved a few panels harder than the antique could likely handle. The box trembled in my hands. Softly at first, then harder until I couldn't hold it still. Off guard, I set it on the floor and stepped back. As if a mounted army were charging down the corridor outside my room, the box bounced on the floor, rattling against the polished tile. Light shot from the cracks, beams brighter than any lantern or torch could provide. As if the sun itself were inside the box.

I shielded my eyes with the crook of my arm.

Then all went silent.

The box remained in one piece on the floor, still now, but with the center drawer hanging open. I picked it up and looked inside for the pieces.

"*Nullae partes*," a feminine voice said.

I jumped, my gaze darting to the sound. A young Egyptian woman stood before me, barefoot, wearing a white linen sheath. A gold-and-turquoise amulet circled her neck. Her hair was black and straight and thick, with a stripe of golden beads around the lower edge. Kohl outlined her eyelids, and black paint had inked a lacy net around her upper arms. Her dark eyes considered me. Her lips were pursed and painted gold.

"What is your name?" I managed to ask, my Arabic terribly rusty. "Where did you come from?"

She blinked slowly, but then looked away, her gaze traveling the room as if seeking escape.

I spoke again, fearful she might leave. This time I tried French. "*Je m'appelle Jean.*" I tapped my chest. "John."

Her eyes flicked back to meet my gaze. "*John es?*"

"Yes." I bowed without looking away from her eyes. "John."

She straightened and lifted her chin, clearly pleased with my manners. "*Mihi nomen est Amunet.*"

As I strained to place those familiar words, the translation struck me suddenly. Her name was Amunet. "You speak Latin." But no one spoke Latin anymore. I had studied it, learned to write it, but the oral language had been dead for centuries. "Where is your home?"

"*Venio ex Rhakotis.*"

My eyes flew wide at this statement. She came from Rhakotis? How could such a thing be? Rhakotis was the original name of the city of Alexandria on the northern coast of Egypt, before Alexander the Great had renamed it centuries ago. Never had I heard anyone refer to the city by that ancient name.

Compelled by the depths of her dark eyes, I clutched the box to my chest and reached out with my empty hand. She flinched, drew back, and stared at me, eyes wide and cautious.

I knew little of Egyptian custom. Women were kept separate from the men until marriage. Perhaps touching a woman was frowned upon.

Yet, after a brief hesitation, Amunet stepped toward me and reached her hand toward mine. Our fingers touched. Her skin was

smooth and hot. I wondered if she had taken a fever. She slid her fingertips over my wrist and up my arm. Her nearness brought the smell of myrrh and balsam. I trembled, captivated by this exotic woman in my bedchamber.

Henry would be so proud.

Amunet's fingernails scraped lightly over the end of the senet box. I held up the box, but the drawer began to slide out. I caught it and shoved it back in.

Amunet vanished.

"What? No!" I dug at the drawer with my fingernails, snapping off one in the process. I dropped the box and shook my hand at the stinging pain.

How? Did she live inside, like some sort of Arab djinn? I crouched and picked up the box. I could still smell her; myrrh and balsam tickled my nose.

"Amunet? Come out," I pleaded to the box, then in my rusty Latin, "*Ego vocarete.*"

No matter what I tried, I could not open the drawer again. Days passed, weeks, months. Had I imagined her? Perhaps my brother's evil spirits were tormenting me. But whenever I held the box, the feeling came over me again as if I could hear Amunet's voice inside my head, saying my name in Latin.

John es?

I carried the box at all times. Henry threatened to take it from me, so I stopped bringing it along to mealtimes, though I felt weary with it so far away. I worried someone would steal it, or that Amunet might return while I was gone, and I would never see her again.

I had to see her again, if only to know I was not insane.

As fall gave way to winter, the temperatures dropped some, and my father took ill. The doctors said it was scrofularia. A humiliating diagnosis. A king afflicted with the disease known as the "king's evil"?

The nobles were in discord over the news, claiming God had set a curse on the Lusignan name. Henry with his falling sickness, Father with the king's evil, and me with my obsession. Though my father asked me to deal with the nobles and assure them all was well, I had no time for bootlicking and flattery, nor could I stomach Father's aides grooming me to be king. They claimed Charles of Anjou vied for Jerusalem and, eventually, Cyprus. They echoed my brother's concerns about traitors and advocated a court of the King.

All weighed heavily on my shoulders, and I convinced myself that if only I could see Amunet again, all would be well. The advisors took their concerns about my lack of duty to my father's sickbed, and I was summoned to his side.

Scrofularia had drained his strength. He looked half his weight, and his fevered skin glistened in the torchlight. When he spoke, phlegm made his voice raspy.

"My advisors say you have an obsession, John. Is it a woman?"

Seeing no reason to lie, I said, "It is, sir."

At this he laughed, wheezing his way into a coughing fit. When it passed, he said, "A prince who could have any woman pines over one he cannot have. Isn't that the way of things?"

I had no answer for this.

"What's her name, boy? I'll have her brought before me, and you shall have her."

Typical of my father to demand things go his way. But I did not want him to know how Amunet came out of the senet box. He might think me mad, might take the box away. "She went to Alexandria."

"Fled, did she? Well, send someone to bring her back."

"I'm afraid only I can do that, sir."

My father wheezed a long sigh. "You see I am unwell, John.

I plan to mend fully, of course, but if my Lord should take me to Him, you must step up to the task. If you do not, Henry will. I would rather not look down from heaven to see Henry iron-handing my people. He is openly opposed to all traitors nearly to the point of being one himself. Watch your back, son."

"Henry doesn't scare me, Father."

"He should. Your brother is ruthless. He twists his falling fits into a gift from God. I know he's beguiled your other brothers to his cause. And they work to convince the nobles. Now then, take a month, go to Alexandria, bring back your woman in chains if you must. Then I need you to assume some responsibilities here. Talk with the nobles. Appease my advisors. Put Henry and your brothers in their place. Guy and Aimery, especially, for they practically worship Henry. Do this for me, will you?"

"Yes, Father. I will."

"That's my son. You'll make a fine king someday, John, so long as you keep your wits about you rather than letting them float loose amongst the clouds."

"Yes, sir."

"I must rest. I will see you when you return. Do not tarry."

"I won't, sir."

And so I set sail for Alexandria that very day.

As my ship made port, I stood on the quarterdeck and took in the ancient city. Wars and earthquakes had destroyed much of it. Alexandria was in a constant state of construction. Pompey's Pillar reached into the sky above the sea of stone buildings. Had Amunet once come here? Gazed at this same view? Was she here now? Did she think of me the way I thought of her?

I prayed for an end to this pining. I had to solve the mystery of Amunet so I could get back to my life.

The Senet Box

On land, I sent out half of my eight guardsmen to look for information. The other four accompanied me as I walked, the senet box cradled in my arms. Nervous about Mamluks, my guards marched on each side of me, boxing me in. I no doubt looked out of place, very Christian, and wealthy. That should cause most Egyptians to treat me well, unless someone suspected I was a prince of Cyprus.

We walked through the marketplace, passed several mosques, and questioned a wide variety of people, but found no clue, no one willing to assist me. Most simply looked confused when my translator explained my needs.

We passed the remains of Saint Mark's Coptic Orthodox Cathedral, which had been destroyed years ago. Though more than half a century had passed since it fell, people placed flowers at the site as if they still mourned its demise. With Mamluks controlling the area, the Alexandrian climate was still too volatile to rebuild a Christian church.

I had been in Alexandria six days before I found my first and only clue. I was standing inside the Kom el-Shoqafa catacombs a short distance southwest of Pompey's Pillar, gazing in wonder at the chambers adorned with statues, burial niches, sculpted pillars, and sarcophagi, when an old Arab fisherman hobbled by. He glanced at my group as he passed, then looked away, but his gaze shot back to the senet game in my arms, and his eyes swelled like an owl's. He continued on his way, though, as if nothing were amiss.

"Sir," I yelled. "A moment of your time."

My guardsmen brought him to me. As my translator explained our mission, the man's eyes grew fearful. He looked at me, glanced at my senet box, then answered, "O holy, foreign lord, may you live forever. I cannot tell you how to achieve this feat, but one of your stature and inheritance can gain nothing but catastrophe by toying with black magic."

When I asked what he meant by black magic, he said, "What you described—a woman coming out of a box—can be none but magic of the darkest kind."

I persisted. I showed him the drawer and asked how I might open it. But he only spoke in circles, repeating himself until my own frustration induced a headache.

I would have stayed in Egypt forever, looking for a way back to Amunet, but a missive from Cyprus summoned me home. My father's health had worsened, and he demanded I return at once. I had no choice. I left that moment for Cyprus.

When I arrived in Nicosia, I could tell that things had shifted in my absence. People looked at me warily, as if I carried some unknown disease. It was the same look most nobles had once cast Henry's way, fearing the demons they believe inflicted his falling sickness.

My father's physician told me that many believed I'd gone mad, thinking myself a player in some mythical story—Henry's doing, no doubt. Not one of my father's advisors would speak to me. The majority no longer favored me for the crown.

I found my father ill indeed. The scrofularia had gripped his lungs in a vise tighter than Amunet had on my heart. His eyes widened when he saw me, and he stretched out a trembling, bony hand. I took hold of it, disquieted by just how frail his grip was.

"You found her, then?" my father rasped.

I knelt at his bedside and clutched his hand to my chest. "I did," I lied, unwilling to admit I had wasted three weeks that I could have spent by my father's side. How had I let Amunet bewitch me from my father's final days?

"Good," my father said. "So now you will be happy, and therefore, so will I." He fell into a coughing fit them, so hard that his body jerked until his blankets slid onto the floor.

I pulled them back over his bony frame.

"Henry tells me I should go to France." Father sputtered again as if trying to clear his throat. "But I would rather die here than crawl before *la maison capétienne.*"

I could only imagine how humiliating it would be for a king of Cyprus to grovel before a king of France, begging for his touch. I didn't know if I believed the rumors that a king's touch could heal. I hated that this superstition was my father's only hope besides a miracle from Holy God. Why was this happening? Why now?

Despite whatever mischief Henry had built up in my absence, my father still favored me as his heir. And as he was still living, none dared oppose him. He immediately began grooming me to replace him.

I was not ready to be king, but I loved my father and would obey him no matter what he asked of me. So over the next few months, my father set my kingship in motion. He received a letter from Charles of Anjou, formally contesting my claim to the throne. Anjou had no reason but his own ambition. Father said that Anjou could get in line behind Henry and my other brothers, whom we knew were still plotting.

When Henry wasn't in seclusion for his falling fits, he barely spoke to me but to deliver sarcastic insults. When he was well, he swaggered about with Guy, Aimery, and his gaggle of noble supporters, shooting me evil glares and murmuring just out of earshot.

I had never felt so alone in my life. That I could not reach Amunet... that everyone seemed to favor my ill brother over me... that my father might truly die... I could not fathom it.

But die he did on the twenty-fourth of March in the year of our Lord, 1284. Hugh III was buried at Santa Sophia in Nicosia. I was crowned king the following May at the *Cathédrale Sainte Sophie.* I was titled John III of Cyprus, John I of Jerusalem. The monarchy was mine to direct. All the riches, land, and women I could desire lay at my disposal. I need only ask.

Yet nothing but Amunet filled my mind.

The absurdity of this did not escape me. Was Henry correct? Was I mad to be so entranced? Had she somehow bewitched me?

I sat on my throne and did my duty, but I replayed that night over and over in my mind. Had I pressed some specific part of the box? Tapped out a combination of some kind? Had I said something—a magic word? Could the time of day have been a factor?

I reached to the small table beside my throne and took the senet box in my hands as I had done a thousand times before. The box was smoother now than it had been that day I had lifted it out of the treasure in the hold of *la Petite Baleine*. My hands had worried the cedar to the same softness I recalled of Amunet's skin.

"What are you doing with that thing?" Henry's voice lifted my chin. He stood in the center of the room, hand on one hip. Two of my guards stood on either side of him, each with a hand on their sword. I nodded to let them know all was well.

"Why do you care what I do with this box?" I asked Henry. "What does it matter?"

"It has you in a trance. You are useless whenever it's around."

Could that be true? I didn't doubt that the box had a hold over me. I stared at it now, sitting innocently on my lap. I slid a panel back, then another one forward, so that both sides matched. I frowned, then slid the first one back. The familiar tremble of the box brought an involuntary cry of anticipation from my lips.

The drawer popped open. And there stood Amunet, looking at me, looking exactly as she had before.

I jumped up from my throne. "Amunet." Her name came out in a breath.

"By the saints' songs," Henry cried, moving closer. "Where

did she come from?"

Amunet spun around to Henry, her black hair flying out like a cape. She looked back to me, her eyes wide, hurt. "*Tu me retrorsum posuit.*"

I shook my head and tried to explain in my best Latin. "I did not mean to put you back. I have been seeking you ever since you left. It has been my obsession."

She smiled then and sauntered toward me. My heart pounded so hard inside my chest it threatened to destroy me from the inside.

Amunet reached out and slid free the loose piece of wood that formed the drawer. She held it between our eyes, and my gaze shifted focus. "This, my protector," she said in Latin, "is the key. Swear to me you will never lock it again."

"I swear to that and more," I said, bumbling over my Latin. "Whatever you ask of me, up to half the kingdom, is yours, fair lady."

Her brows rose, two perfect arcs above her dark eyes. "How is it you can make such offers?"

"I am king of Cyprus and Jerusalem."

"You are a king?" She tugged the rest of the box from my hands. "Well, then, O king, I ask only to hold onto this box so that I may put it somewhere safe. I do not wish to return to its prison again."

"Your wish is my command, my lady."

I called my chief minister and made arrangements for Amunet. She was given the best chamber available, three personal maids, and a new wardrobe.

With Amunet at my side, I ruled like a focused king. I met with the royal advisors, placated the nobles, dealt with a long list of duties that had been awaiting my attention, and asked Amunet to marry me. My advisors and brothers disdained this plan. To marry an Egyptian—unless she was a princess—was foolish indeed. The people would think I had partnered with our enemies.

I did not care. Amunet was all I wanted—all I had ever wanted. She filled me like nothing else.

For several months, life was blissful. What little discord my marriage to Amunet had kindled was quickly appeased by Amunet's charm. The noblewomen adored her. She learned French quickly, moved with the grace of a dancer, and had a way of complimenting anyone who entered her presence so that they left feeling better for having spoken with her.

One night at dinner, Amunet and I began making plans for the one-year anniversary of my coronation. My brothers sulked at the end of the table. I had grown accustomed to their morosity.

Amunet wanted the celebration to be a grand affair, because she had not been there for the real event. "There must be dancers and magicians and athletic competitions."

"What kind of athletics?" I asked, curious.

"Where I come from, we had the *Ptolemaieia*, a competition of great skills. Sword fighting, feats of strength, horse races, swimming—"

A crash turned our heads to the end of the table. Henry had fallen from his chair and lay twitching on the floor. Guy and Aimery stared as if they could see the demons holding Henry down.

"Don't just stand there." I stood and started toward them. "At least move the chair so that he doesn't knock it onto himself." I pulled the chair aside and leaned over Henry.

Amunet's familiar smell drifted over me moments before she spoke from my side. "Will he be all right?"

"He has the falling sickness. It will stop soon, and he'll need to lie down."

Henry's valet entered with three servants. "We will care for him, Your Majesty. Please go back to your meal."

I did as he suggested, but Henry's fit had cast a somber mood over us all. We ate silently and watched the valet and servants move Henry to a litter.

"I'm fine," Henry yelled suddenly, with surprising clarity. "Don't touch me, you fool. It wasn't a bad one. Help me into my chair. I want to finish my dinner."

I shot Amunet a wide-eyed smile, as if there were nothing odd about any of this, and took a long gulp of wine to calm my nerves. Seeing one of Henry's fits always rattled me. The wine helped immensely, and I took a deep breath and finished off my cup. A paste thickened the last few sips of wine. As I peered into the goblet, my throat began to close.

My gaze flew to Henry, who sat staring at me, a crooked half-smile on his face. Aimery and Guy also looked my way.

Traitors. Henry had faked his fit, and when I'd gone to help him, one of my brothers must have slipped poison into my cup. I grasped for Amunet's hand and told her as much. The poison had stolen my voice, however, and I could barely whisper. Dizziness fell hard over me, and I swayed in my chair. Amunet jumped up and called Henry's valet to bring the servants and the litter.

The next thing I knew I was being carried through the castle at a run. My body bounced on the litter. Amunet clasped my hand and ran alongside. The poison did not appear to be fast acting. My throat burned as if on fire. My stomach writhed as if someone had gripped it with a pair of blacksmith's tongs. A chill seized me, leaving my skin cold and clammy. I was dying. I wanted to rage, to demand my brothers be arrested for the traitors they were, but while my mind was strong, my body was powerless.

The servants carried me into my chambers and laid the litter atop my bed. Amunet ran into her room and returned holding the senet box. I had not seen it since that day in my throne room when she had taken it from me.

She stood at my bedside, clutching it in her hands, tears

wending their way down her bronze cheeks. Behind her, Henry, Aimery, and Guy watched from the doorway.

Murderers.

"I will not let you perish," Amunet said. "You shall live longer than any of your brothers."

I wanted to answer her, to tell her not to worry, to ask what she meant, but I could still not summon my voice.

Amunet set the box on my chest, then removed the necklace she wore. She clasped the amulet around my neck, picked up the senet box, and stroked the sides, moving the panels.

I shook my head. I did not want her to go. Not now, when I might be dying. Why couldn't she stay until I was gone?

The drawer popped open as my physician entered the room. Amunet backed away to give him time to examine me. But I could see the truth in his eyes.

Henry had won.

The physician ushered my brothers out of the room, leaving me alone with Amunet.

She sat on the side of my bed and held up the senet box. "In here you will live, perhaps to return to a time where this poison has a cure. Do not fear for me, for I will make sure that Henry is rewarded for his crimes."

Before I could protest, she kissed me deeply and pushed the drawer in.

Darkness came over me, instant night.

"Amunet," I yelled. My voice had returned.

There was no answer.

The smell of cedar overwhelmed me. The hint of Amunet's myrrh and balsam brought clarity.

I was inside the senet box.

How could such a thing be? Had some black magic shrunk me to the size of a mouse? Or had the box somehow grown?

My throat no longer burned, nor did my stomach pain me. I

reached out and slid my hands over smooth cedar on all four sides.

Trapped.

I cannot say how much time has passed since Amunet pushed in the drawer. I do not grow hungry, thirsty, or weary. My beard does not grow. It is as if time has paused whilst I am in this prison, though my mind knows that time has not.

Amunet had claimed to have come from Rhakotis, a city that existed more than 1600 years ago. If she had lived in the senet box that long, so might I.

I wonder, endlessly, whether Henry has taken my place as king, what he claimed became of my body, who he accused of poisoning me, whether Amunet stands beside him as queen, or if she brought some hideous revenge upon him. These thoughts torment me, a constant reminder of my brother's betrayal. And possibly, of Amunet's.

Because the longer I am trapped in this prison, the more theories my mind constructs. Perhaps Amunet was a demon who trapped my soul forever, part of Satan's plunder. Or maybe she was a witch who used black magic to trap me in this cedar casket. Or was the box itself a prison that once held Amunet, and she tricked me into taking her place?

Or did she give up her place in this prison to save my life because she loved me?

I do not know.

I cry out to the cedar walls, "My God, my God, why have You forsaken me?"

But He does not answer. No one does.

Author Note

Although this story is fictional, I used real people to create it. Hugh de Lusignan III, King of Cyprus and Jerusalem—also called *the Great*—was king from 1267–1284. When he died, his eldest son, John, replaced him, only to die a year later, assumed to have been poisoned by one of his brothers. His brother Henry succeeded him and was known as a very ambitious king. Henry had epilepsy, though in those days no one knew what it was, and common superstition held that demons inflicted people with the "falling sickness."

Scrofula (also called scrofularia) is suspected to be a form of tuberculosis. It was known as "the king's evil" and was said to be cured by a king's touch, especially that of a French king.

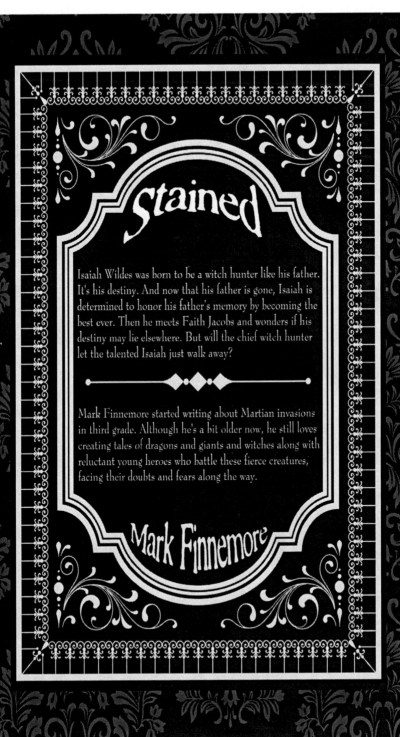

Stained

Isaiah Wildes was born to be a witch hunter like his father. It's his destiny. And now that his father is gone, Isaiah is determined to honor his father's memory by becoming the best ever. Then he meets Faith Jacobs and wonders if his destiny may lie elsewhere. But will the chief witch hunter let the talented Isaiah just walk away?

Mark Finnemore started writing about Martian invasions in third grade. Although he's a bit older now, he still loves creating tales of dragons and giants and witches along with reluctant young heroes who battle these fierce creatures, facing their doubts and fears along the way.

Mark Finnemore

The young woman was all alone, well outside any village, out by an old mill alongside Devout Creek. She held one package-laden mule by the bridle as a second mule bolted across a drought-withered cornfield.

Isaiah Wildes had seen few animals alive in the past two days; the only creatures prospering of late were ravens and flies, both growing fat on rancid corpses of sheep, cows, and chickens. A lone woman was cause enough for suspicion. Add to that the mules.

Isaiah heeled Nan's flanks, and the horse lurched off after the runaway mule, her hooves crunching across the sere field as if it were planted to her fetlocks in quail bones. Where chest-high stalks of corn should be, only quavering ribbons of heat sprouted under the cruel August sun.

When Isaiah returned with the mule, the woman had a terrified look in her eyes. Isaiah wiped sweat from his brow, slowed Nan to a walk, and approached cautiously.

He had heard there was trouble over in New Coventry, so that's where he was headed. He wanted to get there before any innocents got hurt. Or, at least, before too many got hurt.

Isaiah Wildes took no pleasure in his job, not like some did, but he was very good at it. Some said he was the best. His father said he was born to the task. At any rate, Isaiah did have an undeniable gift, though he often wished he'd been blessed with a more mundane talent. But if he didn't do it, someone else would. Better it be done by him. Better it be done right.

Isaiah Wildes could not fly. He could not shape-shift into a raven. He could not make demons do his bidding. What he could do was identify those who were able to do such things. That was Isaiah Wildes' gift.

In many ways, that was also his curse. People were beginning to regard his profession as an archaic relic from an embarrassing past. Rumor had it that Governor Danvers had even convened a counsel to investigate abuses. Isaiah could not blame him. The charlatans, fear-mongers, and revenge-seekers threatened to outnumber honest practitioners like himself. As a result, more people were turning to science for answers. Only when a situation like the one in New Coventry arose did the citizens rediscover their need for people like Isaiah.

Isaiah cocked his head to one side as he fingered the knife at his belt. Yes, there was definitely *something* about this young woman, he sensed that clearly. But it wasn't the stain. So she needn't fear him, though she still faced danger from those who would point the finger for land or to save their own hides, or for plain spite. These were dangerous times for everyone, especially a lone woman.

Isaiah handed over the mule and nodded. "Here you are, Miss...?"

She looked toward the ground. "Jacobs. Faith Jacobs."

Their hands touched as Faith took the mule's reins. Again,

Isaiah sensed something, but it was nothing he'd experienced in his previous eighteen years. He couldn't explain it any more than he could explain the sound of a waterfall to a man born with no ears, or the refreshment of a spring shower to one who had known only drought.

Isaiah laughed aloud and shook his head. His adoptive father, the Reverend Wildes, had often spoken in general, poetic terms about love, but Isaiah suspected the good reverend had never really experienced it outside of poetry. Isaiah certainly hadn't. He was almost convinced it didn't exist. In his line of work, it might as well not.

Faith Jacobs smiled at Isaiah's laughter and reached out to pat Nan's nose before Isaiah could stop her. Isaiah's heart lurched. Nan was a temperamental old girl around strangers, snorting, baring her teeth, stomping the ground. But she stretched her head to meet Faith's hand.

Faith rubbed Nan's graying nose. "She's beautiful. What's her name?"

"Nanna," Isaiah said. He wiped his brow with a dusty handkerchief to hide the heat rising from his heart and into his cheeks. "I found her as a boy." Isaiah bowed in his saddle. "And I am Isaiah Wildes. At your service."

Faith's smile faded at mention of his name, and her blue eyes grew as harsh as the cloudless sky overhead. Isaiah had grown accustomed to this reaction, but to see Faith's face grow cold at the mere sound of his name pained him. He hadn't seen an honest smile since the Reverend Wildes died six years back. And even his father's smile had seemed tentative at times.

Isaiah ignored Faith's frown as best he could, but it was like trying to ignore the scorching sun beating down on them. "Might I escort you home?"

Faith shook her head. "No. Thank you. You've done enough."

"It's no trouble."

"My father and I live at the mill right over there," Faith said. "I'll be fine."

Isaiah watched Faith lead her mules toward the old mill. These were unfortunate times; Isaiah hoped nothing unfortunate happened to Faith Jacobs.

Isaiah reached New Coventry before he realized he was still thinking about Faith. He had grave business to attend to, and daydreaming like a smitten fool could get himself and others killed.

With Faith's image no longer clouding his senses, he perceived the stench of burning flesh and fear, a smell that had been the faintest of bad tastes outside of town, but became pervasive and overpowering inside New Coventry. Smoke covered the town in a filthy haze, and the townsfolk gazed studiously at the ground as if it were more than mere dust.

"Isaiah, thank goodness you've arrived."

Isaiah nodded at his departed father's dearest friend, Thomas Alder, magistrate of New Coventry. Alder reached for Nan's bridle, but the horse snorted and bared her teeth, and he snatched his hand back.

Isaiah dismounted and led Nan after Alder, who walked through town apparently inured to the smell of death around him.

"I have a stew on the hearth," Alder said over his shoulder. "It's on the thin side, and there's no meat in it—hasn't been any good meat in months, nor any animals live-born. But you'd know that, eh? That's why you're here." Alder turned back with a nervous smile. "But dinner will have to wait. Chief Magistrate Ezekiel

Cotton is here. And he wants to meet you immediately."

Isaiah stopped. Chief Magistrate Cotton. No wonder Alder was nervous. Isaiah's stomach roiled, and it wasn't from the stink.

"Come, boy." Alder waved Isaiah on. "We don't want to be caught late. We're enforcing sentence on one of the convicted right now."

Isaiah rarely watched sentences being imposed and never when someone else had made the capture, but with Chief Magistrate Cotton present, he had to attend, although he knew that the woman on the pyre was innocent.

Alder cast nervous glances between the woman and Cotton, who stood atop a granite slab on the far side of the crowd, the smoke and heat of the fire making him appear as a shimmering phantom of vengeance.

To Isaiah's knowledge, none could sense the stain except himself, though he'd never asked anyone except Reverend Wildes, who had ordered Isaiah not to mention it again. But even without the gift, Alder still whispered doubts regarding the guilt of Sarah Goode, a young girl accused by her own husband. Her husband testified that Sarah had sent apparitions to kill him, but rumor said he'd been unable to perform on their wedding night, and Sarah had made the girlish mistake of laughing.

Unfortunately, Isaiah could do nothing about it, not with Cotton there. Vouching for another's innocence after conviction was a sure way to get the finger pointed at yourself.

Isaiah swallowed back acid and closed his eyes. But he could not close his ears to Sarah Goode's screams. The crowd screamed too, cheering the torturous death of someone they'd known all their lives. But she was a witch in their minds now—responsible for the drought, the sickness, the dead animals, the stillborn babies—not some poor girl who had giggled at her husband.

Isaiah silently cursed his gift and wished for the villagers' gift of blind ignorance.

After the fire had died, Chief Magistrate Cotton approached Isaiah. Older than Alder, he wore a lace-flounced jacket with a ruffed collar and a wig of powdered curls. Flanking him were four mercenary horsemen with matchlocks and sabers.

As Cotton neared, Isaiah gasped and took a step back. At the same time, Cotton paused and put a handkerchief to his nose, as though a stench more foul than New Coventry's had suddenly assaulted his senses. He cocked his head at Isaiah before composing himself and lowering the handkerchief.

Isaiah did not know what had possessed Cotton. The only thing Isaiah knew was that Chief Magistrate Cotton was stained!

"Mr. Wildes." Cotton bowed his head slightly. "This territory's finest young witch hunter, I hear. But that does not surprise me. It takes a certain perception into the witch's mind to be successful, don't you think?"

Isaiah mumbled general assent, still shocked by what he sensed in Cotton.

Cotton narrowed his eyes and cocked his head as if trying to come to some decision. "We must proceed with all caution here. These are delicate times, what with the governor and his investigation. There are even those who deny the existence of witches, and I will not stand for that."

Isaiah nodded. He couldn't accuse the chief magistrate of witchcraft. Not here. Not now. Not with four heavily armed horsemen backing Cotton.

"I was present at your birth," Cotton said after taking another whiff of his kerchief. "Right alongside Reverend Wildes and Magistrate Alder. We watched as you arrived into this world in the morning, and we watched your mother depart that same afternoon."

Cotton shook his head. "It is no wonder you have a talent for spotting witches, Wildes, considering your mother was one." He pointed a crooked finger at Isaiah. "I should have never let Reverend Wildes talk me into letting you live. This man is stained. Seize him."

Metal scraped against metal as the horsemen drew their swords. A drop of sweat crawled down Isaiah's back. Alder looked down and stepped away. Isaiah didn't blame him. Alder could do nothing to help him now, or he would share Isaiah's fate.

As the crowd grew silent, Nan stomped and snorted across the town square. Isaiah whirled and shoved through the crowd as Nan galloped toward him, the mob retreating from her bulk and snapping teeth. Behind Isaiah, people screamed as the horsemen charged through the crowd.

Isaiah reached Nan, leapt into her saddle, and galloped off between a tight row of buildings. He hugged Nan's neck as a volley of matchlock shots boomed. Wood exploded from the building beside him, showering him with sawdust and splinters.

At the main road, Nan's stride lengthened. Isaiah glanced back through the dust cloud kicked up by her hooves. With no rain in months, the haze thickened, and the horsemen faded into phantoms. When they finally disappeared behind the cloud, Isaiah pulled Nan's head toward the old mill where Faith Jacobs lived. He had to warn her. He could not bear to have Faith come to the same end as Sarah Goode.

Isaiah circled the old mill, with its rotting timbers and caved in roof. Charcoal and dry rot and emptiness filled the air. It had obviously been abandoned years ago. Faith had lied.

Nan snorted. Isaiah sighed and patted her flank. When his hand came away wet, he dismounted. Blood seeped from a musket ball hole in Nan's side. And yet the ornery old nag had carried him to safety.

"Stupid horse!" Isaiah buried his head against Nanna's neck and fought back tears. "Good, loyal, stupid horse."

Nanna snorted again and collapsed, knocking the two of them tumbling down a hill, crashing through trees and underbrush.

Isaiah's ankle snapped as Nan rolled over him. Agony robbed him of consciousness.

Isaiah opened his eyes to darkness and pain. He tried to stand, but his leg couldn't hold his weight. He fell back to the ground, his scream echoing around him before fading away like a ghost retreating through a catacomb.

He took a deep breath and bit his lip, the throbbing in his head matched only by the throbbing in his ankle, twisted and pinned beneath his calf and swelling to the size and color of a prize turnip.

Overhead, a full moon shone down the hole that had swallowed him. He pushed himself across the damp earth and gravel, his britches soaking up the fetid water beneath him. He leaned back against the cold stone wall of the old well and took another breath. The cloying stench of moldering dirt, like freshly dug graves, assaulted his nostrils, gagging him.

He coughed out muddy phlegm and then whistled for Nan.

There was no answer. He was truly alone now. Nanna was dead. His mother was dead. The Reverend Wildes was dead. And this hole would be his grave.

But at least he hadn't led the horsemen to Faith Jacobs.

And then Isaiah sensed the stain.

Someone—a witch—was out in the underground darkness, watching him.

He drew his knife as a dim light emerged in the distance and grew brighter and closer. Advancing toward him down a rough-hewn tunnel burrowed out from the old well, the light flickered off shadowed walls of dirt and stone.

Isaiah shielded his eyes from the blinding glow with one hand as the knife handle grew sweat-slickened in his other. His ankle throbbed. With his good leg, he pushed his back against the curving wall. The well's crumbling stone pressed into his spine.

A few moments later, a phantom outline appeared. Isaiah blinked dust from his eyes and tightened his grip on the knife. When the light dimmed so that he could see, a little girl stood before him with a dancing flame burning in her palm.

"Get back, witch!" Isaiah hissed as he waved his knife.

"You're hurt," the girl said. "I can help."

"Your innocent form does not fool me. Be gone."

The girl laughed. "You're silly. What's your name? Mine is Destiny. Destiny Jacobs."

"Jacobs?" Isaiah narrowed his eyes. "Do you know Faith Jacobs?"

The girl's smile seemed familiar. "Of course I know her. She's my sister."

Isaiah jerked back onto his broken ankle, and blackness flooded in once again.

Isaiah woke to warmth spreading through his ankle. He opened his eyes. The little girl, Destiny Jacobs, was rubbing his ankle with burning palms.

"Get back." Isaiah jumped to his feet, and the flames in the girl's palms sputtered. He raised his arms to push her away and found his hands tied.

"She helped you, but you would strike her," a man's voice said. "And you call us evil."

Isaiah's ankle was bearing his weight with little pain. Destiny looked up at him with a proud smile, but the two men who stepped out of the shadows had no smiles. And they both reeked of the stain.

"We should kill him now and take no chances," one of them said.

"No, Mathias," Destiny said. The flame grew again in her hand, chasing away the darkness and lighting her earnest face. "Mother said God would send us help, and he dropped from the sky, so he must've come from God."

"From God?" Mathias snorted. "This man is Isaiah Wildes. No man is more surely from the devil. I say we send him back to hell where he belongs."

Destiny looked up at the second man with pleading eyes. "Bartholomew?"

"We must take him to the counsel," Bartholomew said. "And if they decide it, then God or devil, Isaiah Wildes will meet his maker."

Isaiah followed Bartholomew while Mathias trailed behind

with a hayfork. Destiny walked beside Isaiah, passing a flame from hand to hand while babbling endless childish nonsense.

The tunnel eventually opened into a cavern, where people filled buckets from a spring-fed pool circled by lanterns and torches. They watched Isaiah pass, dust-covered children clutching the legs of worn-looking women, men with expressions of hate like Mathias's, and others with no expression save weariness. The whole place reeked of the stain.

"Sit down," Bartholomew said when they reached the far wall of the cavern.

Mathias pushed Isaiah to the ground and chained him to an iron ring set in the stone. Then the two walked off, leaving Destiny standing in front of him, tossing the flame from hand to hand.

"Put that demon-fire out," Isaiah growled. And the fire in her hand vanished.

Destiny's shock turned to a pout. "How did you do that?"

"I didn't do it," Isaiah said. "And if you can make fire, why not do something useful and make rain?"

Destiny's brow furrowed. She cocked her head to the side.

"Destiny," Mathias shouted. "Get home."

Destiny ran off into the shadows, leaving Isaiah alone. He'd rarely encountered more than one witch at a time before, and here he'd stumbled into a whole coven. He needed to escape, so he could convince Governor Danvers that the hunts must continue, starting right here. Then he could reclaim the reputation that Ezekiel Cotton had stolen from him.

Isaiah woke to the bustle of activity surrounding the cavern's pool. A new day must have arrived, but without sunshine it was difficult to tell. In appearance, the place wasn't much different from other villages, aside from being underground and full almost entirely of witches. Shadowy forms came and went with buckets of water. Women did laundry. Small boys tried to swim in the pool while their mothers shooed them away. Some of the braver boys—those not old enough to know to fear and hate him—tried to approach Isaiah, but their mothers called them back.

Mathias knelt in front of Isaiah, blocking his view. "So, the finest of witch hunters is a witch himself?"

"I'm no witch."

"You extinguished Destiny's flame," Mathias said. "That's witchcraft, which makes you a witch. You're in league with the devil. So you must be hunted down and burned. Is my logic correct?"

Mathias shrugged off Isaiah's silence. "When my brother was young he showed a talent for music. My parents were so proud they bought him a fine piano. I tried to play too, but though I could hear the beauty in my brother's playing, all I produced was hideous noise." Mathias laughed bitterly. "I hated him for having a gift that I could appreciate but never master. And so I burned his piano."

Mathias stood and looked down at Isaiah. "You're like that, Wildes. You sense the talent around you, and you hate those who possess what you can never have. I was a child when I burned my brother's piano, so I have some excuse. What is your excuse?"

Destiny came later that day with a plateful of gruel and an apologetic frown. "We have very little."

Isaiah's chains rattled as he took the plate. "Destiny, how did you...get the way you are?"

"You mean this?" Destiny smiled and produced a flame in her

hand. She bounced it back and forth between her palms until it vanished in a puff of smoke. "It's the way I was born. How'd you get so you could blow it out?"

Isaiah shook his head. "I didn't do it."

"Yes, you did. You did it last night, and you did it again now."

"I didn't."

"You did, you did, you did," Destiny chanted while clapping her hands. She flopped onto the ground in front of him. "Teach me how. Please. I'm a fast learner. Really, I am. I'm a faster learner than anyone, even the adults."

She looked around conspiratorially and whispered, "I'm a faster learner than anyone because they don't hardly know any tricks at all. Sure, some of them can do a few little things, but I can do my fire trick, and I healed your leg and—"

"What do you mean they can't do any tricks?" Isaiah interrupted. "I can sense it in them."

Destiny shrugged. "I dunno. They can do some little things, I guess, but it takes a long time, and isn't much anyway. Not like us. No one could put out my flame before. Show me how to do it. Please."

Isaiah frowned. He *had* wanted Destiny to stop both times. And what about the cloud of dust as he escaped New Coventry. Was that just a dry road, or something more?

"I'll tell you what," Isaiah said. "If you teach me your flame trick, I'll teach you to put it out."

A small, flickering flame emerged from Isaiah's palm. Excitement and disgust filled him at the same time.

Destiny extinguished his flame and frowned. "It's more than putting out the fire. It's like your flame goes out too. Like your

talent is gone. Or hidden."

Isaiah nodded. He'd noticed something similar during their practice. When he extinguished Destiny's flame, he could no longer sense the stain in her.

He frowned and shook his head. Using the word *stain* to describe this bright little girl seemed wrong. And the sense of the stain—or to use Mathias' term, *the talent*—was not as offensive as it had been, though it still pervaded the cavern. It reminded him of how tea had tasted when he first tried it— bitter at first, but he eventually grew accustomed to it and even came to savor it.

Perhaps he had subconsciously used this talent when hunting witches, shielding himself against their powers so he could capture them. And Destiny said they could only do little things anyway and that it took a long time at even that, so perhaps their powers were too subtle to be of much use in preventing capture.

He would share this talent with Destiny. Because if Cotton had the same talent that he had, then he would eventually sense all the people down here and—

"Mathias says you're bad," Destiny said. "But I think you're good."

"Maybe I'm both."

"How can you be both?"

Isaiah shrugged. "Your mother taught you to be good?"

Destiny nodded.

"How did she know what's good?"

Destiny shrugged. "Maybe from her mother?"

"Maybe," Isaiah said. "The man who raised me—the one I thought of as a father—taught me that people like you were bad. He taught me that I was doing good."

"Did you believe him?"

"No one told me any differently," Isaiah said. "And maybe I

wanted to believe. I was skilled at it."

"But you don't believe that anymore, do you?" Destiny asked. "You don't think I'm bad?"

Isaiah shook his head. Destiny took his uncertainty as an answer and smiled.

When Faith Jacobs came to see him, she was as distractingly beautiful as Isaiah remembered. He remembered her smile too, though she did not share it with him now.

"How did Destiny get her...talent, if you have none?"

"You don't believe she contracted with the devil?"

Isaiah shook his head. "I don't know what to believe."

"Our parents had the talent," Faith said. "After they were captured and... Well, after that, I ran away with Destiny."

"You must hate me."

"I hate what you've done," Faith said. "I hate what you represent. I hate that my sister must live in a hole. But I don't hate you."

So little to ask for—a mere lack of hate—but it made Isaiah feel better somehow. He'd always been shunned, nearly as much as any witch. People were afraid of him, afraid he would point the finger their way.

"I don't want Destiny to learn to hate either," Faith said. "Blind hate is the reason we're down here."

"I'm sorry."

"Sorry won't allow Destiny to live in the sunshine. All this disease and death you blame us for. Why would we do that? Have you ever considered that it's just a drought, that no one is to blame except the weather?" She sighed and shook her head. "Destiny said you told her that a person could be both good and bad."

"That's the only hope I have now."

Faith studied the people in the cavern going about their tasks and their lives—the men and women working, the children playing, the babies crying. "You realize that none of this was a choice, don't you? No one chose to be what he is, not even you. This is how they were born. This is how *you* were born."

Faith met Isaiah's eyes. "But we all have choices now. We can't blame our actions on the fate of our births."

Destiny ran up with Mathias and Bartholomew close behind. "Men are coming. Lots of them."

Bartholomew raised his arms to calm the growing chaos at news of Chief Magistrate Cotton and a small army marching their way. "Perhaps it is time we stopped running. Times are changing. Governor Danvers is convening hearings. Even Isaiah Wildes is changing. Chief Magistrate Cotton may change as well."

"Cotton will not change," Isaiah said. "Not with a mob at his back. Not with his identity at stake. His power depends on things staying the same. And he will not give up that power."

"Then we fight," Mathias shouted.

Bartholomew shook his head. "We are mostly women and children."

"Run away," Isaiah said. "Hide. Wait for the governor's decision."

"What if he decides the hunts should continue? Won't running prove our guilt to him?"

"Not if nobody knows you were here." Isaiah turned to Destiny. "Remember the new trick I taught you when you showed me how to make a flame: how to shield talent so it can't be sensed?"

Destiny nodded.

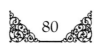

"Could you shield everyone here at once?"

Destiny surveyed the crowd and turned back to Isaiah. "Can you sense us now?"

Isaiah smiled and shook his head.

Destiny grinned back and whispered, "It's easy. I told you they mostly don't know many tricks anyway. Not like us." She winked at Isaiah. "And I'm working on that new trick you mentioned the other day."

"But they have eyes," Mathias said. "They'll see us."

Isaiah created blazing flames in each palm. The people closest shielded their eyes. Destiny smiled, the proud teacher.

"Cotton is the only one amongst them who can sense the talent," Isaiah said. "If everyone is shielded but me, then his sight—and his army—will be focused on me while you escape unseen."

***

Off in the distance, a dog whined. A moment later another answered with a whimpering howl. Cruel, relentless sunshine lanced down on Isaiah, burning his eyes even after he closed them. Beneath him, rough stone scratched at his bare back and buttocks. Sand and gravel scoured his skin.

Isaiah grunted as two men added another stone to the thick oak board strapped atop his chest. He sucked in a rasping breath. The rough-cut plank punctured his skin, and the weight of the stones crushed his chest, forcing the air from his lungs.

Cotton looked down on him with a thin smile. "The record for surviving this test is two days."

"He was an old man," Isaiah wheezed. "Like you."

"Perhaps. But I am in control of how much weight gets added." Cotton motioned for yet another rock to be piled onto Isaiah's chest. "By morning, you will be just another dead nameless witch—like your mother."

Isaiah tried to respond, but he could only grunt. His mouth tasted of blood and vomit.

"You can save your life and your reputation," Cotton said. "Help me track down those witches. We'll go to Governor Danvers with proof that there are covens of witches literally underfoot. And you will be at my side as we bring them to the light."

"You mean...I'll be...your foxhound."

"You will live," Cotton said. "You will thrive even. Things will be as they were. You were good at what you did. You made your father proud."

"He was not"—Isaiah spit out—"my father."

"This is what you were *born* to be, Isaiah."

"No." Isaiah sucked in a wheezing breath. "That's what... people like you...made me."

"Take a stone off," Cotton ordered. "Take two off."

He turned back to Isaiah. "You see, I am not unmerciful. I will be kinder to you than Reverend Wildes was. We are alike after all. We share the same talent. We share the same destiny.

"Do not force me to do this, Isaiah. Join me. After this is over, I'll be the next governor. You'll be my chief magistrate. Think about that."

Cotton strode away before stopping and turning around. "We'll talk again tomorrow. If you're able."

Isaiah coughed out a bitter laugh. Bloody saliva rained back down on his face. Cotton was right: they were alike. A few days ago Isaiah had had the same idea about going to the governor with proof of the witches, convincing him that the hunts must continue. Perhaps their destinies were the same.

Destiny. He smiled weakly, thinking of Destiny Jacobs, her smile so much like her sister's. That small girl had led her people to safety. At least he thought they must be safe. For now anyway. If they'd been captured, then Cotton would have no reason to keep him alive. But they couldn't hide forever.

Someone leaned over Isaiah. He recognized Alder's voice, though his vision was blurring and he couldn't make out a face.

"I'm sorry," Alder said. "You of all people know there's nothing I can do. Please forgive me."

"My forgiveness...doesn't matter."

Alder groaned as if he were the one crushed beneath stones.

Isaiah sucked in air. "You knew my mother?"

"I was there when Cotton passed sentence," Alder admitted. "Reverend Wildes convinced him to stay execution until after your birth."

"What was her name?"

After a moment of silence, Alder said, "I don't remember."

Isaiah sensed Cotton coming the next morning. He could feel the stain in him, though it was weak and Destiny would laugh at Cotton as someone with little talent for learning tricks.

"You've thought about my offer?" Cotton said.

Isaiah nodded weakly and drew in a painful breath. "You offer the same fear and hatred and loneliness I've known all my life."

"But it *is* life. You can change your perspective on what that life means."

"You can give me only one thing."

"Name it," Cotton said with a thin smile.

Isaiah took in a labored breath. "More stones."

"Oh, you shall have them," Cotton shouted. He waved his

men over. "You shall have them all. Your time is up."

Isaiah grunted as more rocks were piled onto his chest. His ribs splintered. "No, your time is up. Without me, you can't win."

"I will win," Cotton said, "when I release your stained soul to hell."

"Release him!"

"Release him!"

Isaiah heard the voice, but he did not know it. Then he heard thunder, or imagined he did. It might have been blood rushing through his ears.

The call came again. "Release him!"

"You heard Governor Danvers." This time Isaiah recognized Alder's voice. "The hunts are suspended. Set Isaiah free."

A drop of rain splashed onto Isaiah's face, and then another. Maybe Destiny had learned her new trick. Or maybe the time for rain had arrived. Either way, the drought had ended. And the hunts had ended. Isaiah smiled and released his final breath. He was already free.

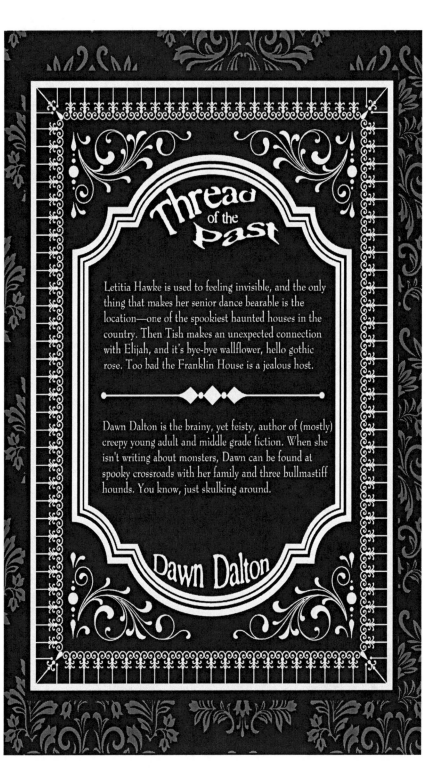

Thread
of the
Past

Letitia Hawke is used to feeling invisible, and the only thing that makes her senior dance bearable is the location—one of the spookiest haunted houses in the country. Then Tish makes an unexpected connection with Elijah, and it's bye-bye wallflower, hello gothic rose. Too bad the Franklin House is a jealous host.

Dawn Dalton is the brainy, yet feisty, author of (mostly) creepy young adult and middle grade fiction. When she isn't writing about monsters, Dawn can be found at spooky crossroads with her family and three bullmastiff hounds. You know, just skulking around.

Dawn Dalton

Cleveland, Ohio – 1999
Franklin Castle

Angry flames poked holes through the gabled rooftop, extending into the midnight sky like Satan's horns.

Loch Craven kicked open the door of the mansion, splintering the wood with a sharp crack. Black smoke billowed out, blurring his vision and filling his throat with the acrid stench of burning flesh. The fire hissed and spit from across the room, deafening. Immobilizing.

Children cried, their soft echoes an eerie siren amidst the snap and crackle of burning lumber. The weight of their screams felt trapped between his ribs, crushing his lungs.

Save the children.

Overhead a giant chandelier swung like a pendulum, threatening to fall. Crystal icicles, pointed at the wooden floor, clinked together in warning. Loch held his arm across his mouth to block the suffocating smoke and choked back his fear. Listened.

There....

Hang on, baby girl. I'm coming for you.

Flames shot toward him like lizard tongues. Tears trailed down his cheeks. He sucked his throat closed and squinted through the fiery smog.

But his daughter did not emerge from the blaze.

The room was empty.

Yet the children still continued to scream.

Cleveland, Ohio – Present Day

Letitia Hawke couldn't take it. One more schoolgirl giggle and she'd start cutting again.

She slid the ribbon cuff of her lace undershirt down to cover the thin vertical scars on her wrists. Not that anyone would notice. She and her classmates were crammed on a school bus like pigs led to slaughter—and if the rumors were true, that might not be far off the mark. The site of this year's after-grad bash boasted a less-than-innocent past.

Ghost stories didn't seem to bother the gaggle of girls in the front. They compared frilly pink dresses and pursed their shiny, glossed lips in admiration.

Or envy.

Backstabbing was a team sport at Cleveland Heights High.

Letitia didn't fit in there. Or anywhere as best she could tell.

While the rest of the girls clung to gold clutches, Letitia's leather pouch hung from one of the chain links around her waist. She wore tall, black lace-up boots instead of ankle-biting heels, clunky jewelry rather than Grandmother's pearls.

And unlike the bulk of her graduating class, Letitia had no suitor to impress. She'd attend the celebration just as she had every other significant event in her high school years—alone.

Suck it up, Tish.

She rubbed at her wrist. The pain had long ago subsided, but she could sometimes feel the sharp slice of the blade across her flesh. Back and forth. Over and over…

And then flashes of blood. So much blood…

Blood the color of the satin wrapped around her body. A tight corset cinched her already small waist, drawing attention to the row of Victorian coins that acted as buttons down the front of the ruby gown. A silver belt hid the stitching where the bodice met the long, flowing skirt, steeping her in a sophistication the school pom-pom pushers could never understand.

And sealing her status as a social pariah.

The ever-wise parent council had thought communal transportation would cut back on drinking and driving, and increase student bonding. But her classmates had given her a wide berth, opting to sit beside—or on top of—one another instead of anywhere near her on the bus. Obnoxious music with indiscernible lyrics blared from the front and back speakers, nearly drowning out the animated chatter of the slightly buzzed.

Almost, but not quite.

Letitia bit back a gag. If not for the destination, she might have skipped the party altogether.

At the front of the bus, Rebekka Eastwood shrugged out of her boyfriend's embrace. "I see it."

Letitia wondered how she could see anything but the whites of Chris Beattie's eyes, considering they'd been lip-locked since the yellow Grad Express pulled out of the school parking lot. She couldn't help but notice, Chris kissed with his eyes open. Loser.

The "it" in question was Franklin Castle, one of the most haunted houses in the entire country, according to Letitia's research. She'd learned the mansion had recently been restored to its natural beauty—the big reveal coinciding with Cleveland High's graduation celebration.

How… lucky.

Letitia peered over the sea of blonde curls as the bus rounded the corner. The stone mansion loomed on the corner of Franklin and 43rd, seemingly alone despite the modern homes surrounding it. Tendrils of ivy snaked their way up the walls to the tall tower window where human shadows sometimes lurked.

Night had settled over the city, and a full moon spotlighted the infamous turret.

Letitia sat taller and craned her neck to scan the window, but all remained still. Her cheeks heated with embarrassment. If her fellow students thought she actually believed in haunted houses, she'd be the laughingstock of the school.

"I heard the last owner took a chainsaw to his whole family," Carter Meade said. The sound of his voice—as if he hadn't quite made it through puberty—always irritated Letitia.

Isabella Carter puckered her lips. "That's gross."

What's gross is the shade of pink on your eyelids, Letitia considered whispering.

Recently crowned prom queen, Isabella had her auburn hair pinned and curled, primed for the coveted cubic zirconia tiara. Letitia had no such ambitions. The glitter would clash with her oversized goggles. Steampunk style had yet to become popular in Ohio.

As the bus pulled up alongside the six-foot wrought iron gate, Letitia's pulse quickened. Students began filing out, crinoline swooshing, animated chatter betraying nerves, excitement, and impatience.

"Don't worry, I brought pepper spray," Ava Smith whispered. At first Letitia thought the popular cheerleader was talking to her, but realized before answering that her comment was meant for David Greene, the senior jock.

He nuzzled his face in Ava's neck and murmured, "Is that to

keep away the ghosts, or me?"

Letitia smirked.

Never mind surviving the spirits. She'd be lucky to survive a night with these tools.

Ava's snubs always stung the worse. Letitia'd yet to form a bond with any of her classmates, but she'd been drawn to Ava. She'd seen the lines across her skin, the telltale scars of a cutter.

Ava had shrugged off the marks as cat scratches, and most believed her. Letitia knew better. She'd once caught Ava in the girl's shower room watching fresh blood swirl down the drain. Ava hadn't acknowledged her existence then, either.

As Letitia stepped off the bus, chills ran along her arms despite the stifling air. A light fog hovered above the fence, and mist swirled from the ground like spirits waking from slumber. A dark cloud slid across the moon's surface. Two antique streetlamps lit the cobblestone path to double front doors, ominous carved blocks of wood with two brass handles. A heavy, ringed knocker featuring the face of a snarling gargoyle was attached to the middle of the left door.

How uninviting.

"Should we knock?" one of the students asked.

But the doors swung open almost magically, revealing a lobby alight with glittering candles and a soft—and familiar—classical melody. A giant chandelier welcomed the graduating class inside, and the students wasted no time entering, jostling and elbowing each other for the best vantage point.

"You're wise to stay back from the herd."

Letitia's breath caught when she turned toward the young man standing before her. A crisp dress shirt was tucked into his white-and-black pinstriped pants. A tailored coat buttoned mid-chest left room for the goggles hanging around his neck. Another steampunk fan. How curious.

Letitia might have pegged him as older if not for the clash of purple dye in his shaggy brown hair. High cheekbones drew her attention to the sparkle in his chocolate eyes.

"Welcome to Franklin Castle," he said, and bowed. "Your dress is perfect."

Letitia looked around, certain his words were meant for someone else, but the giant gates had already closed. She was alone with him at the threshold of the mansion.

"I designed it. I've been, uh, making a lot of steampunk fashion…" She bit her lip against her stammer and lowered her eyelids, certain her cheeks blushed like tea roses. Her breath hitched. "I mean, thank you."

She leaned back on her heels and looked up toward the turret, unable to maintain the boy's gaze. How awkward.

"Such a fascinating home," she said. She looked away from the mansion and into the boy's grinning face, noting the dimples on either side of his cheeks. "Though the history is somewhat vague."

"My name is Elijah Ashmore," he said, offering his elbow. "I'd be happy to answer any questions you may have. Few know more about the castle than I do."

"Letitia Hawke…" She ignored the stutter of her heartbeat and looped her hand around Elijah's muscled forearm, surprised by a jolt of familiarity. Her skin raised in tiny pinprick bumps. "Thank you for showing me inside."

He led her into the lobby. "My pleasure, Ms. Hawke. I've been waiting a long time for you."

The tour guide paused at the landing of the first floor, panting slightly from the exertion of climbing the steps and his tireless fact-sharing, most of which Letitia had already read. She waited

at the bottom of the stairs, trying to hear above the chatter. Elijah stood next to her, close enough that their shoulders touched. His heat gave her comfort in an environment she would normally choose to avoid.

Extracurricular activities with her classmates made her itch.

"Did twenty kids really die in a fire here?" Isabella asked, a quiver in her voice.

The guide's plump face glistened with sweat. He cleared his throat. "There have been two fires," he said. "The first in 1999. Several bodies and bones from the past were discovered throughout the house, but the only death that could truly be attributed to the fire was that of a local man who'd entered the blaze in search of his missing daughter."

"How sad," Letitia whispered, tugging on Elijah's sleeve. "Did they ever find her?"

Elijah placed his hand on her shoulder and leaned close to her ear. His deep voice churned her stomach. "She wasn't in the house. No one was."

"So why enter in the first place?"

"Many believe he followed the sound of children screaming," Elijah said. "Voices have been heard in the mansion for years. Some say they belong to the souls of the dead still waiting for peace."

A shiver crept along the back of Letitia's neck. "That's horrible." She shuddered. "And that poor man…"

"The real tragedy is that his daughter turned up the next day, lost. She'd run away from home. Franklin House was abandoned at the time, so runaways and homeless children often found shelter there. Her father assumed this is where she was."

"You said only the man died in the fire. What about the others?" Rebekka asked the guide. She clutched Chris's hand, her knuckles white.

Thread of the Past

Why had the committee chosen a haunted house for the after-grad party when half the girls squealed at the sight of a spider?

"Death by chainsaw," Carter shouted, causing an eruption of laughter.

"People have many theories," the guide said, offering a tight smile. "I'm afraid chainsaw massacre isn't among them. Come then, let's explore the first floor."

Letitia followed the group up the stairs and into an enormous room yet to be restored. The charred remains of a bed lay broken and dirty in the corner, the mattress soiled. A small wooden carousel, seemingly untouched by the fire, rested atop a damaged dresser.

Isabella pinched her small button nose. "Gross, it smells like rotten eggs in here."

David laughed. "Yeah, because I farted."

"It's cold," Ava said, ignoring her boyfriend's immaturity and wrapping her arms around herself.

She appeared thinner than Letitia remembered. Almost frail, as though she hadn't eaten a solid meal in months.

"This was Emma Tiedemann's room," the guide said. "Her parents were the original owners of Franklin Castle. Some believe she was the first to die here, and that her spirit has not yet come to rest."

"Was she murdered?" Letitia asked.

"Hung by her father," Elijah confirmed, voice grim.

A low groan echoed from the corner of the room. The hair on the back of Letitia's neck stood at alert. Even the guide fell silent when the eerie sound came again, this time in higher pitch.

Save me.

"Did you hear that?" Letitia whispered to Elijah.

The bedroom door slammed shut.

"I don't think Emma likes us hanging out in her old room."

Isabella's voice cracked. "Maybe we should move along."

Ava edged toward the door. "Yeah, let's get out of here." She tugged on her boyfriend's arm, but he didn't share her urgency to leave.

"You could just haul out your pepper spray," David said. Smirking, he used his index finger like a trigger and made a spritzing sound.

Ava kicked at his shin. "You're not funny. I'm serious. Let's go."

Elijah's voice dropped to a whisper. He trailed a finger along Letitia's arm, freckled with goose bumps. "Come on," he said. "This guide doesn't know what he's talking about. I have something I want to show you."

"I shouldn't lea—" Letitia started, but Elijah had already opened the door and slipped into the hall. She glanced at her classmates, still joking with each other. Would anyone notice if she left?

She almost laughed. Why would they start now?

Letitia ducked out of the room and followed Elijah up three flights of stairs, amazed at the ease with which he climbed. He all but floated, occasionally glancing over his shoulder to ensure she hadn't lagged too far behind. Captivated by his twinkling eyes and flushed cheeks, she ignored the dull ache of trepidation thudding in her chest.

He stopped at the entrance to the turret, a large wooden door blocked by crisscrossed two-by-fours. KEEP OUT was crudely painted across the front in red. Blood tears dripped from the lettering where too much paint had been used. Letitia's pulse spiked.

"Why is this room closed to the public?"

The sparkle in Elijah's eyes dimmed. "It's the site of a great tragedy," he said. "An ancient mystery unresolved. I'm sure you know the story."

"Only what I've read on the Internet." She traced the door with her fingers. "Tell me what happened."

"A young girl committed suicide in this room after her sister, Emma, was hanged. She slit her wrists." His eyes bored into her, nearly piercing right through. "Some say she was a rare beauty, trapped in the turret by her evil father. Betrothed to another and forbidden to be with her true love."

"Like a princess," Letitia said, thinking of her own scars. Had this girl felt pain or relief when the suffering ended?

"And what about her true love? Did he marry someone else?"

Elijah's eyes met hers. In his she found sadness, and longing. "No. He never stopped loving her."

She wetted her lips. "Even in death?"

"Especially in death."

Letitia pressed her cheek against the door and inhaled the scent of birchbark and the faint odor of smoke. "This room wasn't destroyed in the fire?"

Elijah reached for her hand and held it. "It remains almost as it did in 1879." He caressed her hand with his thumb. "Would you like to see inside?"

Letitia stared at the way his fingers moved across her skin, somehow comforted by his touch. She tucked a stray strand of hair behind her ear to allow more time to find her voice. He seemed to have a knack for stealing it. "But the door is barricaded."

"The house is a labyrinth of passageways." He pulled her toward another small room adjacent to the turret. "You just have to know what you're looking for." He motioned to a wooden hatch, almost camouflaged in the corner amidst a broken table and miscellaneous pieces of plastic and glass.

Elijah pulled on the handle, and the door creaked open. He offered a boyish grin. "Through here."

How could she resist when her own spirit craved this kind of adventure? For so long she'd felt trapped in boredom, lulled into depression by memories that came in coughs and spurts, but offered no true meaning or resolve.

Gathering her skirt in her hands, she followed Elijah, allowing herself to laugh. Such a foreign sound. She giggled like Isabella and Ava, absorbing this brief moment of joy before emerging on the other side of the passageway, where her smile faded.

Moonlight streamed through the window, casting an eerie blue-tinted glow. Her eyes traced the path of its wide beam to the center of the room, where an antique sewing machine rested on a wooden cabinet with wrought iron legs. The large handwheel appeared brushed in silver.

The most beautiful thing Letitia had ever seen.

Her skirt swished against the hardwood as she walked to it. Her fingers traced a line through the thin layer of dust across the top of the cabinet. Someone had recently used this machine.

Elijah pulled back a chair so she could sit. "It won't bite."

"I love it," she whispered. "Was it hers?"

At Elijah's nod, she grinned.

"I wonder what she sewed. Perhaps Victorian? Something about that era calls to me…" She laughed, catching sight of his formal wear. "I guess you'd know all about that."

Letitia ran her hand along the top of the sewing machine and wrapped her fingers around the wheel. Her hand molded to its form.

Somewhere in the background, an organ played a familiar tune. Letitia hummed its melody while her hands explored, barely registering Elijah's voice in tune with her own. Her fingers knew just where to touch, and her foot slid along the ornate pedal as though it belonged there.

"Go ahead, try it," Elijah said, his breath like a soft kiss on

her cheek.

"But I have no material, no thread. And it's so old. I don't even know if it works."

Elijah positioned her hands on the wheel, his body pressed against her back. The warmth of his skin awakened a memory. "Close your eyes and pretend," he whispered over the rising crescendo of the organ's song.

Its final note ended with the shattering of glass and a piercing scream from below.

Letitia gripped the staircase and whirled down the steps, one hand pressed against her heart.

Elijah begged from behind, "Please, Letitia, stop. You *must* stay with me."

Another anguished scream pierced the night. A classmate, a blonde girl whose name she couldn't recall, ran past Letitia. The girl covered one side of her face with her hand. Blood dripped between her fingers, over her chin, and splattered her pale yellow dress.

"Nobody move," someone shouted. "Remain calm."

Letitia crossed into the darkened ballroom.

"Is everyone okay?" she asked. "What's going on?" Her questions went unanswered.

"Someone turn on a light," Carter's high-pitched tone called.

Letitia ran her hand along the wall in search of a switch. Her fingers brushed the edge of a knob. She turned it, but instead of light, the room filled with deafening music. Quickly, she turned the dial back.

"What the hell was that?" someone called. "Is this a joke? I'm not laughing."

"Turn on your phones," suggested another faceless voice.

Isabella. Letitia would recognize that quaver anywhere. "We can use them to find our way out."

Pockets of glowing smart phones emerged from the dark, providing enough light to highlight a pile of broken glass in the middle of the room. The giant chandelier had plunged from the twenty-foot ceiling and shattered.

Beneath the rubble, lay the outline of a small female body. Blood speckled her frilly pink dress.

Ava?

Letitia's hand flew to her mouth, but not in time to stop the scream. She lifted her gaze, searching the confusion for another light switch or something to further illuminate the room. Instead, she spotted Elijah in the corner. His entire body appeared translucent, nearly glowing in the dark shadow of chaos.

She waved at him, motioning for him to do *something*, to help Ava. But he remained still, staring at her with such intensity her soul burned.

Why wasn't he doing anything?

She ran to the center of the room and knelt before Ava's scratched and bloodied body. Ava's chest heaved, signaling life, though the girl's thin face was milky white. Letitia smoothed a strand of hair from Ava's forehead and whispered, "It's going to be okay." But she didn't know how true her words were. Blood dribbled from Ava's mouth, outlining her lips.

"Somebody call an ambulance," Letitia shouted. She wrapped her hand around Ava's cool wrist, covering the scars she knew all too well.

"Call 911," David echoed. He rushed to his girlfriend's side and pushed away the glass surrounding her. Other classmates lifted the broken chandelier and heaved it aside with a grunt. But its imprint remained on Ava's dress, leaving a permanent dent in her ribcage just below her heart.

"Baby, stay calm. I'm going to carry you downstairs," David said.

"Maybe we should just wait for the ambulance," Letitia began, but her words were drowned out by the deep monotone of an unfamiliar voice.

Leave this place.

The warning echo brought the sound in the ballroom to an abrupt halt. The words vibrated in Letitia's eardrums.

Leave. Now!

"Letitia, come with me."

Not a request. She shrugged Elijah's hand off her shoulder. How had he crossed the room so quickly? "Do you hear that voice? We should all go."

He pulled her to her feet, spun her around, cradled her face in his hands. "The ghosts of Franklin Castle are unhappy. Please, follow me. I know where we will be safe. There's no time to waste."

"I can't leave, Elijah. These are my…"

Friends?

No, that term was too generous. Not one of her classmates had called out to her, responded to her questions. To most of them—maybe all of them—she was as good as invisible. What had caused the chandelier to fall? If Elijah was right, the spirits would not stop until everyone left—or died. That realization clawed at the back of her throat.

Elijah offered her safety.

She couldn't accept it. Letitia turned back to Ava. A crowd of people now blocked her view, confused and concerned voices merging into one indiscernible buzz.

Elijah wrapped his hand around her wrist, covering her own scars borne out of loneliness and confusion. His touch seemed to erase the pain, leaving only unanswered questions. "Help is on the way for Ava. For all of them," he said. "There is something I must show you before you leave."

His eyes pleaded for trust, and her heart dared her to resist even as her mind begged her to retreat.

"But Ava—"

"Will be in good hands," he said, locking her within his gaze. Desperation shone in his eyes. "You can't even get close to her. Please. Come with me."

After another glance at the crowd surrounding Ava, Letitia nodded for him to lead the way. In the light of the hallway, she stopped and inhaled. Once. Twice. Again.

Elijah pushed aside a bookcase to uncover another secret door. "This way, Tish. Please, I will not hurt you."

His use of her nickname gave her pause, but she continued to follow him. The hole was too small to walk through, so she sank to her knees, bunched up her dress, and crawled after him. Slowly, and then faster as the panic of claustrophobia bubbled in her throat. Elijah was already well ahead, but a dim glow guided the way. Only when she almost bumped into him did she realize the light emanated from his body.

Her stomach roiled and turned. This couldn't be happening.

But it was real, as real as the human bones her hands brushed against as she groped through the muted light. As real as the fear building in her esophagus, blocking her own scream. As real as the scent of burning flesh that hovered in the air.

Oh God, what now?

So confused by the vividness of her senses, Letitia didn't realize she'd crawled to the end of the tunnel.

Elijah stood and faced her, his expression so sincere and caring, her apprehension almost melted away. He held out his hands and lifted her to the cold cement floor, the space empty save for a chair spotlighted by a single light bulb. Something was silhouetted from behind.

A hanging form…

Letitia moved toward it, covering her mouth with one hand. The smell of death was ripe, so overpowering she gagged. With each step she saw more details. Blonde hair. A pale yellow dress. A long, crooked neck within a noose and dangling feet capped with high heels.

Emma.

The girl's name came to her.

Letitia let out an anguished cry and shook the lifeless body. "Help me," she pleaded as tears slid down her face. She worked tirelessly at the rope above. Her fingers grew raw.

Elijah laid a hand on her shoulder, his touch calming the panic inside. "There is nothing you can do," he said. He spun the rope so Letitia could see the girl's face, the lifeless eyes that stared back. "Your sister has been dead a long time."

"My sister?" Letitia shook her head. "No. I don't have a sister…"

She backed away, her palms, pressed against air, rippled with fear. "Why did you bring me here?"

How stupid to have followed him. She'd trusted Elijah to protect her, to lead her to safety, not to…

"I didn't know how else to tell you, how else to make you believe…"

"Stay away from me," she said."I don't believe your lies. Just stay away."

Letitia spun and ran back toward the passage. Hazy flashes of memory glided past her eyes, now stinging with tears. She pushed them away, dropped to her knees, and groped through the darkness. Without Elijah's light, she relied only on touch and smell to guide her. Her nostrils filled with the pungent scent of dust and mold. She rolled her tongue along her teeth to prevent grit from settling in her mouth.

"Holy hell," shouted a muffled male voice. "Fire!"

Panic pressed Letitia forward. Her hand struck something damp. She stifled a scream and focused on getting to the blaze. The mansion was a web of hidden passages and trap doors. If the exits were blocked by smoke and flame, would she and her classmates be able to leave the mansion before it was engulfed by fire?

She cursed at her stupidity. Why had she followed Elijah?

At the other end of the passageway, she pushed open the hatch and spilled into the hallway. People stormed toward her, racing for the stairs, screaming, crying, desperate for escape. Vines of smoke chased behind them.

"Yes, run. Get out of here," she shouted. "Be careful on the stairs…" Her classmates stampeded past, not even acknowledging her as she pushed in the opposite direction to enter the ballroom.

A curtain at the back of the room had ignited. Flames wove upward toward the ceiling, flickering with each gasp of oxygen.

She snatched the punch bowl from the buffet table and rushed toward it. The flames hissed and roared but did not fan out. The scent of peaches and ginger ale sailed on the tendrils of smoke that burned her eyes. Balloons and streamers lay in a tangled mess. Shards of glass littered the floor, smeared in blood.

Ava's blood.

In the center of the room, David remained hunched over his girlfriend's limp body.

Letitia ran toward them, dodging flecks of ash that swirled around the room. "Let me help you," she said. "We have to get out of here. We can carry her together."

David looked up at Letitia through tear-streaked eyes, but he did not acknowledge her presence. He stared past her—perhaps *through* her—toward the door. His lower lip tightened with grief, and then slackened as two emergency workers charged into the room carrying a stretcher.

"Get to safety, young man," one of the EMTs said. He laid the stretcher on the floor next to Ava's body and patted David's rigid shoulder. "We've got this."

Letitia reached for David's arm. "They'll take care of her." But her fingers closed into a fist around air.

David glanced backward with longing and then disappeared through the exit.

The emergency crew seemed to move in slow motion as they loaded Ava onto the stretcher and covered her body with a blanket. One of the men withdrew a walkie-talkie. Through the crackle he said, "Clear."

Clear?

Letisha ran after them while they carried Ava's body down the stairs toward the exit. She called out for them to wait, but neither spared even a backwards glance. Through the windows, she saw her friends scrambling onto the bus. An ambulance was parked at the front entrance, lights flashing.

Elijah waited in the foyer, standing beside the double wooden doors.

Letitia yanked on a handle, but the door wouldn't budge. "I have to get out of here. The whole house will soon be on fire."

Elijah didn't move. She pulled on the handle again, cursing as it refused to open. In the side window, she glimpsed the bus and ambulance pulling away from the street. Isabella's tear-streaked face peered out from the back, her boyfriend's arm wrapped protectively around her shoulder.

"No," Letitia shouted, banging on the glass with both fists until her hands were bruised and her throat raw. "Doesn't anyone realize I'm missing? Am I invisible to them?"

Elijah pressed his hand on her back, comforting. This time she didn't push him away. "I'm afraid you are invisible, my darling Tish." His voice was thick with emotion. "And you can't leave, my love. Not now. Not when you've finally come home to me."

PrESENT

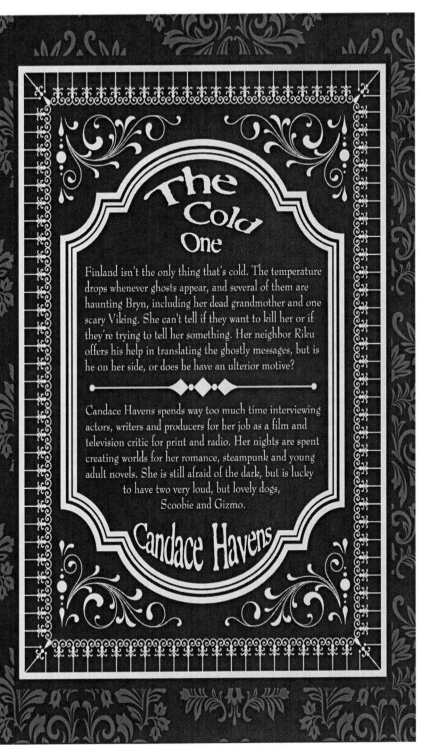

The Cold One

Finland isn't the only thing that's cold. The temperature drops whenever ghosts appear, and several of them are haunting Bryn, including her dead grandmother and one scary Viking. She can't tell if they want to kill her or if they're trying to tell her something. Her neighbor Riku offers his help in translating the ghostly messages, but is he on her side, or does he have an ulterior motive?

Candace Havens spends way too much time interviewing actors, writers and producers for her job as a film and television critic for print and radio. Her nights are spent creating worlds for her romance, steampunk and young adult novels. She is still afraid of the dark, but is lucky to have two very loud, but lovely dogs, Scoobie and Gizmo.

Candace Havens

Bone-chilling cold and secrets.

Those are the two things I'll take with me when I leave Finland.

If I leave.

I have serious doubts about my future. From the moment we stepped into my grandmother's house, I've had a strange feeling. Something weird is happening, but I don't have a clue what it might be. I just know I'm in danger. Maybe I sound like a paranoid freak, but that curling anxiety living in the pit of my stomach is a sign I'm not wrong.

The visions don't help.

My grandmother died five days ago, and yet I've seen her around the house several times washing dishes and knitting. She smiled at me once. Not a sweet grandma kind of smile. No, this was a creepy one that almost made me pee my pants. Her eyes are milky white, and the jerky way she moves sends my heart thumping every time she's near.

One minute she's at the sink, the next she's standing over me making a weird slashing motion against her neck as if to say I'll be the next one to die. Oh, and she visits my dreams every night.

The Cold One

She's trying to tell me something, but she only speaks Finnish, and I only *do* English with some Puerto Rican thrown in. All I understand is "Brynja." That's my name. Sort of. Everyone calls me Bryn, because Brynja is freaking lame.

My grandmother isn't the only dead person I see around here.

There's the Viking. At least I think that is what he is—a giant scary-looking guy with a big beard. He carries a sword and has a seriously mean face. From what my mom says, we're the descendants of a powerful Viking family. I always thought the Viking part of my heritage was cool, until troll dude showed up. He keeps pointing to my neck like my grandmother does, and he's very scowly.

I want to tell someone, but Mom and the great aunts are too busy sorting through my grandmother's house. And I'm afraid they'll think I'm crazy. Mom's been through enough with the guilt about my grandmother. She hadn't seen her mother in twenty years, and Grandma died two hours before we arrived from Miami. I've heard of people feeling as if their souls had been crushed, and that's exactly what happened to my mom. I've never seen her so sad.

"Bryn, do you need an extra blanket?" Mom steps into the room she gave me when we arrived. It's cheery with a huge, cushy bed and would be welcoming—except for the ghosts.

"I'm fine." I try to smile, but my teeth are chattering—more from the fear of the dreams that will find me once I fall asleep than the cold.

She pulls out a heavy wool blanket from a trunk at the end of the bed and lays it over the eiderdown. "The house is warm, but I guess you're taking a while to adapt to the weather here. Are you feeling all right? You look flushed."

I'm scared to death, but other than that I'm great.

"Do you have any idea when we'll be able to go home? School

starts in three weeks." Luckily, or not, depending on how you look at it, my school took a month off for the December holidays. It's the only reason my mom brought me with her. That and I think she needs the moral support.

A shadow crosses her face as she pushes her blonde hair behind her ears. People say I look like my mom, but she's so beautiful that it isn't anywhere close to the truth. She's tall and model thin. I'm not.

"Sorry. I didn't mean to push."

She pats my arm. "No, you have every right to ask. I promise I'll have you back in time, but we have a great deal of work ahead of us. And I need to find a renter for the house."

"I thought you were going to sell it." She'd said that a few days ago, and I was glad. I never wanted to come to this place again.

She shrugs. "I feel my parents here. It's the last thing I have of them, so I don't know if I can do that."

I don't just feel them. I see them, well at least my grandmother and the Viking.

Every time the ghosts show up, the temp drops and a chill slithers down my spine. It's a feeling I've come to dread.

Just tell her the truth. If you're going crazy, you need help.

But the last thing Mom needs to worry about is her daughter being insane.

I have no plans to sleep, but after cleaning all day I eventually pass out.

"*Havahduttaa jalkeilla apulainen.*" The words are so loud I jump out of bed and hit my head on the slanted roof. Groaning, I rub the top of my head.

Grandmother stands at the end of the bed pointing at me. "*Havahduttaa jalkeilla apulainen.*" She says it again.

"I am up," I grumble. I can see my breath the room is so cold.

"Wait." I sit back on the bed. "I understood you. You said, 'Wake up, girl.'"

"He's coming. Save me." *Poof.* She's gone. I mean, like I blink, and she's no longer there.

"Who's coming?" I whisper. I glance at the clock on the wall. Two in the morning. But I'm wired. No way I'll be able to go back to bed any time soon.

I pull on one of the big sweaters mom bought me for the trip and go downstairs. It's even chillier in the living room without the fire. The crazy thing about houses in Finland is that everything is white—the walls, the counters, the floors, and even the cabinets. The house reminds me of a hospital. In the kitchen I fill a glass of water from the tap and chug it down.

Thump. The sound against the basement door sends the glass clattering into the sink.

My breath catches as the door opens. Screaming and moving seem like great options, but my body freezes. My reflexes take a hike.

Maybe this is one of my crazy dreams. And...

"Good, you're awake." A guy's blond head pops out of the darkness. He steps into the kitchen, and I can see he's probably only a year or two older than me. "I can use your help. We're almost out of time."

"Who-uh-who are you?" My voice sounds strangled. He's more solid than the ghosts, so I assume he is real. Though, around here anything can happen. But how did he get in?

"Riku. I'm helping your grandmother. She won't leave me alone. Come on." He waves me toward the basement stairs and then disappears.

Bad things happen in basements. In every horror movie I've ever seen, people die when they go to the basement. Sometimes it's

the devil. Other times it's zombies or evil spiders. But they always die. There's a strange guy I didn't know in grandma's house, and the smartest thing I can do is tell my mother. Or call the police.

Do they have 911 in Finland?

Then something he says clicks in my brain.

Before I realize it, I'm halfway down the stairs.

"My grandmother is dead," I say as I step into the small area where my grandfather used to have his workshop. He died when my mom was my age. The rest of the place is used for storage. Mom and I have been bringing up boxes the last few days and going through each one with the aunts. It's cold and moldy smelling and the last place I want to be. Yet, I can't make myself leave.

"Yes, and if we don't help her, she's going to be stuck here forever." He has a slight accent, but his English is nearly perfect.

"I—what are you talking about?"

He stops sifting through a box to stare up at me. His right eyebrow is up.

"You know what I'm talking about. Your grandmother has been telling you for days what would happen to her if you didn't find it. Haven't you felt her growing weaker?" He frowns and gives me the *are-you-some-kind-of-idiot?* look.

I sigh. "I don't understand anything, except that you must be as crazy as I am, because I see my dead grandmother too. But until tonight, I haven't been able to understand her."

The puzzled look on his face is exactly how I feel.

When he gazes at something behind me, I shiver and turn slowly.

My grandmother points at me spewing Finnish so fast I can't pick up any of it.

Riku taps his temple with his forefinger. "Ah, she didn't understand that you're on a different frequency until tonight."

"Then why can't I understand her now?"

He shrugs. "She knows I understand her, and it doesn't drain her so much trying to communicate. She wants me to explain, so you will help her."

This is all too much. My brain feels like I stuck my finger in a light socket and fried it. "I'm not sure I want to know," I say as I pull myself onto my grandfather's workbench.

"Your grandmother was a Draugar—you come from a long line of them. They have great powers."

"And a Draugar is?"

He waves a hand to silence me. The lighting isn't great, but if he wasn't so arrogant, I might think he was cute. Maybe.

"Since the time of the Vikings, the Draugar have been responsible for protecting the treasure of the great warriors. Using their magic, they also find any stolen treasure. Each generation has taken on the duty. Now it is your turn."

"Oh no." I point a finger at him. "I can't have a job. My mom won't even let me work at the mall." It's an insane thing to say. The last thing I want is a job that involves taking care of ghosts or treasure. I have enough trouble taking care of myself. "And if it goes from generation to generation, then my mom or my Uncle Sig should be next up."

"Your Uncle Marcus, who was killed many years ago, was a great Draugar. He died returning treasure that had been lost for more than eight hundred years. His death meant your grandmother had to return to her duties and protect the treasure."

I never knew my Uncle Marcus. He died before I was born. "I don't want to do this. I mean it. The Viking guy who keeps following me around will have to find some new Draugar."

"You don't get a choice. The magic has already been passed to you. That's why you can see the dead. The other powers will manifest within you in a matter of days."

I shiver. Magic?

No. No. No.

"If you can see them," I point out, "then you're one of those things too. You can help them."

"I have since my mother died five years ago."

That stops me. "How old are you?"

"Seventeen."

He's been taking care of dead people's treasure since he was twelve? I mean, I have a hard time dealing with this, and I turned sixteen months ago. I can't imagine being twelve and seeing dead people.

"Luckily for me, I've been preparing for the job since I was born. When my mother died, her magic found me. I'm helping you, because your grandmother hasn't been able to pass down her knowledge to you."

"I don't have any magic, and I don't want any. You can tell her she'll have to find someone else."

He shakes his head. "If you don't help her, she'll be caught here on this plane until she fulfills her duty. She can't do that if she's dead. And your Viking will haunt you until you die."

No freakin' way would I let that happen.

Find the treasure and you'll be free. The message is loud and clear.

I take a deep breath. "So why are you digging through my grandparents' things?"

"There is a necklace of fire known as the Brising. It has great powers and was stolen from one of the graves more than three hundred years ago. Your grandmother spent her life searching for it and finally found it a few months before her death. She became ill shortly afterward, so she couldn't return it as she'd hoped. Now King Harald wants his treasure back, but it's lost again. Your grandmother says it's somewhere in the house, but she can't remember where."

"Who is King Harald?"

Riku points to the left, where the Viking's giving me a mean look. The temperature drops even more.

As much as I want to, I can't turn away from the scary dude. I'm his Draugar. I think the words, but they make no sense. I'm numb from my head to my toes, and my brain is a pile of runny scrambled eggs. I pray this is some lame dream. I'll wake up, and the world will be normal again.

Normal? You see ghosts. That's so not going to happen.

My gut tells me this is my crazy destiny whether I want to accept it or not. I hate my gut.

He snaps his fingers in my face.

"Rude." I huff.

"Your eyes glazed over for a moment. I need to make sure you're still with me," he says.

I stop myself from snorting. He might be seventeen, but he acts and talks like some grumpy old professor.

"She left the necklace in one of the magical safes your grandfather built into the house, but I checked before you and your mother arrived, and I haven't found it in any of the places she remembered."

"Well, if she can still see what's going on, why can't she find it?"

"She wasn't in her right mind the two weeks before her death. She was in and out of consciousness. She thinks she might have moved the piece when she was in a trance. She couldn't have left the house without someone seeing her. That's why we feel certain it is still here. If you tuned into your powers, you'd be able to sense it."

I shift uncomfortably on the wooden bench. I feel guilty for not having some kind of spidey sense, which is ridiculous. "If you have powers, why can't you sense it?"

"You have so much to learn. Your magic is tied to the families you protect. Mine is useless in this situation except for communicating with the dead."

"Okay, so you want me to help you go through boxes?"

He nods. "But first, I'd like to try something."

I eye him warily.

"Here." He motions to a rocking chair in the corner. Using a rag, he dusts it off. "I want you to sit here and relax for a moment."

"I'm comfy here." That isn't true. My body has long passed the frozen stage, and I'm fairly certain frostbite will destroy my hands and feet.

He frowns again. "Yes, but if you go into a trance, you might fall off."

"Trance? Uh, no. I won't be doing that." I point at him. "I may have just found out I'm a—whatever the heck that Draugar is—but I'm not into your crazy woo-woo stuff. You can su–"

"You are in a calm place, Brynja." The words flow over me like a soft rain shower.

The ocean is in front of me. Waves slide onto the beach, tickling my toes. The warm water relaxes me. I'm home. I take a deep breath and look back. Our white beach house is there with the deep blue chairs on the front porch. I love our house. No matter where I might live the rest of my life, this is home. I turn back to the water.

Grandmother yells at me and points a finger. The words are Finnish, but something clicks again. "He doesn't understand. If he touches it, he will die. The power will corrupt."

Boom! A flash of fire burns my eyes. I'm fairly certain my brain has exploded.

Darkness consumes me. A chill settles over my skin.

So this is what happens when you die.

Boom! Another flash of fire.

117

The red haze clouding my vision clears. Grandmother appears to be sneaking out of her bedroom. The milky eyes are gone, and she seems normal. Outside her bedroom door she stops and cocks her head as if she hears a noise. She's nervous. I can feel her fear deep in my belly like a giant cloud of dread. She's worried about being caught, but after a long pause, she creeps along the hallway to the bathroom. Before easing the door shut, she peeks out. Just before the *eww*-factor of possibly seeing my grandmother use the toilet kicks in, she kneels and reaches for one of the stones on the floor. Tapping it three times, she whispers something. The stone rises as if by magic, and a golden necklace with a fiery red stone slips from her fingers into the space below. She taps the stone again, and it gently slides into place.

Something punches me in the gut. I double over gasping for air. Everything goes black.

"Bryn, baby, wake up. Wake up, honey." Mom sounds worried.

I try hard to open my eyes, but they won't budge. Someone has taken a lawnmower to my brain. It's in shreds. The pain is like nothing I've ever experienced before.

"Owww."

"Oh, thank God. You're conscious." Mom squeezes my hand.

"I think I have a migraine." I crack open one eye and wince at the sliver of light that shines through.

Something pricks my arm. I try to pull away.

"Hold still," a man's voice says. "This will help with the pain."

Wait, that's—

I force my eyes open. "Uncle Sig?"

He winks at me. "I was in Geneva at a medical conference, and it seems I arrived in the nick of time. I found you passed out

on the couch downstairs. When your mom and I couldn't wake you, I realized something more might be going on." He opens a container for the hypodermic and drops it in.

I hate shots, but the instant relief of the excruciating pain only makes me grateful. Whatever was in the syringe works.

The fuzziness fades, and I sit up.

"Looks like our little Bryn has been talking to ghosts."

The look on my mom's face tells me she knows exactly what he's talking about. Her brow furrows, and worry shows in her eyes.

I'm just about to spill all when my grandmother pops up behind Uncle Sigs' shoulder with her milky white eyes and shakes her head violently. She doesn't want me to tell the truth. A tiny tendril of a memory whips through my brain. She's shown me something in a dream, but it's floating around, and I can't quite grasp it. I have the same problem with algebra equations during tests.

"Ghosts? Now I know you're messing with me. I think I forgot to eat last night. I was really tired. I woke up hungry and then…" I didn't like to lie, so I let it go.

"I'll fix you a late lunch, honey. You've been out for several hours." Mom runs to the kitchen.

"I know about the ghosts, Bryn. You can tell me the truth."

The Viking appears and points to my uncle. Pulling out his sword, he makes a stabbing motion.

Okaaaay.

They don't want me talking to Uncle Sig. I can't imagine why. He's the nicest guy in the world. My mom and grandma never communicated, but Uncle Sig was around for the December holidays every year. He and my dad were best friends until my dad died.

"Are you sure you're feeling OK?" I raise an eyebrow. "Ghosts? Really?" I smirk.

There are more lines around his face than I remember from the last time I saw him, and much like my mother, there's worry in his eyes.

"Fine, if you don't want to tell me, but I know you're the next in line."

I want to talk to someone, but the stares the ghosts are giving me are enough to cause the heebie-jeebies. "I'll tell Mom to fix you something too. There's definitely something wrong with your blood sugar."

That evening, I bundle up in my coat, desperate for some fresh air. Mom has been hovering all day, and I need a break. I also hope to see Riku. I remember something about my grandmother telling me not to trust *him*. But I didn't think she meant Riku. I mean, why would she tell him everything if she didn't trust him? No, I think she meant Uncle Sig. They obviously didn't want me to tell him the truth.

Out on the street, I look left and right, trying to decide which way I should walk. Snow is piled high in all the yards and looks like what I always thought the North Pole would be.

"Do you remember the vision?" Riku comes up behind me.

I jump. "I wish you would stop that. You keep popping up out of nowhere."

"Well, do you?" He has a knit cap over his shaggy blond hair, and his face is even more handsome in the twilight. Crystal blue eyes stare at me beneath some of the longest lashes I've ever seen.

Really? This is not the time to start jonesing after some boy.

"What vision?"

"The one where you passed out. I think she took over your body for a minute. That drains your energy faster than anything else they do to you."

120

Do to me? I didn't think they could do anything but yell and make scary hand gestures.

Great.

"I remember talking to you in the basement, and then it's all kind of foggy. I do remember the Draugars. And I disagreed with you about being one. Then zip—"

Riku sticks his hands in his pocket. "Do you drink coffee?"

I pull up the hood of my coat to save my ears from frostbite. My parka is warm, but this cold is bone-chilling.

He points down the street. "Come on, there's a place around the corner. You're going to freeze if you don't get inside."

A few minutes later we have some awesome looking pastries and the strangest coffee I've ever had. It tastes more like hot chocolate.

"I want you to be calm." Riku's blue eyes are intense.

My breath slows and I relax. "You did this to me last night, and I passed out."

"No. Well, yes. But it wasn't because of what I did. You let your defenses down, and your grandmother took things into her own hands. Do you remember anything? Give into my magic. It will help you."

It's useless, but I close my eyes and focus. At first all I can hear are the noises in the café. People talking and dishes clanking. The smell of pastries and—

A red haze covers my eyes as I whirl into a vortex. I blink to clear my vision. Grandmother places a necklace into the hole under the stone. Then the magical words she says are "Brynja find me. Brynja find me. Brynja find me." The vision ends, and I'm back to the sounds of the café. Stomach roiling, I open my eyes.

The pastry that had seemed so delightful before threatens to make me ill. "I don't understand. If she knew where it was, why didn't she do that in the first place?"

Riku raises his hands as if he doesn't know. "My guess is she needed the memory space you gave her—like extra RAM on a computer—to help her remember. That's never happened to me, so I have no idea how it works." He pauses. "So does that mean you know where it is?"

Excitement runs through me, giving me more energy than I've had in days. "Yes. But she told me not to trust *him*. I don't know if she meant you or my uncle."

Riku's brow furrows. "I see. I'd like to say you could trust me, but so much magic and power lie within this treasure, it's probably best if you don't test it."

Somehow doing this without him is the scariest prospect of all. "Even if I can do the magic to get the safe open, how do I get the necklace back to where it belongs? I don't know where the graves are, and I wouldn't have any way to get there. I have magic, right? In theory, if you try to take the fire necklace, my magic will stop you."

He sits back and eyes me. "How do you know that?"

I stop to think. "I have no idea. But I know it the same way I understand everything you told me last night was true. I have to do this." A weird electricity spreads through me. I'm on the right track.

"We have to go now. Like now, now" I stand up and don't wait for him to follow.

In front of the house, grandmother appears in the window. She waves as if to signal me to stay away.

"What the— She's been bugging me to do this and now…"

"It's a warning." Riku's hand is on my arm.

No way can I feel the heat from his touch through my bulky jacket, but I swear I do.

"There's something— No." The last word came out as a curse. "What is it?"

The dark expression on his face scares the hell out of me.

"We have to protect you." He waves his hand, and a shimmering gold mist covers me. "It's a protection spell. There's something in the house that has nothing to do with your grandmother or the king. It's evil, and it has attached itself to someone. My guess is your uncle. He probably isn't even aware of it."

Lovely. "So I go in there with some big, bad evil thing lurking around, snatch the necklace, and then what?"

"I'll have the car waiting."

"You've got to be kidding me." I make the crazy sign with my mitten. "I'm not going in there without you."

"It will be difficult to explain my presence, and we can't make your uncle suspicious. He may not even be in control of his mind. Whatever is in there is strong. It's best if you pretend to be clueless." He pauses for a moment. "Yes. Clear your mind completely. Don't think about the necklace until you retrieve it. We don't know the magic this entity carries. If it senses you know something…" He stops again.

"What?"

"It might try to use you. The spell I did will keep it from attaching itself to you, but it doesn't protect you from any magic it might throw at you."

Hands trembling, I wrap my arms around myself. "No. I'm not doing this." I'm creeped out beyond belief. And then it strikes me. That horrible thing has attached itself to my poor uncle. And is in there with my mom.

Mom!

Unwrapping my arms, I steel myself for what I must do. "Give me an hour. If I don't show up, you'd better come in with all your magic and save me. Got it?"

For the first time since I met him, Riku smiles. "Got it."

I move past him toward the house.

"Bryn?"

He uses my nickname. He hasn't done that before. "Yes."

"I have great faith in you and your power. Your magic will protect you."

I can't hide my smile. And I stand a bit taller as I walk through the door.

My uncle must be in his room, and my mom is in the kitchen making herself a cup of tea. "Did you have a nice walk?"

"Yep. I went to the little café on the corner. We need to figure out how to get some of those pastries sent home."

She smiles, a rarity the last week. "That's one thing they do well here." She yawns, which makes me yawn.

"You go on to bed. I'll clean up." I offer.

"Thank you, honey. See you in the morning." She kisses the top of my head.

My nerves send my stomach into spasm. "You are calm." I whisper to myself. Every time I even began to think of the necklace, I sing, "la, la, la, la." Or a lame version of *Row, Row, Row Your Boat*. I can't think of anything else to distract me.

In my room I make noises as if I'm going to bed. I pick up a warmer sweater and an extra pair of socks. I don't have any idea where I'm going or for how long… I stop myself. "La, la, la," I sing in a whisper as I stuff an extra pair of jeans and money into a bag. When I'm sure Mom is sound asleep, I creep into the bathroom in much the same way my grandmother did in the dream.

The house is eerily quiet. I shiver as I close the door. Sitting on the floor near the clawfoot tub, I try to figure out which floor stone it was. Through a process of elimination and a whole lot of guessing, I narrow it down to two. No one is more surprised than me when the stone lifts the first time I try.

A flash of light almost blinds me. As the brightness dims in the small floor safe, I find a necklace decorated with brilliant, fiery rubies. I remind myself to breathe. An intricate weaving of tiny leaves pressed into gold encircles each stone. Touching it is the only thing I want to do. But I'm genuinely afraid of the magic it possesses. Using one of my socks to pick it up, I wrap it in the sweater I brought with me. I carefully stuff it into the small backpack. After I tap the stone three times, it returns to the floor.

I'm positively smug. I've done it. Now all I have to do is get the treasure to the— Oh, no. I haven't protected my thoughts.

What if the creepy, bad ghost is listening?

Stomach churning with fear, I turn off the light and slip downstairs.

"Hmmm," something growls.

I accidentally bite my lip, and the coppery taste of blood hits my tongue.

The kitchen light flicks on. Mom stands in the doorway.

Great.

That's what I get for being smug.

But at least it's my mom and not the scary thing in Uncle Sig.

"Where are you going?" Her normally sweet tone is dark and gravelly as if she has a sore throat.

Slipping off a mitten, I stick it in my pocket. "I, um, realized I'd left one of my mittens at the coffee shop. They're the ones Cari gave me before we left. For good luck." So much for not telling lies. Well, she did give them to me, but she'd said something more like, "You'd better wear these so your hands don't fall off from frostbite." She was cheery that way. It went with her whole Goth vibe. In fact she would love all this ghost mess.

"You can go in the morning." Mom turns so the light hits her face.

Nausea burns my throat, and every muscle in my body

tightens. Those are not Mom's eyes. They're black. Her head is at a weird angle, which is something right out of the *Devil's Spawn* movie my friends forced me to see last year.

Cripes. My mom is possessed.

I have no idea what to do.

Okay, magical powers time to kick in.

I don't feel any different.

Come on magic.

Nothing.

Where the heck is Riku? He probably could zap her and be done with it.

"I really, really don't want to lose it." I mention the mitten again.

"Give me the necklace, girl."

Oh heckssss. Mom's voice is replaced by an evil devil one.

"Don't know what you're talking about."

It—Mom—moves toward me. I try to run past, but it catches the sleeve of my jacket and shoves me against the wall.

Mom has never touched me in anger, but this thing inside her growls as if it's ready to rip me apart.

"Where is it?" the demon voice demands. Angry fire lights its eyes and sends me reeling.

Heart pounding as if it might explode from chest, my body once again takes a hike. I can't move my extremities no matter how hard I try.

The thing slams a hand against my throat, and tears well in my eyes.

Oh, crap. It's going to kill me.

I don't want to die.

Stop panicking. Tap into your powers.

I clear my mind.

You are calm. You are calm. You are calm.

126

Grandmother's voice penetrates the hazy fog taking over my mind.

She keeps repeating the same phrase.

I can't understand you.

Evil dude yanks hard on my backpack trying to tear it from my shoulder. Hot pain sears through my body. I whimper. I can't help it.

Grandmother screams the words louder.

Realization dawns. I repeat exactly what she says.

The thing howls, but lets go. My wobbly legs no longer hold me. I slide down the wall.

I never stop saying the phrase.

Half crawling, half walking, I scramble for the door.

As I reach for the knob, the door bangs open. Riku pulls me outside.

The cold air is a welcome relief.

"Mom just tried to—" I can't say the horrible words.

Riku shoves me into a car the size of a refrigerator. I don't care as long as it can outrun the scary evil dude.

The door to the house flies open. Mom stands there snarling before stepping onto the snow-covered path. She lurches forward until she's pounding on the window of the car.

"Go, go, go!" I scream.

Riku floors it.

Luckily, the tiny car has some get up and go.

Mom runs alongside for a short bit, and I worry the thing will smash through the window.

I say the words again, and it falls back.

"She has no control, and she'll have no memory of it. I'm sure she never meant to hurt you." Riku tries to comfort me.

True. *But it won't keep me from having nightmares.*

Hands shaking uncontrollably, I squeeze them together.

"How far is this place?"

"Maybe a quarter of an hour."

A nervous laugh escapes my throat. "I thought it would be some major journey up the mountains."

"No, the town was established by the king to protect the graves of the warriors."

"Hmmm." A chill rushes through me.

Is something following us?

I glance around. No one else is on the road, but that doesn't mean the evil creature isn't near.

What if it's taken over Riku?

Forcing my breathing to slow, I grab the door handle in case I need to bail.

Riku notices and shakes his head.

"You're safe. I shielded myself from the magic in the necklace. I won't harm you."

After what happened with my mom, I didn't see me trusting anyone, anytime soon. "Okay," I say hesitantly. "But I'm more worried about that creature possessing you."

"Ah, I can't blame you. I've protected myself from that too. It's something I do every day as a part of my ritual."

I want to ask him about that, but we arrive at a big gate. Riku gets out of the car and punches in some numbers. The gates slide to the side, and we drive through.

"This is the fanciest cemetery I've ever seen, and how do you know the code?"

"Each of the Draugars has a code. You'll learn yours once you're blessed by the elders."

I roll my eyes. "Hey, I'm done with the whole treasure thing. My plan is to give the Viking his treasure, and then I'm back in Miami in a few weeks."

Riku has a glint of a smile as he says, "We shall see."

He pulls up in front of a giant, creepy looking building. I mean, this thing is straight out of *Dracula*.

"Wait, why are the graves inside a building? I thought the Vikings were around like 1032 or something. They wouldn't have had anything like this."

"It was built around the gravesite to protect the treasure and the site. No one but the Draugars are allowed inside. There are fake graves a few miles away for the tourists, but we have always protected the real ones. Most people believe the majority of warriors are buried in Norway, but only a few know the truth."

As we near the door, I notice a panel. Four more doors and four more panels later, we reach a cave-like area filled with dirt. Massive stone statues fill the inner sanctum. Hundreds of them.

"This the resting place of the great warriors."

Power permeates the room, sending the hairs on my arm to attention. My favorite cranky Viking stands next to his statue, which is an amazing likeness. For the first time he doesn't yell or make cutting gestures.

"Don't I need a shovel or something?"

Riku laughs. "No. Place the necklace at the base of the statue."

Bending down, I carefully shake the necklace loose from my sock, and it hits the ground softly. A flash of light momentarily blinds me, and when I glance down the necklace is gone.

Weird. And cool. Definitely cool.

I exhale as the Viking fades away.

I've completed my mission. The drama is over. Maybe my grandma would even be gone when I returned.

I smile.

Then I remember—that scary thing that tried to kill me was still in my mom.

Guess I'm in the kicking-ghost-butt business after all.

Death
Becomes Her

Willow Martin's life is a fairytale. Only problem is she's
Cinderella before Prince Charming shows up. She has a
real life evil stepmonster and stepsister, who take great
pleasure in making sure Willow's story is a nightmare.
As her dance draws nearer, a dress and a haunting spirit
forever change her story. Will it be a Happily Ever After?

Kitty Keswick enjoys a good ghost story but, finds a little
romance more rewarding. A professed romantic, Kitty
believes in the power of love, for it has the power to
transform.

Kitty Keswick

Willow Martin scurried off the Market Street bus and made her way downtown. Spring had come in with a force, threatening to pull summer in sooner than expected. Sweat snaked along the collar of her shirt and down her back. She swept her forehead with the back of her hand, then hiked her backpack higher on her shoulder as she continued down the cracked and gum-marred sidewalk.

For the third time that afternoon, she counted the money she'd earned babysitting the Warren twins. She'd earned every penny. The twins were brats. They'd deleted the songs on her MP3 player and colored in her history book. Willow wasn't certain she'd break even. Yet, having the cash to buy a dress at Rêve made it all worthwhile. She'd placed the dress of her dreams on hold three days ago. Shermer High School's Spring Fling was this Friday, and she was going with Cole Bradley.

Willow slipped the money back into her wallet and crossed the street to the storefront window. A male mannequin dressed in a black tuxedo knelt before a female in a short sequined dress. He positioned a glass slipper inches from her foot. Willow placed her palm on the glass.

A woman's reflection wavered in the window. She wore big round sunglasses and a scarf covering her hair. "They really have us programmed, don't they? But, what they don't tell you is, not everyone gets a happy ending."

Willow turned, but the woman was gone.

Strange.

"Willow!" Abby Logan crossed the street, her ponytail swinging, and hopped over the curb.

Willow checked her phone. Nearly four o'clock. "You're late."

Abby tugged Willow into a smothering hug. "But worth the wait."

"I'm so excited," Willow said.

"Me, too!"

Abby opened the door, and they both entered the shop. The fragrant smell of expensive French perfume, a soft rose scent mixed with something spicy, filled the air. Rêve's decor was sparse with spotlights that featured a sole purse or shoe as if it were an object of art. Willow swallowed hard. She never shopped here. This was her stepmonster Sky's type of store, but for the dance and Cole, Willow wanted everything perfect. She wanted the fairy tale.

No matter how cheesy that sounded.

Abby squeezed her hand as they walked up to the counter.

"May I help you?" the saleswoman asked. Dressed in a white suit, she wore her hair pulled back in a tight bun, which might have been the reason for her pursed lips and sour expression—suffering for her fashion.

"Willow Martin. I'm here to pick up my dress."

"One moment." The saleswoman disappeared into the back.

Willow tapped her finger on the counter. A few minutes later the woman returned empty-handed. "There seems to be a problem. We no longer have your dress. No money had been put down on it, so it was sold."

"What?" Willow had been dreaming about how this night would be perfect. The dress was the key. She'd spent weeks selecting it and even longer working for it. She'd built up huge expectations—how she'd float down the stairs to greet Cole, how his dimples…

This wasn't happening.

"I do apologize."

Abby patted Willow's shoulder. "It's okay, Willow, let's pick another."

It wouldn't be the same, but what choice did she have? Willow turned from the counter and stopped. The racks no longer held formal wear. "Um, where is all your…" She paused, trying to keep the tears from forming. "Evening wear?"

"I'm very sorry, but we've sold out. Most girls purchased their formals weeks ago."

Willow's sight became glassy. "Ironic naming a store *Wishful Thinking*. Things sound sweeter in French. Maybe that lady was right, not everyone gets a happy ending."

"What lady?" Abby asked.

"Just someone on the street. She made a comment when she saw me drooling over the window display." Willow plopped into one of the plush chairs. "All the other boutiques have probably been picked cleaned, too. It wasn't meant to be." She fought to keep her bottom lip from quivering.

"I have an idea." Abby looped her arm in Willow's. "Just call me your fairy godmother."

"Isn't this place great? This thrift shop is a treasure trove. I'm sure

we'll find something here." The metal hangers clacked as Abby trailed her fingers along the racks of clothes.

Willow thumbed through a rack of coats. "I bought my Halloween costume here when I was in sixth grade." She grimaced. The place had a faint scent of mothballs and eau de old lady. Surely she wouldn't find a dress here that would make Cole's jaw drop.

"You have to keep an open mind, *darling*." Abby draped a feather boa around her slim shoulders and struck a dramatic pose. Taking a purple shawl from the rack, she wrapped it around Willow's shoulders and shimmied the sides back and forth until Willow laughed.

Placing a sure hand on Willow's shoulder, Abby said, "They keep the new arrivals in the back. They know me here. Let the treasure hunt begin."

Abby's enthusiasm was contagious. Willow actually smiled as she followed Abby's long strides.

After exchanging a quick hug with an employee named Kara, Abby pointed to Willow and filled her friend in. Kara led them to an antique dresser in the back room of the shop. Atop it sat a pile of goods and a price gun, its roll of price stickers trailing down the dresser.

"This came from an estate yesterday. We received a large donation. Mostly furniture, but this might help Willow." Kara lifted the lid off a white box, pulled out a robin's egg blue chiffon dress, and gave it a good shake. "I don't think it was ever worn. It looks brand-new." Kara held the dress against Willow. Her glasses slipped from the tip of her nose to dangle from their beaded chain as she tilted her head to study Willow. "Blue is your color."

Abby cooed and clapped her hands. Kara beamed like a stage mom at a beauty pageant.

"Take it. It won't bite," Kara said. "There's a mirror against the wall."

Willow padded across the back room to the mirror. She held the dress up. It draped perfectly and fell just below her knees. Abby gently piled Willow's hair up, letting a few dark tendrils fall around the nape of her neck.

"I have these fabulous silver hair clips you can borrow. And my mom has tons of earrings," Abby said.

"It's beautiful." Willow caressed the fabric taking care not to dislodge any of the jewels that glittered on the skirt. She spun toward Kara, "Is there a place I can try it on?"

"The mop closet is over there. It's empty if you want to give it a whirl." Smile lines formed around Kara's warm eyes.

Willow smiled back, opened the door, and slipped inside. When she came out of the dressing room, she couldn't help but do a little spin and a tiny skip, trying to keep her smile from exploding. "I love it." Willow twirled in front of the mirror. The diaphanous fabric was so soft, it floated around her like a symphony of butterfly's wings. It fit as if it was made for her every curve. "How much is it?"

"Today's your lucky day. The dress is going for thirteen dollars," Kara said with a wink. "Get dressed and I'll meet you at the cash register. You have to promise me a picture. My daughter never went to any dances."

"Deal."

Willow turned her key quietly and inched the door open. She made it to the middle of the stairway before her father called out, "Is that you, Willow?"

Worrying her lip, she clutched the box with the dress to her chest. "Yes, Daddy. I know it's late. I went shopping for my dress."

"It's rude to yell." Her stepmother followed her words into the foyer. "Dinner is almost ready. I need you to clean up the kitchen. It's your turn."

Cleaning the kitchen, scrubbing the toilets and showers—everything really—was always Willow's turn. Her stepmother enjoyed her role as purveyor of the inequitable distribution of chores. The only reason Willow didn't mind was that, when she was cleaning, her stepmother didn't nag her. Willow could escape with a scrub brush into her own alternate universe.

Her stepmother eyed the large white box. "What's that?"

Willow grasped the box more tightly. "My dress." When her stepmother reached for it, Willow added, "I got it from the thrift store."

Immediately her stepmother withdrew her hand and curled her lip. "You're going to wear a...used dress?" She raised her nose in the air.

"Yes."

Willow scurried up the stairs to her room. She removed the dress from the box, then shook it out. Kara was right. It looked as if it had never been worn. Willow padded across the worn carpet, hung the dress beside her floor-length mirror, and turned to go downstairs.

"Give it back," a female voice whispered.

Willow turned. The room was empty, but a slight breeze toyed with her curtains. She went to the window she had left open slightly. Her neighbors, the Warren twins, were playing outside in the yard, arguing over whose turn it was to play with a stuffed dog. Their voices must have carried. Willow shut the window and went downstairs to the dining room where her family was already seated.

"Mom and I went to Nordstrom's," her stepsister Sky gloated. She twirled a long blonde curl around a manicured finger. "I found the most divine little dress." A white gold charm bracelet dangled from Sky's wrist and jingled with her movements. "It's champagne and beaded. An exact copy of the dress Leslie Lyle wore for the Oscars."

Leslie Lyle was this month's Hollywood *it girl* as well as Sky's obsession of the month. Sky slapped an open magazine over Willow's plate. "There's Leslie wearing my dress. Mom said I was worth every penny."

"It's nice." Willow pushed the magazine off her plate.

"Nice? You know nothing of fashion." Sky narrowed her hazel eyes as she took her magazine back. "The only other one I would have wanted is the blue floaty number Leslie's going to wear to the premiere of *The Mirror*. But Pierre hasn't released any photos of that one to the public… yet. I look amazing in blue."

An hour and a half after dinner, Willow was exhausted. Her stepmother had made spaghetti and meatballs and succeeded in getting flour and tomato sauce everywhere. Willow had had to scrub the tile grout with a toothbrush. No doubt Stepmother had done it on purpose. She and Sky enjoyed making messes for Willow to clean. Willow had given up fighting them. Her father seemed oblivious.

"Only four more months until college," Willow said to herself as she climbed the stairs and made a quick stop to deposit Sky's toothbrush back into the holder. She dragged herself into her room and had just collapsed on her bed when someone knocked on the door.

Dad poked his head around the door. "May I come in?"

Willow nodded, and her father entered carrying a small box. She sat up and leaned against her padded headboard as her father settled next to her.

"I know how important this dance is to you, sweetheart. I'm sorry I didn't get you a dress. It's just that your mother—"

"Stepmother."

"Our credit cards are maxed to the limit right now, and Sky is... very..."

"Demanding," Willow finished. "It's okay. I love the dress I bought."

"Is that it?" Her father motioned to the dress hanging next to the mirror. "Your mother looked nice in blue too." He pushed the box across the comforter.

"What is it?"

"A tiger," Dad teased.

"It's an awful small box for a tiger," Willow said on cue. They had played this game since she was small.

"Then you'd better hurry and let him out." Dad patted her hand.

Willow opened the box. Inside was a pair of silver high heels. Thin and strappy with little rhinestones that sparkled like stars in the night. Willow pulled them out of the box.

"They were your mom's," Dad murmured with moisture shining in his eyes. "I thought this way your mother could be with you."

Tears pooled in Willow's eyes, threatening to ruin her mascara. Her mom had died three years ago. Willow still missed her. So did her dad, even though he had recently remarried. Willow hugged her dad and then slipped on the shoes. She teetered as she took a few tentative steps. The heels were higher than she was used to wearing. Once she got her balance, she sashayed a few waltz-like steps to the dress and held it against her. "They're a perfect fit. Thank you so much, Daddy."

Her father cleared his throat, but his voice still sounded hoarse. "I'm glad." Standing, he rubbed his eyes. "Good night, sweetness."

"Daddy?" She sniffed back a tear.

He paused studying her, "What is it, Willow?" When she hesitated, he added, "You can tell me anything."

She only wished that were the truth. They used to be so close, but ever since her father had remarried, he was…different. Ruled by her tyrant of a stepmother. Willow just couldn't bring herself to tell him what the past few years had been like for her when he was obviously suffering too. She buried the pain under all the heavy emotions she had been shouldering since her mom died.

"'Night." Willow crossed the room to give him a peck on the cheek.

As soon as the door closed, she returned the shoes to the box, slipped them under her bed, and padded into the bathroom she shared with Sky. After locking the adjoining door, she opened the jar of makeup remover, scooped a bit onto a washcloth, and scrubbed her face.

A thud sounded inside her room. Willow peeked around the open bathroom door. No one was there. She finished washing her face, brushed her teeth, and changed into her comfy drawstring pants and tank top. Her routine completed, Willow exited the bathroom and climbed into bed.

"Give it back," whispered a female voice. Was that the same voice she'd heard earlier? Or had she dreamt it?

Willow threw the covers over her head. Slowly, she peeked out from under the wadded edge of her blankets and surveyed the room. The branches of the oak tree outside her bedroom window created long, gnarly shadows in the moonlight. Willow paused and listened, waiting for the voice to return. The only sound was silence. Perhaps she'd only imagined it after all.

Willow hardly slept. The next morning she rushed about, getting ready for school. She hastened to the kitchen and placed a slice of bread into the toaster. Her father was watching the morning news. The newscaster's voice carried into the kitchen from the living room.

Sky elbowed her way to the counter and added a slice of bread to the other slot. "You kept me up late with all that noise you made last night."

Willow hadn't made any noise last night. She ignored Sky, opened the refrigerator, and took out a carton of orange juice.

Sky grabbed the container from Willow and poured herself a glass. "Oops. That's the last of the OJ. I guess you get milk." Sky grinned.

Willow was allergic to milk. She ate her toast and then rushed upstairs to retrieve her backpack. Opening her bedroom door, she froze. Her clothes were strewn about her room, and the dress she had bought yesterday was stretched out on her bed as if someone had fallen asleep atop her comforter. She was about to yell for her father when she caught sight of her floor-length mirror.

Scrawled across the glass in red lipstick were the words: *Give it back.*

Willow grabbed her backpack and raced from the room, slamming the door behind her. She trembled as her heart thudded against her padded bra. Fear morphed into anger.

Sky had been known to throw temper tantrums, but this seemed a bit beyond her normal realm of let's-torture-Willow-because-I-can-get-away-with-murder. Willow had had it with Sky and stormed down the hall to confront her. She pushed open Sky's bedroom door just as someone shrieked. She scurried downstairs.

In the living room, Sky was sobbing loudly, her face against Dad's suit. His hand hovered over Sky's head as if he wasn't quite sure how to console her.

"What happened?" Willow asked.

Sky lifted her head. Mascara streaked her high cheekbones

and Dad's lapels. "It's terrible. She was so young, so alive."

"Who was?" Willow asked.

"Leslie Lyle. She's dead!" Sky screamed and raced up the stairs. Her bedroom door slammed, rattling the pictures on the living room wall.

Dad patted Willow lightly on the shoulder. "Sky's staying home from school today." He handed Willow the TV remote. "I'm going to change. Am I giving you a ride to school?"

"Yes, please." Willow turned up the volume on the newscast.

Actress and socialite Leslie Lyle was found dead in her Beverly Hills mansion last week. The cause of the death is still being investigated. Authorities haven't ruled out foul play. The body of the twenty-two-year-old actress was discovered by her personal trainer. At the request of the family, a private funeral was held three days ago.

Lyle was known for her ravishing beauty and even hotter temper tantrums. A fickle supporter of the fashion scene, Lyle was recently detained for the alleged destruction of the entire spring line of French fashion designer, Pierre. Her on-again–off-again boyfriend, Pierre, later dropped the charges. Fashion Forward praised the tattered chiffon dresses.

On a related topic, the dress Leslie Lyle was to be buried in has disappeared. The gown is rumored to be the only original Pierre gown not destroyed by the actress's outbursts.

More news after the break.

Dad came into the foyer wearing a fresh suit. "Are you ready? I'll drop you off on the way to the office."

Willow clicked off the TV. "Sad. She was very young," she said to the empty television screen.

"Willow!" Abby jumped up and down, waving her hand above the crowds in the hallway.

The lunch bell always created a mass exodus. Students flooded the hall, a sea of multi-colored fish, and Abby was going against the flow. As usual. Abby ducked in and out, weaving through the throngs of students. When she finally reached Willow, she shoved a tabloid into Willow's face. "Do you see it?" She shook the paper.

"I could if it wasn't smashed up my nasal passages." Willow took the magazine from Abby.

"That's it!" Abby tapped the glossy paper. "Your dress. It's Leslie Lyle's missing dress!"

Willow studied the pen-and-ink stylized drawing, the type fashion designers favored, with a rail-thin model striking an unnatural pose as fabric flowed around her, almost seeming to dance off the paper. It did resemble her dress. The color, sleeves, and bodice were the same, but, this dress was much longer, complete with a frilly faux train.

"It's very similar," Willow said. She handed the magazine back.

"Similar? Willow, cripes it's *the* dress. Designers often make changes to the final product. The article said it was custom fit to Leslie Lyle and she's a bit short—"

Willow shot her friend a hard look.

Abby patted Willow on the shoulder. "Not that you're short, really. But can you believe that *you,* Willow Martin, will be the only girl at Shermer High going to the dance in a *Pierre* original? It's worth fifteen thousand dollars," Abby squealed and hugged Willow with such force they both collided into the lockers.

Willow nibbled her fingernail. What if it *was* really Leslie's dress? Had she imagined that voice? Maybe Sky hadn't trashed her bedroom? And the lipstick note? Willow grabbed Abby's shoulder and steered her into a quieter part of the hall. Colorful posters announcing the dance decorated the walls.

"Abbs, I have to tell you something really strange." Would

144

Abby think she was crazy? Was she crazy?

Abby's smile faltered, and her brows scrunched together. "Okay, sure." She placed a hand on her friend's shoulder. "You can tell me anything, Willow. What are best friends for?"

Willow brushed her eyebrows with her finger, debating on the least ridiculous version to tell. She decided the truth, all of it, was the best action.

"I think Leslie Lyle is haunting me."

"What are you doing in my room?"

Sky spun around, clutching Willow's blue dress against her chest. It flowed with her movement like silk dancing on water. A coy smile slid across her glossed pink lips. "You aren't good enough to wear this dress. I know what it is, who it belonged to."

"Get out of my room." Willow tossed her backpack next to the dresser and stalked toward her stepsister.

Sky backpedaled and skirted out of her way, stopping in front of the full-length mirror. She held the dress against her, running one hand along the skirt, letting it flutter beneath her fingers. Suddenly Sky gasped and pulled back her hand as if she'd been bitten by a snake. She flung the dress to the floor. "Your dress pricked me!" A small dot of blood pooled at her fingertip. She sucked on it and looked fiercely at Willow.

"Serves you right," Willow said. "Now get out of my room." She pointed toward the door.

"Did you steal it, Weeping Willow? I bet you did." Sky sashayed closer to Willow.

Willow clenched her teeth as Sky's minty breath puffed against her flesh. She hated her stepsister's pet name for her. She wanted to say so many things, tell Sky off for good. But Sky ruled the roost. A sad fact, and nothing Willow did would change that fact. Even her father usually sided with Sky and her stepmother. There would be no happily ever after for Willow Martin.

"Don't be ridiculous. I bought it at a thrift store."

Sky narrowed her eyes. "I bet Father would love to hear my version of how you snagged a fifteen thousand dollar dress to wear to the prom tonight."

Something inside Willow snapped. She refused to give in to Sky again.

"Get out!" Willow squared her shoulders and pointed toward the door.

But Sky leapt on Willow, knocking her to the floor. The two girls rolled in a tangled mass of flailing arms and legs. As Sky kicked out, the standing mirror crashed onto the floor. Then Willow's head slammed into the dresser. The room spun, tilted.

Sky fled.

Willow sat, but the movement caused an intense pressure in her head. She closed her eyes and clutched her temples, willing the room to stop revolving. When she no longer felt as if she were on a tilt-a-whirl, she opened her eyes.

The dress was gone.

Willow's bedroom succumbed to the gray shadows of dusk. An orange glow from the outside security light shone through the blinds. Willow still sat on the floor stunned by what had happened, the fight with Sky, the missing dress… She wished this day were over. Clothes, shoes, and her coverlet littered the floor. She crawled to the toppled mirror. A jagged crack ran diagonally across the glass. The mirror had belonged to her mother. Whenever Willow glanced into the looking glass, she believed her mom was there watching her, looking out for her, sharing her life. Willow knelt in front of the glass, placed her hand on the surface, and righted the mirror.

"Mom, I miss you so much." A single tear dropped onto Willow's arm.

A knock sounded at her bedroom door.

"Come in," Willow choked, wiping her eyes. She stood, but the inside of her head was like a jar of marbles, all wobbles. She placed a hand on the dresser to steady herself.

Abby rushed in holding a small purple duffel and carrying a garment bag over one shoulder. She skidded to a stop. "You haven't showered yet? What's wrong?"

"I'm not going." Willow dropped onto the bed with a heavy sigh.

"Nonsense." Abby hung her dress up on the closet door and dropped her duffel beneath it. She sat next to Willow. "Where's your dress?" Abby brushed Willow's hair back. "Have you been crying?"

Willow's lip quivered as she nodded.

"Is this about Leslie? I wouldn't let a little ghost scare me from a wonderful evening with Cole. Besides—"

"It's gone. The dress is gone, and I don't have another. I'm not going. Could you please call Cole? I don't have the heart to do it."

"You're going." Abby frowned. "Sky's not here. Nobody is. I let myself in." She stood. "I have an idea. Wait here."

Minutes ticked by. Willow made her way into the shared bathroom and swiped at the dark streaks of mascara on her cheeks. She wasn't sure why she was bothering, but a little light of hope filled her. When Abby had a plan, there was no stopping her. Willow smiled. She added some cleanser and washed her face completely. Deciding she was up for a shower, she stepped into the refreshing stream. The rhythmic dance of the droplets renewed her spirit. Sky wouldn't win this fight after all. Willow was going to the Spring Fling, with or without the cursed dress.

Willow exited the bathroom dressed in her robe and found her best friend grinning at her. Abby waved her hand, indicating dresses in a variety of colors and styles covering the bed, including Sky's brand-new Leslie Lyle knock-off.

"I raided Sky's closet. If I'd known the riches buried in her room, I would have suggested it earlier," Abby said with a glint in her eye. "Your sister is a mall."

"Stepsister," Willow corrected. She picked up a light blue dress. Her heart had been set on the color. It was a fairy princess gown with a heart-shaped bodice that cinched at the waist. The skirt billowed with layer upon layer of taffeta and netting. Tiny rhinestones twinkled like stars on the bodice and skirt. "This is the one. I hope it fits."

"It will. I'm playing Fairy Godmother after all."

An hour later Willow and Abby stood in front of the dressing mirror, hair piled up in long cascading curls, faux jewels dripping from their necks and ears. Willow's smile was back on her rouge-colored lips.

Abby rested a hand on her friend's shoulder. "You look marvelous, my dear," she said in a funny little voice as she twirled Willow around.

"So do you." Then Willow's bottom lip quavered as she pointed a trembling finger at the mirror.

Abby shifted her gaze from Willow to the elaborate mirror. A shrill scream escaped her. She stepped backward, dragging Willow with her.

A girl stood in the cracked mirror. Her face was ghastly white, and dark hollows ringed her eyes. Her hair was stringy and dull. Willow had seen that face a thousand times, plastered on every tabloid and fashion magazine. Leslie Lyle was hard to forget. Even

148

in death, she was unmistakable. The spirit took a step forward, escaping the mirror. The temperature in the room dropped. Willow shivered as her breath came out in little puffs.

"Give it back," the phantom moaned. "My dress, I want it back."

Pictures thrummed against the wall. Objects in the bookcase toppled and fell. A gust of wind scattered loose papers in a small cyclone.

"Give it back."

"I don't have it," Willow shouted.

The ghost clutched Willow with her bony hands. Abby screamed and flung a book at the ghost, but Leslie flicked a wrist, and the book hit the wall.

"Death. The dress is death." Leslie's voice was hoarse as if she was having trouble speaking. Her needle-like fingernails burrowed into Willow's shoulders.

"I don't have it. My sister stole it."

"Po…i…sss…on," Leslie hissed.

Abby took several steps back. "What???"

Leslie croaked out the word once more. "Poison."

"The dress is poisoned? Is that how you died?" Willow asked.

The ghost nodded. "The jewels…" She faded from view.

"One of the stones pricked Sky earlier. She could die!" Willow raced to her nightstand. Fingers shaking, she picked up her cell phone and dialed Sky's number. "I got her voice mail!" Willow gasped. "Sky, take off the dress! It's poisoned! Leslie was murdered!"

"She isn't going to believe you." Abby dug her own cell out of her purse. "We need to call someone else."

"Who?"

"I'll text Alex while you try Sky again."

Willow dialed Sky's cell a second time.

"What do you want?" Sky snapped on the third ring.

"Sky, take the dress off. It's poisoned. Leslie was murdered."

"Nice try. It looks fabulous. Much better than it would have on you. Don't worry, Weeping Willow, Alex is dying to get the dress off me too." Sky giggled.

"Sky, I don't care about the dress." Willow tried to keep her voice calm. "You're in danger. Come home now!"

"No." Sky's voice was a bit slurred. "I don't…bel…ie…v."

"Sky," Willow shrieked. "Don't hang up! Sky!"

Muffled movement sounded on the other end of the line. Willow's heart thrummed in her throat. It was all her fault, if she had never bought that dress…

A beep indicated the end of the call. The line went dead.

Abby took the phone from Willow and hugged her. "Alex didn't answer. Sky's probably fine."

"Leslie tried to warn me, but I didn't listen."

Someone flung the front door open downstairs. Heavy footsteps pounded into the house.

"Hello?" a panicked male voice shouted. "Mr. Martin? Someone help me!"

Willow and Abby raced down the stairs. Alex gently laid Sky on the floor. "We were outside talking in my car, and she… collapsed…"

"Call 911," Willow ordered.

Sky's eyes fluttered open. "Wil…low…help…me…" Sky's breathing grew shallow. "I'm sorr…" A tremor shook her body. Then she went inert.

Willow placed her ear on Sky's chest. "She's not breathing. We're too late."

Willow stood under the big black umbrella and shivered, but not only from the cold. Rain ran down the slick granite of the tombstone. The graying sunlight obscured the newly carved name. Tears slid down her cheek as she placed a single white rose on the freshly turned earth.

A hand caressed her shoulder. Willow didn't turn, but leaned back for support. The symphony of steady droplets drowned out their soft sobs.

"So sad, taken in her prime. She was so young."

"Yes." Willow muffled a cry. She brushed the raindrops from the stone. Her fingers lingered as she whispered words only the dead could hear.

REST IN PEACE

"Thank you for saving me," Sky murmured.

"What are sisters for?" Willow leaned toward the headstone and added, "And thank you, Leslie, for saving both of us."

Leslie Anne Lyle
1990–2013
Beloved actress and friend

Willow glanced up at a movement by the bank of trees. Even in the rain, the figure was distinct. Head covered in her trademark silk scarf, Leslie Lyle lowered her sunglasses and winked.

Leslie had been right. Not everyone had a happy ending. But some people did.

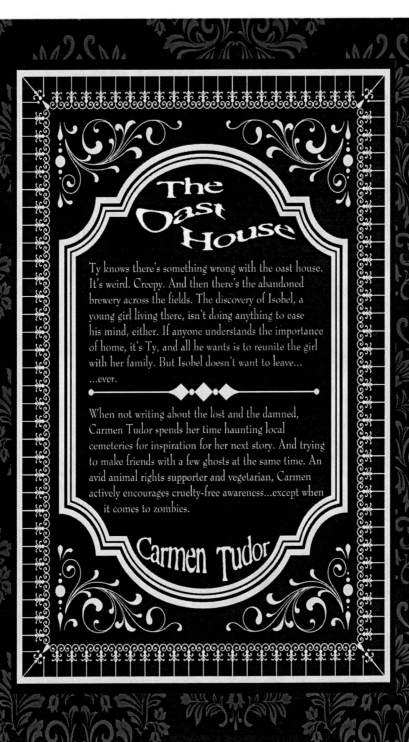

The Oast House

Ty knows there's something wrong with the oast house. It's weird. Creepy. And then there's the abandoned brewery across the fields. The discovery of Isobel, a young girl living there, isn't doing anything to ease his mind, either. If anyone understands the importance of home, it's Ty, and all he wants is to reunite the girl with her family. But Isobel doesn't want to leave...

...ever.

◆◆◆

When not writing about the lost and the damned, Carmen Tudor spends her time haunting local cemeteries for inspiration for her next story. And trying to make friends with a few ghosts at the same time. An avid animal rights supporter and vegetarian, Carmen actively encourages cruelty-free awareness...except when it comes to zombies.

Carmen Tudor

The scattering of fallen oak leaves sheltered a thin layer of frost covering what little grass hadn't already been scorched by the pale autumn sun. Every step toward the oast house sent my feet sliding forward as if I were hurrying home. But the oast, I knew, could never be my home.

The three-story octagonal rag-stone building had been sitting in the heart of the Chapel Hill fields since before my grandparents were born. The slate roof rose like a spire piercing the sky, and although the place had been converted to a dwelling nearly half a century ago, sometimes the acrid aroma of dry hops overwhelmed me when I walked through the front door.

The derelict brewery to the south of the oast had undergone no such conversion, and the numerous windows kept vigil over the fields, now the color of golden wheat. An avenue of oaks lined the drive up to the oast house. Years before, the tree limbs had been pruned to form a cathedral-like canopy, and even now, after the leaves had fallen, the sight still awed me. I shuddered from the cold and reached the mudroom entrance just before the rain started.

"Did you get them, Ty?" my father asked. He didn't look up from where he sat with his crossword puzzles at the kitchen table. I threw a small paper bag down to him, and several washers spilled out and rolled in circles. Like him, I didn't offer a greeting. Like him, I didn't know how.

Lately the only sound that broke the silence between us was the incessant dripping of the bathtub faucet. We had been here for close to three weeks, and every night I'd lie awake as the drops of water pinged into the enameled cast iron tub. I'd tried spreading a towel in the bath, but the muted impact of the water pounded on the soaked material. One more night of the infernal dripping would drive me insane.

I climbed to my room on the second floor. Most of my things were in boxes in the attic, but I still had my music, so I put my headphones on to drown out Dad's silence.

When I came out of my room at dinnertime, the soft pattering of rain against the window on the landing was accented by a dull gust of wind that made the leaves on the oaks shiver and flitter. Across the fields, the brewery loomed like a hulking shadow. Seeing it swathed in the eerie glow of dusk reminded me of the stupid stories circulating at school about ghosts and hauntings. But at the end of day when the building was reduced to a barely-standing pile of rubble, it was easier to believe the only ghost around here was me.

And then it hit me. Silence pervaded the oast. He'd replaced the washer.

I headed into the bathroom, where time and neglect had transformed the once-white tiles to a mottled gray, and the constant dripping had eroded a permanent rust stain through the enamel of the tub. As I stared at myself in the mirror, the grime and smokiness of the glass gravitated toward the center and nearly obliterated my reflection. Soon I wouldn't be able to see myself at all.

But by that time we wouldn't be living here. The oast house was only temporary. Once she'd sorted out her problems, she would tell me and Dad to come home. She had to.

When I got down to the kitchen, Dad was putting dinner on the table. As usual he'd only set one place. He took his work jacket from the back of his chair and walked to the door.

"Lock up after me," he said.

I nodded, but it was too late. He'd already gone.

Dad worked nights as a security guard and usually got home after I'd left for school. He seemed to like it that way. He'd never worked nights when we were back home, but we all had some changes to get used to. Some just seemed easier than others.

The hours ticked by slowly, and by the time I'd finished all of my homework, I could hardly keep my eyes open. I stumbled upstairs and collapsed onto the bed. Moonlight stole in through the window, battling the darkness.

As I relaxed and drifted toward sleep, something tugged at my consciousness. My eyes shot open. *Plink. Plink.* The sound wound its way from the bathroom and along the hall to my room. *Plink.* The dripping seemed to be growing louder.

I debated about ignoring the drip, but after a few moments, annoyance got the better of me. I groaned as I hauled myself from the bed and staggered through the darkened room.

Panic quickened my pulse as my fingertips fumbled over the hand-hewn beams and the grittiness of the lime mortar while I searched for the light switch—like when I was a kid and nearly freaked every night that something horrific and unseen was hiding in the darkness. *Plink.*

I found the switch and flicked it on, lighting the room and blinding my eyes. The tiled floor was icy cold against my bare toes as I walked to the bathtub. I grabbed a towel from the rack and was about to place it under the faucet to soften the noise of the water, but the tub was dry.

I stood still and waited. Had I imagined the dripping?

I bent over the tub and ran my hand along the rim. Definitely dry. I must have been dreaming. Or maybe the rain had started up again.

I flicked off the light and returned to my room. The sound of the rain—the slow, steady rhythm that often reminded me of a heartbeat—always calmed my nerves. Especially when I was younger and she was having one of her episodes.

But tonight no rain fell.

I closed my eyes again. I didn't want to think of her.

When I awoke the next morning, I ran over a mental to-do list. Saturday meant no school, but I had a million boxes upstairs to unpack, the brewery to explore, and maybe I'd catch a movie in town. I also had to study Horatio's lines in *Hamlet* for the upcoming school production. Whatever I ended up doing, I had to get out of this place. The ceilings were too low, and the dark beams too oppressive. That biting scent of hops, whether real or imaginary, made it hard to breathe, and I wanted out.

After the matinee finished, I trudged back toward the oast. The avenue of oaks signaled that I was nearing the house, but I bypassed the drive and wandered straight through the middle of the fields.

Although the rain had held off all day, the sky remained heavy with clouds. The brewery doors were bolted closed, but I couldn't resist taking a look inside. Just this once. I easily climbed through one of the front windows and landed with a thud on the wooden floor. I had never been inside before, and the overwhelming quiet lingered differently from the silence in the oast house.

The brewery was in ruins. Dodging holes in the floor as I walked, I scanned the now-familiar lime plaster, most of which had crumbled off the walls long ago. High windows let the light in, but darkness pervaded the building, and many rooms remained steeped in a state of perpetual night.

Only shadowy markings remained of where the original fittings and machinery once stood, which gave the brewery the desolate look of an empty shell. What hadn't been stolen or broken by neglect had been damaged by squatters and tramps.

I tried to make out some of the crazy writings on one of the walls, but the lighting was too low. I left the massive front rooms and wandered deeper into the brewery. I wasn't sure if the old stairwell, or even the rotting floorboards, could be trusted, but I had the entire evening to kill.

The vast rooms seemed to grow as I wandered from one to another. Toward the back of the brewery, I found an old sign pointing to the stairs.

I glanced up the stairwell. No sunlight reached this dark corner, but something about entering the unknown thrilled me. The hair on my arms rose as I ascended.

I slid my hand along the wall while my feet guessed at each step. Finally I felt a landing underfoot and reached out. My fingers grasped a doorknob, and I sighed with relief as a single shaft of pale light shone from under the door.

The door was much heavier than I'd anticipated. At first I thought it was locked, but I struggled with both hands to reach the light that would surely be waiting on the other side. Just as I was about to give up and make my way back downstairs, the door creaked under my weight and swung in.

The light filtering through the high windows momentarily blinded me. I took a step forward, clamping my fingers over the doorknob until my focus returned.

As I was now at the rear of the brewery, most of the space here was open plan. All the north-facing windows were boarded up. This left only the south and the west facing windows to light the room.

The space was entirely empty. And yet... And yet I got the feeling that I wasn't alone.

I took a step backward. I scanned the space one last time to make sure I hadn't disturbed someone living in one of the dark corners. A hazy flutter in my peripheral vision had me spinning around so fast I nearly lost my footing. I expelled a string of expletives and clutched my hand over my heart. Sweat beaded my brow, and I shook all the way to my fingertips.

"Sorry I scared you," she whispered.

Adrenaline coursed through my veins as I stared at the girl. She couldn't have been more than eight or nine years old.

"What are you doing in here?" I asked.

"I let you in," she said.

I nodded uncertainly. "Do your parents know you're here? I don't think it's safe to play in here."

The girl considered me. She cast her eyes down swiftly before looking up again. "I'm Isobel," she said quietly. "Who are you?"

"I'm Tyler. I live over there." I pointed toward the boarded-up windows. "In the house across the fields."

Isobel's eyes widened slightly.

"I didn't mean to frighten you," I stammered. "I was just taking a look."

She gave me a furtive once-over.

"It's going to get dark soon. Maybe you should go home too."

Isobel glanced around the room. "But I live here," she said. "I am home."

A million thoughts ran though my head. Was she a runaway? Was she making up stories? Was she homeless? Abandoned? What should I do?

"Do your parents know you're here?" I repeated.

I stepped back into the light of the room, and Isobel followed. She didn't look as if she'd been living in a deserted brewery. She was dressed kind of weirdly in scruffy old clothes, but otherwise she seemed okay. Although I had to admit, I hadn't exactly had much experience with the homeless.

"It's okay," Isobel assured me. "I could tell you weren't like the others."

"What?"

"The other people. I didn't like them."

"I think you should go home now," I said. I started for the stairwell again, but Isobel stayed where she was.

"I told you," she said, "I live here."

Her eye contact was unnerving, and I was beginning to think she was telling the truth. I wished I knew what to do. Should I call someone? Inform the authorities? Would anyone even care? "Isobel," I asked, keeping my voice casual, "how long have you lived here?"

She thought about it and shrugged.

"For a long time?" I pressed.

"I don't know. I can't remember."

"I go to high school. I just joined the drama club. What about you? Do you go to school around here?"

Isobel shrugged again.

The setting sun streamed an orange light over the wooden floorboards and illuminated a million dust motes flying through the air. It also cast a clearer light on Isobel. Her hair was pale like the sunburnt grass in the fields, but her eyes were forlorn and as dark as the empty stairwell. She smiled, but it wasn't a happy smile. It was something else entirely.

The Oast House

That night as I lay in bed blindly staring up at the ceiling, images of Isobel alone in the brewery, hiding in the darkest, coldest recesses, flashed through my mind.

I'd tried to get her to leave. I'd offered to take her somewhere, but every time she had refused my help. Even though she was probably hiding out, I couldn't forget the look in her eyes. The dullness of resignation and the spark of need. God knows, I'd seen that look before.

Earlier when I'd come inside the oast, Dad was at the table with his crosswords. I stood in front of him wondering if I should tell him there was a little kid out in our fields. When he looked up, he just said, "Dinner's in the oven."

I knew then. He wouldn't be able to help either of us.

Isobel was my problem.

I got out of bed and went to the window on the landing outside my room. I squinted, trying to see the brewery in the darkness, to see anything at all. The world was in shadow, and Isobel was hidden in the bleakest one of all.

As I walked back to my room, the familiar *plink, plink* from the bathroom beat out a slow and somber meter that chilled me to my bones.

I got up early on Sunday morning. I grabbed a duffel bag from the corner of my room and filled it with blankets from the hall closet. On my way out I raided the fridge and threw in a couple of bottles of water and whatever I thought a little kid might eat.

With each stride across the frosty field, grass crackled as the weight of my steps snapped the frozen blades. When I reached the brewery, I tossed the duffel bag through the same window I'd entered the day before. The bag's impact sent up a cloud of dust that greeted me as I jumped down from the stone sill.

Picking up the bag, I strode through the rundown rooms

toward the stairs in the back. I placed my palm against the stone wall of the stairwell and slid my hand against its length as I climbed to the top. I knocked once on the door.

Then I waited. Not a single sound stole out from the other side of the door, no indication that anyone was even there. "Isobel," I called. I knocked louder this time. "It's Tyler. From yesterday." I leaned against the door and placed my ear to the cold surface. Still I heard nothing.

The door creaked open slowly. I jumped back, so I wouldn't fall forward. Isobel stood before me.

"May I come in?" I asked.

She smiled and stepped aside. The brewery, which had been icy downstairs, wasn't any warmer up here. I set the bag down and unzipped it. Isobel stood over me and watched with interest as I unpacked the blankets.

"What are these for?" she asked.

"For you. Yesterday I noticed you didn't have any. I brought you some food too." I left that in the bag as Isobel didn't seem interested.

She picked up one of the blankets and ran her fingers along the corner where my initials had been hand-sewn many years before. "Thank you," she said.

I sat in the stream of light from one of the windows, and Isobel did the same. She watched my every movement like a little bird and seemed to be waiting for something startling to follow.

"We have to figure out what we're going to do with you," I said. "You can't stay here."

"Why not?"

"Your family must be worried about you. Don't you think we should let them know you're okay?"

"No." Isobel's face fell. "We can't."

"Sometimes if we do something wrong, we worry that we

might get in trouble. But it's not always as bad as we first thought. If you're hiding because you've done something wrong, I can talk to your parents about it. Or whatever."

Isobel shook her head. "I don't have any parents. Or brothers and sisters."

I nodded, though I wasn't any closer to understanding her than I had been the day before. "Tell me about the other people who were here. You said yesterday that there were others."

Isobel turned away from me. "I don't want to talk about them," she said. "Tell me about your family."

I leaned back against the wall and stretched out my legs. "Well, I just moved here."

"Do you have any sisters?" Isobel asked.

I smiled. "No. It's just me and my dad."

Isobel tilted her head to the side. "Don't you have a mother?"

I cleared my throat. "She's not well."

"Where is she?"

I didn't usually discuss this with anyone, but Isobel leaned closer and studied me intently. She tilted her head to the other side and blinked expectantly.

"She was in a hospital for a while. She's out now, but... Well, she just needed some time by herself. So my dad and I moved here."

Isobel lowered her gaze. "Will you leave when she gets better?"

"I don't know. Why? Don't you like being on your own?"

She shook her head. "I like it when you're here."

I had an idea. "Why don't you come to my house? It's right across the field."

"I've been there before."

My brows rose. "Really? I've never seen you around."

"Not since you've been there," she said. "Before. I don't know when, but it was a long time ago."

"What did you do there? Were you, like, playing?" If she was homeless, she might have been squatting in the oast house before my dad and I arrived.

"I didn't want to go. They took me there. Then I came here."

"Who made you go?" I asked.

"I don't want to talk about it," she said. She jumped up and ran toward the stairwell.

"Isobel," I called, and ran after her. I reached the stairwell and descended to the ground floor. The room before me was empty. I marveled at her speed. I ran through the remaining rooms and out toward the front of the brewery, my footfalls echoing loudly in the empty space.

Isobel had disappeared. Had she gone out the window? I walked to the ledge and peered out over the fields. They, too, were empty, but she had to be here somewhere, hiding within the walls of the abandoned brewery. "Okay," I called. "I get it. You're scared. We don't have to talk about it right now, but you can't stay here. I'm gonna go home and think about this for a while. It's going to be okay."

I sighed and climbed onto the sill with one sad thought tumbling through my mind: how do you help someone when they don't want you to?

Later that night recurring dreams tormented me. Over and over I raced through the fields, chasing Isobel and calling her name. She ran toward the brewery, but the building swayed on its foundation, threatening to collapse. As the stones crumbled, a giant haze of dust rose into the air and hovered above like an ominous storm cloud. But Isobel kept running. When I finally reached her, I grabbed her wrist and spun her around. But it wasn't Isobel. It was my mother.

Plink.

The dripping broke my restless sleep. It seemed to be calling to me.

165

The Oast House

I stumbled out of bed and reached for the light switch, but something stopped me. Whatever spell had been cast on me and the oast house would be broken by the intrusion of light. Experience had taught me truth was best discovered in the dark.

The oast house, like any old building, had been standing long enough to harbor many secrets. Whatever mysteries were buried deep within these walls had been suppressed for too long, denied for too long. But while I lived here, the oast fed on my energy, taking it all, draining me until I had nothing left to give. The heart of the oast was beating out its broken rhythm one drop at a time.

I staggered forward as the oast pulled me toward the truth. I passed the light switch on the landing but left it untouched.

I passed my father's empty room.

I passed the window that overlooked the fields and the brewery. *Plink.*

The oast house was steeped in darkness. I wasn't afraid of the unseen horrors of my childhood tonight—no hands would grab me, no shivering breath would tickle the back of my neck. Whatever was here was real. And it waited for me now.

A shaft of moonlight from the window marked the bathroom doorway. Although it was only a small offering of light, it would have to suffice.

I crept closer until I stood at the doorway. I entered the room with my eyes squeezed shut, pressing my toes against the cold tiles one small step at a time

The dripping stopped the moment I walked through the door. I envisioned my mother the last time I had seen her. She'd lain in the tub with her back toward me, her hair spilling out over the rim of the bath. The water ran red with her blood as she lay across the thin line between life and death.

I opened my eyes and wiped away tears as I tried to make sense of the scene before me.

The floor wasn't tiled as it had been the last time I'd entered the bathroom. Instead, the floor was untreated oak. The walls were stone, and in the air hung the thick, bitter smell of dried hops.

Everything as it had been had disappeared. Nothing remained except for the body on the floor.

"Isobel," I breathed.

I knelt beside her battered body and smoothed the hair from her face.

I checked her cold skin for a pulse, but felt none. The little girl lay dead, surrounded by broken beer bottles in the aftermath of a drunken and violent frenzy.

A muffled creak like a door opening downstairs, startled me, and I left Isobel to check it out. I fought panic as I peeked over the railing to the entrance hall below.

"Ty?" my father called up.

I stared back blankly.

"What are you doing up so late?" he said.

"I... What are you doing here?" I glanced from him to the bathroom.

My father sighed. "I forgot my ID."

I could think of nothing to say to him in that moment. My thoughts were with Isobel alone, and I stepped back through the door to the scene of her demise.

The room had returned to normal. I flicked on the light and faced nothing more than the dirty tiles and the frosted mirror.

"Isobel?"

The tears on my face had dried. Was I losing my sanity? First my mother, then the girl from the brewery. It had all seemed so real.

My father's boots clomped on the tile as he approached. I was slumped on the floor next to the bathtub. I didn't even realize I was crying again until Dad crouched next to me and placed a hand on my shoulder.

"It's going to be okay," he said. He took me by the arm and led me away from the bathroom, away from my memories. I lay down on top of my bedcovers and closed my eyes. The oast house was silent, but it rang with the echo of my father's voice: *It's going to be okay.*

When I woke the next morning, I had more pressing matters to deal with than algebra. As soon as I'd dressed, I ran straight across the fields to the brewery. I didn't stop to catch my breath as I headed for the stairwell and the upstairs room where I'd found Isobel hiding before.

"It's me. Open the door," I called.

The door opened, and Isobel stood before me as she had done previously. She smiled, but I couldn't return the gesture.

"What happened last night?" I asked.

Isobel's brow creased. "What do you mean?"

"You were in my house." I folded my arms across my chest.

She shook her head. "No, I wasn't."

I sighed and ran a hand through my hair. "I don't want to play games, Isobel. I don't know who you are—or what you are—but I saw you." The word *dead* was on the tip of my tongue, but I couldn't bring myself to say it. "Come outside with me." I reached for her arm, but she sprang back.

"No," she cried.

I stepped closer to her and held out my hand. I took another step. Isobel retreated farther into the corner of the vast room. I strode forward. I needed answers. Isobel stopped only when her back hit the wall.

"Come with me," I said.

Tears streamed down her face. I forced myself to remain unmoved. "You either *can't*, or you *won't.*"

"I tried to tell you," she whispered. Her tears continued to

flow. "Ever since the other people... I've been stuck here. Please help me. *Please*."

Leaving Isobel, I ran back through the fields to the oast house. Her secret lay within those walls, and I intended to discover it even if it killed me.

I grabbed a crowbar from the mudroom and took the stairs two at a time. *Plink.* My footfalls on the treads of the stairs matched the pounding rhythm of the dripping in the bathroom. *Plink. Plink.*

I hoped my father would understand what I planned to do. I'd need an explanation that wouldn't get me grounded for life. *Plink.*

The dripping grew louder and louder, reverberating in my eardrums as I entered the bathroom. I cried out in pain. Dropping the crowbar, I pressed my palms over my ears to block out the noise.

Clenching my fists until my fingernails pierced my skin, I braced myself. I snatched up the crowbar. I struck at the tiles. Some of them resisted and merely cracked. Others fell and shattered on the floor. I smashed at the wall until I broke through the plaster and reached the ancient laths underneath. The thudding in my ears was almost unbearable.

Part of the bathroom had been insulated. I tore out sections of foamy insulation to find nothing. I moved on to other sections of the wall. Nothing. I slid to the floor, exhausted. "What am I supposed to do?" I raked my hands through my hair.

When the sun, light as the sunburned fields, shone through the window, one golden ray landed in the center of the mirror. Swiping plaster dust from my eyes, I jumped up.

With the crowbar, I wrenched the mirror from the wall. The glass shattered as it hit the floor. I smashed through the plaster and then tore pieces away with my hands. The sink blocked my way, so I moved to the side of the vanity and yanked away chunks of plaster with newfound energy, barely noticing the gap made by the missing oak laths here. My heart was pounding. When the hole was large enough, I put my foot through and stepped inside the wall of the oast house.

The drips ceased, plunging the room into a silence that enveloped my whole body. I blinked more dust from my eyes as they adjusted to the dark.

I plunged forward in the small space. The hollow was less than six feet wide, but without light the space seemed as immense as a bottomless pit. The stonework of the walls was the same as I'd imagined it, and I could make out an indistinct mass lying on the floor.

With shaking hands, I leaned down to pull away the crumpled sheets covering it, but stopped. Lying on the ground was a shoe. Small and dusty. A child's shoe. I didn't touch the sheets. I didn't want to see Isobel that way.

I visited my mother after the inquest. I told her about school and the drama club. I told her about the color of field grass when the frost burns it white. But I didn't tell her about the brewery or the oast house. My mother needed to hear stories about life and living, and Isobel's story was not yet finished. Her death remained unsolved. It would only be complete when she chose to tell me about it.

Since the day in the bathroom, Isobel hasn't reappeared.

Even cold and empty, the brewery hints at stories it wants to tell, and although Isobel no longer hides behind its crumbling walls, she has to be somewhere nearby. After all, she needs my company. And I need hers.

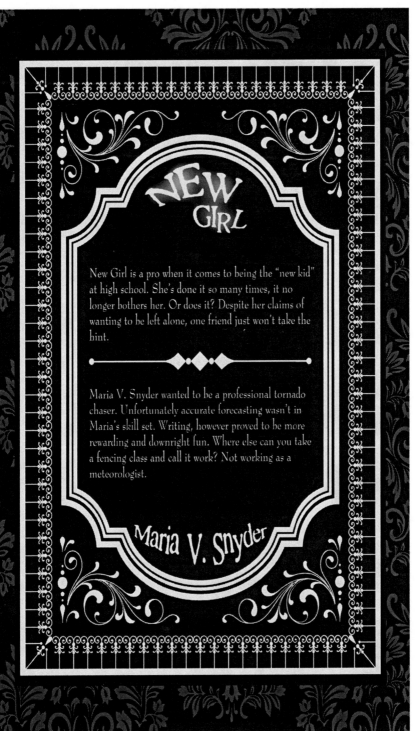

NEW GIRL

New Girl is a pro when it comes to being the "new kid" at high school. She's done it so many times, it no longer bothers her. Or does it? Despite her claims of wanting to be left alone, one friend just won't take the hint.

◆◆◆

Maria V. Snyder wanted to be a professional tornado chaser. Unfortunately accurate forecasting wasn't in Maria's skill set. Writing, however proved to be more rewarding and downright fun. Where else can you take a fencing class and call it work? Not working as a meteorologist.

Maria V. Snyder

I'm the new girl. Always am. Don't worry, it doesn't bother me anymore. I'm a pro. It's so easy to ignore the stares of the other students as I stand on the steps leading into the main entrance of another Dead President High School. I'm in some town in Wisconsin. Or is it Minnesota?

All I know is, it's cold and bleak here, my mother's still dead, and there's nothing to distinguish this place from any other town in the Midwest. Just like the school. It resembles the one I attended before and the dozen I attended before that. I can predict my first day here without fail.

One of the type-A cheerleaders will show me around. She'll be friendly, bubbly, and introduce me to all my teachers. And then she'll abandon me 'cause I'm not one of her "people." She will have determined my place in the high school hierarchy thirty seconds after meeting me by assessing my average—i.e., not designer—clothes, my generic backpack, and well-loved purple sneakers. She'll rate me slightly better than the freaks, geeks, and invisible types, but far below her own exalted station.

I'll try not to laugh at her, 'cause I've seen her type in every high school across the United States. There's nothing special about her or anyone in this place. Millions just like them are forming the same cliques, dealing with the same problems, and all believing they're special.

In fact, nothing will surprise me today. The jocks, the goths, and the teachers will meet my low expectations. The faces and names might be different, but that's it. I'll attend my classes amid whispered speculation, rude stares, and I'll see that hopeful gleam in a few girls' gazes. You know the type—the fringers who don't have any friends. They'll see the new girl as a potential new BFF.

I'll ignore them. It's kinder this way, trust me. If we become BFFs, I'll only break their hearts when I leave to attend the next Dead President School or Dead Humanitarian School. 'Cause I will leave. That's a guarantee.

Maybe not for a month or two, but my dad will find another job too good to pass up, and off we'll go.

So I know you're wondering why I still bother with school. I'm sixteen and could just quit. But, you see, attending college is my goal. Why? 'Cause college means I get to stay put for four whole years. When I'm in college, I won't be dragged from place to place, and I can make a friend without worry.

And as I predicted, my day plays out like it has too many times to count. At the end of the first day, I retreat to the library. Sorry, I guess I should say the Learning Resource Center, or the Media Center, or the IMC. Doesn't matter what it's called, it's my place to study and hang out until my dad picks me up.

I'd rather be here than in some hotel room. Wouldn't you? I find a spot that's hidden and quiet and make it my temporary home.

Except this time, my spot isn't quite as hidden as I'd thought.

"Hey, you're the new girl, aren't you?"

I stare at the "genius," deciding between a sarcastic reply or cold silence to drive him away. He looks like a fringer, but he could be one of the invissies. I opt for silence, but he doesn't get the hint.

"I'm Josh Martin." He plops in the chair on the opposite side of the table. He points to my open textbook. "I have Algebra Two with Mr. Kindt."

When I don't respond, he leans forward and says, "So what do you think about our school?"

I consider my options. What will drive him away the fastest? "Did you know there are forty-seven other high schools with the same name across the US?"

"Really? Wow. How do you know that?"

I suppress a groan and shrug. "Internet."

"Cool." He smiles at me.

Josh has freckles, a few pimples, and grayish green eyes. His shaggy brown hair curls at the ends. He's wearing generic jeans, sneakers, a gray hoodie, and an L.L. Bean® backpack. At least he doesn't have his initials stitched on it—that's so lame.

Before I can tell him to get lost, he asks my most hated question, "So where are you from?"

I refuse to answer. Always will. Instead, I say, "Look, John—"

"Josh."

"I have lots of work to catch up on."

But he's sixteen and male. Which means he's denser than a dwarf star and unable to pick up on subtle hints. I try a more direct brush off. "Jack—"

"Josh."

"Go away. Shoo!" I wave my hand.

But the idiot just gives me a goofy grin. He pulls out his Algebra Two textbook, flips the pages, and works on the assigned problems.

Whatever. I ignore him and concentrate on my own work.

But he can't keep quiet.

"Number five is tricky," he says.

"What did you get for number nine?"

"Avoid the taco salad. It's poison. But make sure you try the school's french fries," he says.

I don't answer, but that doesn't seem to matter to him. He gossips about the other students despite the fact I have zero interest.

"Uh, Jake—"

"Josh."

"Don't you have to be home?" I ask.

A brief flash of pain creases his face before he shrugs. "Not really."

"Oh."

At five o'clock the librarian kicks us out, and Josh disappears. Typical. When my father arrives, he knows better than to ask about my day. We eat at a local diner and return to our hotel room. I sit by the window reading my book and watching traffic as my dad laughs at one of those ridiculous reality TV shows. Reality is *not* entertainment.

You'd think Josh would ignore me after my rude behavior, but you'd be wrong. He shows up in the library after school again.

I don't say a word or encourage him in any way as I do my homework. His stream of chatter seems endless.

"Michael Klein asked Jenna to the prom, and she said no," he says.

"Do you know Mr. Hedge can do fifty one-arm pushups? That's awesome for an old dude."

"Death Kombat Ten is coming out this Friday. And I'm gonna have the whole Prez's day weekend to play it. Three days of heaven. I can't wait."

I look up at this last comment. "Uh, Joe—"

"Josh."

"President's Day was two weekends ago. Today's February 28."

"Oh." He stares at me for a few uncomfortable seconds. "My friend Matt's addicted to video games. You're sitting in his favorite seat. He says it's the only place where the librarian can't see you."

A rough edge in his voice catches my interest. And despite my promise not to encourage him, I ask, "Matt? What's his last name?"

"James."

"Is he in any of my classes?"

"He used to be the captain of the swim team, and it bugged him I never learned how to swim."

He didn't answer my question. "Did he quit the team?"

Josh fiddles with his pencil. "No."

"Did he get cut?"

"Oh, no. He made the state finals last year." He notices my confusion. "He just doesn't swim anymore."

"Why not?"

"There was an… incident." Josh looks down at his homework. "What did you get for number ten?"

Matt was probably caught doing 'roids or drugs. And since I've learned it's best to stay uninvolved, I flip my Algebra folder open.

After a few weeks in town, my father rents an apartment with a loft. Now before you get too excited, he's done this a few times in the past, and it doesn't mean anything. It's not a sign that he might want to stay here for more than a couple months. Not at all.

"Look, sweetie," he says, raising the blinds in my "new" room, which is basically the loft. "You have a view of the river. I know how much you love a view."

I do. Tight quarters don't seem so bad with a decent view. And I'm surprised by how much I like the loft and having my very own level. I'm missing it already.

Despite my best efforts Josh doesn't give up, so I now have a friend. He manages to get a few personal details from me. Only child. Mother dead. Father unable to stay put.

In the library after school, I warn him. "Look, Jim—"

"Josh."

"I won't be here long. And when I leave, I'm not going to do the whole text/Facebook thing. I know how it goes. Lots of texts at first, and then more and more time will pass between replies until we're apologizing for not getting back to each other sooner, and then the messages will stop all together. Not worth the effort."

"Cold turkey, huh?"

"Yep."

"Do I get a warning, or will you just not show up one day?" he asks.

"You'll get a couple days notice. That's all I get." I try to keep the bitterness from my voice.

Josh looks glum and twirls his pen on the table. "Better than no notice. It sucks when you don't get a chance to say good-bye."

The librarian rounds the bookcase. Her annoyance causes the wrinkles on her face to multiply. Considering she's at least a hundred years old, I didn't think she had room for more lines. Go figure.

"Cell phones are not allowed in the Media Center, miss. Please turn yours off or leave." She stabs a gnarled finger at the exit.

I spread my hands wide, showing that they're empty. "I

don't—"

"Don't get smart with me, young lady. I might be old, but I know all about those ear things."

But she can see my ear, because my hair is pulled into a ponytail. It's straight and brown, so there's not much else I can do with it. I turn so she can see my other ear.

She squints and huffs. "I heard you back here talking so don't play cute with me."

She's lost her mind. I glance at Josh. But he's gone. Stifling a laugh at his cowardice, I apologize to her. She leaves muttering about "kids these days." Josh doesn't come back. Chicken.

"So why won't your father stay in one place?" Josh asks.

We're at our table in the library, doing homework. I consider ignoring the question—he's getting better at reading my moods and won't press the issue. But I'm curious to see what his reaction will be. Especially since I've never shared my theories with anyone.

"I think he's running away from grief," I say, keeping my voice low so the librarian doesn't accuse me of using my cell phone again.

Josh sits a little straighter in his chair. "Really?"

"Our nomadic existence started right after my mother died, and I recovered from my head injuries. I think the…excitement of moving, meeting new people, and starting a new job keeps him from thinking about my mom. But after the newness wears off, he has nothing to distract him, and so…we move again."

"Wow. That sucks for you. Running from grief…" He pulls a sketchpad from his backpack. The cover is almost torn off, and the metal spine has seen better days.

"I didn't know you liked to draw," I say 'cause this isn't what I expected.

"I don't. I doodle." He sketches two figures. One looks like

179

a zombie-wolf hybrid that you'd see in a manga comic book. It's chasing the other who appears to be a normal guy.

"Who's that?" I ask, pointing to the monster.

"It's Grief."

I lean back. He's lost his mind.

"Like a personification," he says. He gives me his goofy grin. "I learned that in Comm Arts last week. A personification is… like Death. He's always a skeleton wearing a hood and black robe, carrying a scythe. Grief is his…younger brother. What weapon do you think he'd carry?" Josh looks up. "A knife?"

He sees the answer in my expression.

"Dumb question," he acknowledges. "Of course he'd have a knife. 'Cause Grief always goes right for the heart. One thrust and you're done." He gives Grief a long, wicked-looking dagger.

Josh's had some personal experience with grief. My mom's been gone two years, and when I think about her, it's like Josh says, a cold steel blade stabbing right through to my backbone. But I don't want to commiserate with him or anyone.

So I quickly backpedal. "The whole running-from-grief thing is probably nonsense. I'm sixteen. What do I know?"

My joke falls flat. There's a strange shine in his eyes. "A lot can happen in sixteen years. For some people, it's all they get."

Oh crap. Is he talking about his ex-swimmer friend Matt? Maybe the "incident" wasn't 'roids, but something more dire. I decide to stick with the original topic. "Well, I learned about people avoiding their feelings from the Internet. My dad fits the profile for someone in denial. But that's just some website. It's probably wrong."

"The Internet knows everything," Josh says with a reverence only a sixteen-year-old boy could have. "Humanity is so screwed when the Internet becomes self-aware. You do know that, don't you?"

He sketches another mutation that's half human and half computer with big pointy teeth.

"You do know you're insane, don't you?" I ask.

"Oh yeah." He gives me a sad smile. "My friend Matt used to tell me that all the time. He also called me a genius." Full-out sorrow erases his smile. "Too bad I can't talk to him anymore."

Awkward. Very awkward. I don't want to know anything about Josh's personal life. That makes it harder when I leave. So instead, I say, "If you're such a genius, then why are you failing Algebra Two?"

"Albert Einstein had trouble in school."

"You're no Albert Einstein. At least, not yet. You need bushier hair."

"Tell that to my mom. She was nagging me to get it cut."

With that, we return to normal.

The next day, he asks, "Why don't you tell your dad how much you hate moving?"

"He knows how much I hate it. Doesn't matter."

"How does he know? Did you do the girlie thing?"

"What girlie thing?" I demand.

"You know. The silent treatment. Pouting. My mom does it all the time. Well, at least that's what my sister says she does."

"No. I'm not like that."

"Then how does he know? We guys can be pretty dense sometimes."

"I already know *that*, Jeff—"

"Josh." He grins.

I think back to all our moves and really can't recall telling my father how unhappy I am. We also never talk about Mom. Am I running from grief too?

New Girl

That night during dinner, I tell my dad about Josh. Since I never talk about school, he's surprised. But he's smart enough not to make a big deal about it or question me too much.

"Why don't you invite him over to watch a movie or something?" Dad asks. "We'll order pizza and wings."

"I can't."

Dad waits. His bushy eyebrows hover at the midpoint of his large forehead. Poor guy has only a few hairs doggedly clinging to his scalp. The silence goes on a little too long. I didn't realize how hard this would be.

"I can't be friends with Josh," I say. "'Cause, you know." I wave a hand.

"No, I don't know."

He's denser than Josh, and I didn't think that was possible. I huff. "'Cause we'll be moving in a couple months. No sense making friends. It's pointless."

"You can always email."

"And how many of *your* friends do you email?" I ask.

The answer is in his haunted gaze. Communicating with friends reminds him too much of Mom.

"As I said, pointless. Unless…"

He focuses on me.

"Unless we stay. I really like this place and the school. And I really…hate moving." There I said it!

"We'll stay. For a little while at least." He bustles around the kitchen, cleaning up the dinner dishes.

"How long?" I rub my temples.

Dad won't say.

The next day, I wake up with one of my migraines. Since the accident, I get them from time to time. Stress-related, or so the doctors claim. They might not be too far off—talking to my dad is always stressful.

After downing mass quantities of caffeine and aspirin that will dull the pain from OMG-I'm-ready-to-spew bad to just plain rotten, I head to school. It's better than hanging out in our lonely apartment all day.

When classes are over, I round the bookcases at the library and say, "Well, I took your advice—"

I stop. Josh isn't there. Some blond-haired guy is sitting in my seat.

"Took my advice?" he asks.

He's wearing a blue swim team hoodie, black jeans, and high tops. A jock. So what's he doing here? Is he Josh's friend?

"Sorry, I thought you were someone else."

He gives me the once over. His blue eyes are as pale as the winter sky. "Are you the new girl?"

"No, I'm the *newer* girl. The new girl is now the old girl."

Completely missing my sarcasm, he smiles and pushes the chair across from him out with his foot. "Have a seat."

"That's Josh's seat." Yes, I know it's a stupid thing to say.

His humor is gone in an instant. He surges to his feet. Anger pulses off him as he stares at me. I shrink back. He's tall, and the only other person in the library is the hundred-year-old librarian.

"You're one sick girl." He hefts his backpack and strides away.

I watch him go. That was…odd.

Josh doesn't show up the next couple of days. I'm not worried. I never see him during the day. Well, I don't usually look for him. I was just…concerned. I pay more attention to the school gossip than I usually do, hoping to hear if Josh is sick or something. But talk about an upcoming swim meet fills the halls, and how losing Matt really hurt the team.

When I spot Josh at his usual seat in the library, I pause a moment in relief before joining him. He's been gone three days.

"Hey, where've you been?" I ask.

"Did you miss me?"

"No. I enjoyed the quiet."

"Yeah, right. You were bored."

Pretty much, but I'm not gonna admit it. "Oh, not at all. Some jock was here. He asked me to the prom."

Josh laughs. "Yeah, right."

"He was sitting in my seat. Maybe it was your friend Matt?"

His humor disappears. "No. Matt doesn't come around here anymore."

I think back to Josh's earlier comments—the ones I paid attention to anyway. "Why not? Isn't Matt's your friend?"

"He was."

"Why aren't you friends anymore?"

"I did something...really stupid." Josh doodles on a clean page of his sketchbook. The jagged lines resemble waves.

"Does it have to do with the incident about the swim team?"

"Something like that," he mutters.

I know what I said about not getting involved, but I like Josh. "Is there some way you can apologize? If you've been good friends, I'm sure he'll forgive you."

"No. I ruined...everything." He shakes his head. "It's not possible." His pencil point breaks off. "Crap." He pulls out a pencil sharpener.

"What did you ruin?"

Concentrating on his pencil, he ignores me. I shrug and pretend to work on my homework as I listen to the crunch-squeal of the sharpener. The smell of pencil shavings reminds me of my

childhood. Getting ready for my very first day of school, I filled my pencil box and tucked my favorite book into my backpack. I love books. My mother used to read to me when I was little. All my childhood books are packed in a box that we lug from place to place. I never have time to unpack them.

As if Josh can read my mind, he asks, "Did you tell your dad that you hate moving?"

"Yeah."

He waits.

"Didn't change anything."

"Did you say it like a dozen times?"

"No, why?"

He rolls his eyes. "It takes at least that long for stuff to sink in. Even when my mom makes me repeat back to her what she just said, I've no idea what she wanted me to do."

"My dad was paying attention."

Josh flips to the page where the mutant zombie/wolfman is chasing my dad. "Did you explain your theory?"

"No. He's not gonna listen to me and my Internet diagnosis."

"How about talking to the school counselor? I hear she's pretty good, and she can—"

"Not gonna happen."

"Then you'll be moving soon. And when you're in your *new* school, talking to another nobody, you'll be sad that you didn't listen to my advice."

"I'll make sure to note it in my agenda that day." I pretend to write. "Jay. Was. Right."

"Josh." He smiles. "You're gonna run out of *J* names pretty soon."

"Not gonna happen."

The boxes show up after I've been at Dead President High

School for three months. They're scattered around the living room. Some are half full. Others packed and piled. I stand in the doorway half expecting to see Josh's mutant zombie/wolfman hiding behind the pile, waiting to ambush my father.

Dad strolls from his bedroom carrying two more packed boxes. He pauses when he sees me, but drops them onto the floor before he starts in with his lame excuses.

"...better opportunity for advancement...benefits...exciting challenge...almost double the salary..."

"I don't want to move," I say.

"Sweetie, this job—"

"Sounds like the one you have now. I like it here. Can't we stay until I graduate high school? Please?"

A queasy expression creases his face. He glances at the pile of boxes and tugs on his shirt. "No. Sorry, sweetie, but we have to go. We can't stay."

"You can't stay, but I can." I rush to explain. "With the next job, you can afford to rent this place and your next...whatever. I'll finish high school and then hang out with you the summer before I go to college. I can even get a part-time job this summer."

So many possibilities! I can get a library card and join a school club or team. My excitement rises until I see my dad twisting the bottom of his shirt as he stares at me in panic.

"You can't stay here all alone," he says

"I'll be seventeen soon. And you know I'm responsible."

"But...but...you'll be *all alone*."

Which means, *he'll* be all alone, and the answer is *no*. I swallow the lump of emotions lodged in my throat. College. I console myself with the knowledge that I can do all those fun things when I get to college.

"When are we leaving?" I press my fingertips into my temples, hoping to stop the migraine from building.

"Friday morning."

Three days to pack. Josh's words, *it sucks when you don't get a chance to say good-bye*, sound in my mind. At least, I'll be able to tell Josh.

Except the next day my migraine and Matt are back, and Josh is nowhere. I search the library just to be sure. Nope. Matt is sitting in my seat, but he's staring at the floor and playing with a blue and yellow scarf—the school's colors—pulling it through the fingers of his left hand.

I retreat to another table and take out my homework. I'm worried Josh won't show up before I leave. Then I won't get a chance to say good-bye. I realize I don't even have his cell number, home phone, or an address. What's the point in getting all those when you have no intention of using them?

"Hey, New Girl," Matt says. He's standing next to my table. "Sorry I yelled at you last week. When I heard Josh's name..."

"That's okay." What else could I say?

"Yeah, well..." He looks around. No one's here except the ancient librarian. "Lots of kids are named Josh." He shrugs. "I shouldn't have gotten mad."

"That's okay." Yep, I'm the queen of conversation.

"I should have known better. I mean, you're like a ghost around here. You wouldn't know Josh Martin."

"I'm a ghost?" It's all I can manage. I'd like to see you do better.

"You don't talk to anybody. Hiding in the library, talking on your cell phone. Friends from your last school, right?"

Too surprised to do anything else, I nod.

"You should try and make friends here," he says.

"I have a friend, and I do know Josh Martin. You used to be good friends. Right? But now you're mad at him."

His mood changes in an instant. "I could never be mad at Josh. You're crazy." He storms off.

Confused is an understatement.

But Matt's comments won't disappear, and when I combine them with Josh's, a scary thought forms in my mind. A shudder rips through me, sending my migraine to stratospheric levels of pain. I rest my head in my arms. Matt is right. I'm crazy.

The next day, I ask a couple of fringer girls about what happened between Josh and Matt.

They give me these shocked looks.

"Something about the swim team?" I prod.

"You've been here three months and don't know? How lame is that?" the redhead with five nose piercings asks.

"Did you even *see* the memorials?" the other girl demands.

Fear curls inside my stomach. "Uh, no."

Redhead rolls her eyes. "You want to know what happened between them? A fall through the ice and death happened over Prez's Day weekend last year. Death tends to end a friendship *permanently.* Come on, Sara." She pulls her friend away.

I've been talking to a dead guy. *Yikes* isn't a strong enough word to describe how I feel. And I know what you're thinking. It's impossible. Yeah, well, I'm not going to worry about it right now. If I'm crazy, they'll put me away, and I won't have to move. Win-win.

My father isn't the only one running from grief. Josh's been running, too. That's why Josh liked talking to me—'cause I didn't know about Matt.

After school, Josh is once again missing in action. And I'm frantic. Which is funny, considering I didn't want to get involved.

But I have one day of school left, and I need to say good-bye to Josh. Yes, *need* to. For all my disdain about nobody being special, Josh is special.

He should know Matt isn't mad at him. Maybe then he won't pretend his friend is still alive. I log onto the library's computer to find Josh's address. Google, the search engine of last resort.

"Most of your stuff is packed, but you'll need to finish up tonight, so we can get an early start in the morning," my dad says when we get home.

"Tomorrow? But what about school?"

"I'll call them in the morning."

"No," I tell my father. "Not tomorrow, I need—"

"I'm not asking. We're leaving. Go pack." His tone borders on anger.

My own fury rises, and I see red. Which is way more than a visual thing. Although everything appears to have a reddish tint, my blood boils, and an intense surge of energy consumes me as well.

I yell and call him a coward for running from grief. "Eventually, Dad, it will catch up to you. By then, I'll be gone, and you'll be all *alone*. No friends. No family. Nobody." I throw my backpack down and rush out the door.

Sprinting through the streets, I have no idea where I'm going. I ignore the dull throb in my head, hoping it won't explode into another migraine. Eventually I end up walking along the river. Chunks of ice tumble in the quickly moving current. The edges of the river are slushy. Our neighbor last year warned me not to trust a frozen river, even if the crust appeared to be sturdy. I was polite enough not to tell her that every northern Midwestern school I've attended made students aware of the dangers of thin ice.

Up ahead, a white cross stands out against the surrounding gray twilight. My insides clench as I draw close. Plastic flowers, stuffed animals, and half-burnt candles cluster around the base of the cross. I glance at the name carved into the wood. A memorial for—

"Hey, New Girl."

I yell and jerk in surprise. Matt is standing behind me. His hands are tucked into the pockets of his hoodie.

"Sorry," he says. "I thought you heard me."

Too scattered to reply, I just gape at him.

Matt squats next to the memorial, straightens a couple teddy bears, and fixes a bouquet of flowers. "Why did you think I'd be mad at Josh?"

The big block letters on the cross consume my vision as black and white spots swarm in front of me.

"Are you all right?" Matt grabs my arm as I sway. "You better sit down."

My legs fold under me. I suck in deep breaths, hoping I don't pass out.

Josh's name, not Matt's marks the cross.

I've been talking to the wrong dead guy.

"You're an odd chic…girl," he says, settling next to me. We're near the edge of the steep bank.

He gazes at the river. "I've been thinking about what you said. And, you're right. I'm pissed at Josh. He knew better than to fool around on the ice. And he should have learned to swim." Matt picks up a rock and flings it into the water below us.

I regain my composure. "It wouldn't have mattered. It would have been too cold to swim. You only have—"

"That's bull. I get hot when I swim. I should have—" He fires another rock as if he can punish the water for taking Josh's life. "I should have jumped in after him."

"But you would have—"

"No, I wouldn't. I'm the fastest swimmer in the state. I could have pulled him out in seconds." He launches a few more rocks. "Instead I called 911 like an idiot and flagged down help." Sighing, he looks at me. "And why am I telling *you* all this?"

"'Cause I'm the new girl?"

He huffs in amusement before standing up. Wiping the dirt off his butt, he offers me a hand. "My mom will freak if I'm not home soon."

If Matt doesn't forgive Josh, Josh will be miserable and all alone when I leave.

"Wait," I say, stopping him before he walks away. "Josh is upset that you're mad at him. I know. You think I'm insane, but I've been hanging out with Josh—or rather his ghost in the library these last three months."

"No, you're beyond insane. You're a grade-A sicko." He turns.

"Then how do I know Josh liked to draw manga figures and play Death Kombat?"

He pauses. "Someone at school told you."

"Who? I haven't talked to anyone but you and Josh. You said it yourself."

"You're lying."

"Why would I lie? I'm leaving tomorrow for I-don't-even-know-where."

He spins back to me. "Then why do you care?"

"'Cause in the last two years, I haven't met anyone I've wanted to say good-bye to. And he won't come back until you're not mad at him."

"Stay away from me." He growls before striding away.

But I won't give up. I'm not going to slink back to the apartment to finish packing and leave without saying goodbye. Not this time. I'm done running from grief.

I race after Matt and grab his wrist. "Just listen, please."

"Get lost!" He breaks my grip with ease and pushes me away. Hard.

My feet slip on a patch of ice as I move to chase after him, throwing me off-balance. How did I get so close to the edge? I pinwheel my arms, but the next thing I know I'm falling, and waves rush up to greet me. The shock of the impact steals my breath.

I flounder before I remember I know how to swim. Except the icy water saps my strength. My legs turn numb as the river tosses me around. Panic sets in. I thrash, but with frozen limbs, it's too hard to swim. My soaked clothes pull me down.

"Hey, New Girl," a voice calls over the drum of the river.

Matt is cutting through the waves as if he's Michael Phelps. "Come on, move," he orders, grabbing my arm.

I make a few weak attempts.

"You going to give up, New Girl? Can't hack it, can you? You're beyond lame!"

I know *exactly* what he's doing. But it works. Anger fuels my efforts, and I kick to keep our heads above water.

The current drags us along as if we're a couple of bath toys. Matt holds me tightly, and we try to swim for shore. But the river is stronger. We're in trouble. My fear is dulled by the bone-aching numbness. All I want to do is give up and go to sleep.

A yell cuts through my icy stupor. People on the bank are waving and calling to us. A rope flies through the air. Matt catches it, but when the men on the bank pull, it slips from his hand.

Another attempt fails. But on the third throw, we both catch it. Clinging to the rope, we're fished from the river and wrapped in blankets by our rescuers. Shivers take control of my muscles. I plop onto the ground so I don't fall down.

Matt pushes through the press of people. He kneels next to me with an alarmed expression. "Did I—"

"No. I slipped." My teeth chatter. "You…c-couldn't…have saved him."

A wild look shines in his eyes.

"Water…c-colder last year. Josh…c-couldn't swim. I *can*."

192

A smile tugs at his lips. "You call *that* swimming?"

"I'm out…of practice."

"You. Are. Insane."

You know what happens next. Police, ambulance, hospital, and my father's panicked face as he barges into the ER. Questions, questions, and more questions. I make sure everyone knows Matt saved my life. I stay overnight in the hospital and spend the next day at home. The upside to all this is my dad stops packing. The downside is he keeps asking me questions about the swim that wasn't.

And a strange thing happens. We stay. My dad keeps his current job. The only annoying thing is we have weekly sessions with the school counselor. Boring.

The rest of the week, I go to the library, but Josh hasn't returned. It's quiet and lonely until Matt's swim practice is over. Then he shows up smelling of shampoo and chlorine. We attempt to do our homework, but always end up talking or going to the coffee shop down the street instead.

Two weeks later, I head toward my spot in the library and stop. Josh is there. I'm not sure if I should be scared or glad to see him. "Hey Jared—"

He laughs. "Josh."

"So where ya been?" I ask.

"Around."

I sit and take out my Algebra Two textbook. Just because he's dead doesn't mean we can't hang out. "How did you do in last week's chapter test?"

"An epic failure. You?"

"Not bad."

He looks at me. "So I guess you took my advice," he says.

New Girl

"You're no longer the new girl."

"Yeah. Thanks, Joel."

"Josh." Grinning, he pulls his sketchbook from his backpack and rips out a page. He pushes the sheet across the table toward me as if it's a huge effort. When he lets go, a high-pitched pop sounds. "For you."

I pick it up. It's a drawing of Grief lying on the ground with a dagger through its heart. Standing over it is a girl with her fist raised in triumph. I meet his gaze.

"Grief's not dead," he says. "But round one goes to you."

"What about you and Matt?" I ask.

"We're good. Thanks for your help."

I shrug. "That's what friends do, right?"

"Right. And you'll soon have lots of friends. Matt knows everybody." He glances at my Algebra textbook. "So what did you get for number three?"

A couple things click, and I realize Josh hasn't been hanging around to copy my homework.

"Do your own work, Josh."

"You called me Josh!"

"So?"

"You know what that means, don't you?"

"That you don't have to worry about Algebra Two anymore?"

"Yeah, and it's time for me to say good-bye."

"But I'm not leaving."

"I am."

"Oh." I swallow. "Thanks for the picture and for…everything." Tears threaten to spill.

"That's what friends do, right?"

"Right."

"Good-bye, Emma."

"Bye, Josh."

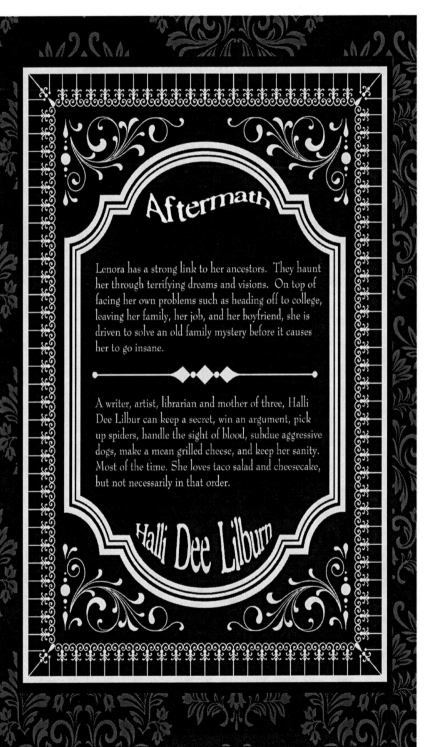

Aftermath

Lenora has a strong link to her ancestors. They haunt her through terrifying dreams and visions. On top of facing her own problems such as heading off to college, leaving her family, her job, and her boyfriend, she is driven to solve an old family mystery before it causes her to go insane.

A writer, artist, librarian and mother of three, Halli Dee Lilbur can keep a secret, win an argument, pick up spiders, handle the sight of blood, subdue aggressive dogs, make a mean grilled cheese, and keep her sanity. Most of the time. She loves taco salad and cheesecake, but not necessarily in that order.

Halli Dee Lilburn

Someone is haunting me. I see her in my dreams. She stands amidst a cluster of other girls, their filthy white dresses flowing around them, looking over the edge of a dusty cliff. Her green eyes tunnel into me, and I become her.

An alarm rings. Air raid! I run to the nearest pile of rubble to hide from the German bombers. This burnt-out building is all I have for protection, but it isn't enough. I cry out, knowing my life is about to end.

"I will take my secret to the grave. Basil must never be told the truth."

"Lenora, you'll be late for work." My mother's sing-song voice floats in on the morning breeze.

I freak out. I jump out of bed staring at the sky blue wallpaper and track lighting. How did this building survive the last blast? Where is the fire? Is the air raid still on? How can my mother still be alive?

Mom stares at me as if she doesn't know me. The alarm is still ringing. My reality slides back into place.

"I'm up." I yawn and fall back onto my forget-me-not blue duvet as Mother pads down the hall.

Work. I work at the sub shop down on Fourth. I have two weeks left before I move to Tallahassee to begin pre-med at Florida State. I don't live in war-torn England with someone named Basil. I don't have those bouncing blonde curls she has, the ghost who haunts my dreams each night.

I can't share this with anyone. I can't even share it with my boyfriend, Dylan. He knows I get these crazy dreams—giant spiders or gory axe killers. It bothers him how much I dream. He doesn't need to hear any more.

These dreams I can't escape. While I'm sitting at work, counting out slices of meat, doing dishes, or anything mundane, my mind reverts back to the ghost. Images flicker past my eyes like a badly edited movie, a war movie with choppy frames and a sepia tint. *Dirt is everywhere. Men fighting and trucks loaded with sullen-faced people. Bad teeth. Ripped wool scarves. White lace. Red lipstick.*

"Lenora, you there?"

I blink. The salami is still in my hands. "Sorry, I was trying to remember something."

My co-worker, Tracy, sits at the cash register, texting on her pink phone. "Like the day's count for salami?"

Mornings are always slow.

The door chime jingles as Dylan walks in. He usually stops by before his shift. What will he do when I leave for college? Will he carry on a long-distance relationship with me? So far he hasn't hinted at anything, and I'm starting to worry the next two weeks might be our last. The thought catches something inside my memory as if I've been through this before. *A group of miners with headlamps shuffling into the bright summer sun. One turns back and winks at Tracy. I look over to the cash register, and it's her. Blonde curls in pink ribbons. She returns the miner's wink before he vanishes.*

"Hey, good to see you too." Dylan leans against the glass sneeze-guard.

"What?" I look hard at Tracy. Her cell lights up with a new message. The ringtone is a church bell tolling.

"I said 'good to see you too.' You're a bit preoccupied with who knows what. Save any burnt cookies for me?"

Sometimes Tracy and I will overbake the cookies on purpose, so we have to throw out the whole batch. They taste just as good. "Uh no, sorry."

"Hmm. Well, I'll call you when I'm done work. We'll catch a flick or something." He backs up, waving. "See ya, guys."

Tracy waves without looking up.

"Hey, wait." It takes me a moment to realize he's leaving. "I'm sorry. I was hungry this morning. I'll burn a new batch..."

He's already pushing the door open with his back, the chime jingling. "No worries."

Tracy's phone tolls. *Dong. Dong. Dong.*

The movie is disturbing. It's about a girl who gets committed to an insane asylum.

"You always take things too personally," Dylan says.

"What do you mean?"

"You are not the girl in the movie."

I change the subject. "What do you know about the World Wars?"

"Which one?"

"I'm not sure..."

He chuckles. He does that when he doesn't understand me.

Aftermath

"Look it up later. Want some more popcorn?"

"No thanks." I will find out later. I'll be learning all about it in my dreams.

Hands twist in pain. Blood stains her dress. Long fingernails break as they scratch into the dirt. Letters emerge in the hard ground. D-o-l-e-. A name. An old family name she doesn't want forgotten.

I focus on the girl's ghostly white face, trying to keep the dream from fading. I want to ask who she is, but I already know. She is one of my sisters.

The rest of us watch helplessly as the stain on her dress spreads. She raises her head. She cannot speak. Her mouth is full of dirt. She has no eyes. I shudder. Her head falls back into the dirt, lifeless. Her finger's still stuck in the earth where she carved the name. Dole.

My eyes snap open, and I draw in a shaky breath. I stumble downstairs to the display case in the living room where we keep the Hansen family Bible. My father usually keeps the case locked, but I am in luck. Today he must have cleaned the glass and left the latch undone. It isn't that I'm forbidden to touch it. He just wants to keep it well preserved. One touch, and the oil on my fingers will slowly erode the parchment. I wear gloves when I take the display cover off. Elaborate oak branches dance across the parchment with ancestral Hansen pictures nestled between the foliage. When the dates precede photography, the faces become drawings of Hansens. And records. Hansen's father and his father's father. How much land they owned and how it was divided when they died. The wives' names are written off to the side.

When my mother enters the room, I jump.

"Did your father say you could take that out?" she asks.

No point in hiding it. "Do we have any Doles in the family tree?"

"Not on my side. But I'm sure there are some in there." She peers over my shoulder and pushes a page back with her sleeve.

"There." She points. "Sarah Hansen was a Dole. Her son Basil was your great grandfather. They came to America after the Great War."

I stare at the portrait. Her hair is curly blonde, but too short. Too much flesh on the cheeks, but close enough to my ghost to be a relation.

The Folkestone mine is dark and tight.

"Fill yer boots, mates." The man's voice echoes through the darkness.

The boys are laying rail tracks to haul out carts of ore. Water drips steadily down the black walls. Twice it douses a lamp. The horse shivers. He's restless, stomping and snorting. He'd buck if there were room.

"You hold the horse. I'll set the track." The man hands off the reins.

"Thanks, Garret, you're a corker," the boy says.

Garret swings his hammer high overhead and brings it down hard. He drives the nail into the bedrock with a loud clang. The impact sends water spraying onto his coveralls. Something is wrong. There's too much water.

"Bring the lamp will you, lad?" Garret has the boy hold it as close to the tunnel's end as he dares. He punts the hammer hard against the rock. The wall of the mine cracks like gunfire. Water sprays onto his boots.

"This will be the last load tonight, boys. Mary Anne will be wanting me to head home. This shaft may be flooded by the morrow. We'll need to pump it out." He passes the lamp back and encourages the horse to back up the steep shaft.

I wake, holding my arms up for protection. Protection from what, I can't remember. I check overhead, expecting something to fall on me, but nothing is there.

The truck grinds gears trying to downshift. Its tires spin in the mud as it claws its way over the rise. The town of Folkestone is lost to the fire. Mother and Father never made it out. My sisters' dresses are soiled. The white lace that once gleamed is now gray and will forever remain that way no matter how hard they scrub. Men in wool uniforms offer their hands to help us up and into the bed of the truck. I bump into a toothless stranger in a worn top hat. He eyes me as I sit on the floor of the cab. A homeless woman with two children under her cloak, and two scantily clad girls from the red-light district are sitting too close. I turn up my nose at the foul odors of sweat and urine.

I wince. "Sisters, let us pray this ordeal will be but a moment. When we arrive safely at uncle's, everything will be in order, and we shall think no more of this small sacrifice."

"If we arrive." Mary Ann moans, cupping her hands over her enormous belly. "I would prefer it be with my child still inside."

I don't have time for this. My summer is coming to a close. My life is about to change forever. I should be packing my stuff, getting my textbooks, and breaking up with Dylan, but the ghosts are too strong.

I cry just thinking about it. I have no way to solve my problems let alone the unfinished business of my ancestors.

I sit in front of my computer, my head nearly falling onto the keyboard. I am so tired. I am trying to find information about a trek across England during World War One. There are so many sites with guns, bombs, green wool uniforms, red poppies, muddy trenches. Everything I could ever dream of reading, yet nothing helps. The battles, the enemies, the victims are organized into lists a mile long. It's hopeless. Where is the image I saw last night? Of dark, dead trees lining an abandoned lane? Of the truck pulled over in a muddy ditch, the driver smoking while a woman, hidden in the tall grass, lies screaming? According to history, my dreams are not a documented part of the war. Apparently, the Internet doesn't know everything.

My fingers hover over the keys. My eyes are unfocused. *Mary Anne's baby cries, but Mary Anne is silent.* Silent as a one hundred-year-old grave. I change my search. I type "Mary Anne Dole death before 1920." A thousand pages pop up. Genealogy sites, British censuses, fruit manufacturing... I rub my sleepy eyes.

The alert beeps on my cell phone. It's Dylan.

U up? Wada u doin?

Some genealogy

That war stuff?

Yep

Y so keen?

I pause. It's not really a secret, so I tell him.

My gr8 grandmothers ghost is haunting me

Huh?

Actually my gr8 gr8 gmother

I dont get it

Can't get it out of my mind even when I'm awake. Talk about it l8tr?

U ok?

Just tired.

And petrified to go to bed, petrified of what I might find in the tall grass in the ditch.

Nothing is left of the Dole family's flat on Harper Street. The foundation isn't even intact. Only a black crater remains. Am I even on the correct street? Yes, I must be, the fishmonger is still across the way. And there's the chapel on the hill, minus a roof. Will Garret come looking for me? Where do I go now?

I wake up, and my hands are dirty and cold, like hers. They're holding a baby.

"Agh!" I kick out. I hit my head on the headboard. As I bring my hands up, the baby in my arms wakes up. He floats into my face, and I scream again, boosting myself onto my pillow. The baby floats right through my head. His cry seems as if it's coming from inside my ears. I hit my head a second time.

I look down and see blood on my forget-me-not blue sheets. Mary Anne's blood. Forget me not.

The sun has not yet broken the surface of the horizon, but I won't sleep now. I tiptoe down to the computer and connect to the Internet. Hunched over the keys, I start at the top of my search list and slowly make my way down.

An hour later my mother enters the room in her housecoat.

"Aren't you going to get ready for work?" she asks.

"I called in sick. Tracy will take my shift."

"Oh, what's wrong?"

"I haven't been sleeping enough."

"Well, why don't you go back to bed?"

My bottom lip trembles at the thought. I hide behind my dark hair, hoping she won't notice. How can I tell her I'm afraid to sleep? Afraid to be awake? Afraid I'm crazy?

"Lenora, you don't look so good." Dylan is here. Tentatively, he stretches his arm out, but if he's aiming for my shoulders, he misses and slowly rests it on the back of my chair. "I spoke with

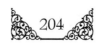

your mother—"

"What? Why did you do that?" I rub my eyes, but I don't look at him.

"Because there's something we need to talk about. You've been avoiding the topic, but there's no time left."

I had to tell him. "Dylan, I am so freaked out."

"So am I."

"I don't know why I'm having these visions. They're making me crazy."

"Am I losing you?"

I stop. My heart flutters like it is dying. I breathe out, hoping in the next second or two I can breathe back in again. "What do you mean?" I ask.

"It's a simple question. Am I?"

Yes. My mind is not my own. It's lost with a wandering girl holding a baby that is not hers. My heart is not my own. I'm standing in a muddy ditch somewhere I've never been by a road outside London.

Yes, I am going away to university. Going to focus on my future education and career where there is no room for petty high-school crushes. Time to grow up. Time to earn my independence. I'm going to miss you, Dylan.

My insignificant problems are nothing compared to those of Sarah and Mary Anne Dole.

"Can I show you something?" I ask. He thinks I've changed the subject or evaded his question, but I haven't. I need to explain my answer because it's so complicated. It's not a *yes* or a *no*.

He nods. I lead him downstairs to the Hansen family Bible. This time the case is locked, but the Bible is open to the same page that I last flipped to. Even though I wore gloves, I can practically see my oily fingerprints imprinted on the parchment, eating at the pinched leather like acid. I imagine the sizzle as steam rises from

Hamen Family

Richard Hamen
1881-1932

Sarah Dale Hamen
1904-1967

Annie Hamen Honeberg
1922-

Edward Honeberg
1920-1979

Basil Hamen
1918-1989

Lolita Gonzales Hamen
1920-1999

Darwin Hamen
1945-2006

David Hamen
1945-2004

Basil Honeberg
1952-

Gloria Montez Hamen
1939-

where I interfered with the eternal state of my family tree. One telltale print lies right under the name Sarah Dole Hansen.

Dylan studies the names scrawled on each green leaf. He looks confused. "Is that who's haunting you?"

"I don't know. There's this girl, Sarah. I see her hiding in a church with no roof. She's holding a tiny baby that her sister died giving birth to. She's waiting for a man named Garret to come and save her, but he never comes. She's going to starve to death if she stays there."

I blank out.

My white shawl is a tattered mess. The baby squirms and kicks it off. Doesn't he know he'll freeze if he keeps doing that? I tie it more tightly around him. I stir a mixture of flour and water in a fish tin with my finger and stick it into his mouth. He pulls away, kicking at the shawl, but this time the knot holds. He arches his back, and I almost drop him. Where is Garret?

A car engine rumbles somewhere down the street. I pray to God that it's him. I struggle to stand, limping from lack of circulation. I step over the broken threshold of the church and look out. A black Model T is winding its way through the rubble—an American car? Garret can't afford a Model T. It can't be him. I sit on a broken slab of concrete and sob. No, no, no.

A strong hand softly touches my cheek. I look up through my tears. A man in a tan trench coat and fedora stands in front of me. He has an old flashbulb camera strung around his neck. His dark brows are creased with worry.

"Garret?" I shake myself awake.

"Who is Garret?" the man asks.

I blink. It's Dylan. He's wearing the hat, trench coat, and camera. I gasp, blinking him back into his jeans and T-shirt. I'm lying on the floor, and my head is pounding.

"You fainted and hit your head. Lenora, you need to see a

doctor." Dylan scoops me up and puts me on the couch. "Don't move. I'll get your shoes."

"Right now?"

"Yes, right now. The walk-in clinic on Eighth Street is open on Saturdays."

"No, wait! Dylan, you have to understand. I'm not sick. There's nothing a doctor can do." The horrific visions are exposing something mysterious and unresolved in my family history. Even though I desperately want them to stop, I feel obligated to solve them.

He comes back and kisses my forehead, "What then? Do you want to talk to a psychic or something?"

"I don't believe in psychics." I groan with the pulsing pain in my head. "Can you get me some aspirin?"

"You'll be OK?" he asks.

"Sure." I fake a smile.

As soon as he leaves the room, I close my eyes, calling back the memory that isn't mine.

"Excuse me, miss, I'm with the New York Times. *I'm doing a piece on the aftermath of the war. May I take your photograph?"*

I don't answer him. Despair cascades over me like a heavy downpour. He sets up his camera and flashes a couple of shots. Something inside of me snaps in sync with the click of the camera.

"Will you take me with you?" I plead.

He lowers the camera. His eyes are as deep as the English Channel. "Are you married?"

"No."

"Where is the child's father?"

"He's not coming back."

We look at each other in silence. He breaks from my gaze and looks around to see if anyone has noticed us. The streets are desolate. We are alone. "What is your name, miss?"

"Sarah. And this is Basil."

I glance down at the baby in my arms, but he is gone. I panic for a second until I realize I'm back in my own body. I am my own self, Lenora Hansen. I mustn't forget that.

"Come on. We're going." Dylan helps me to my feet.

"Going where?" I ask.

"If you don't believe in psychics, then we'll go visit someone who does."

He doesn't have to tell me who he means. I already know.

Dylan's truck follows the main road out of town. He turns at a familiar corner onto a dirt road that leads up the side of Cemetery Hill. It's creepy that Gramma Hansen lives beside the cemetery. She says it's the safest place in town. But then, Gramma Hansen is crazy.

The ride jostles my brain inside my skull. I rub my temples. Branches whip against the windshield until a clearing opens in front of us. Gramma is out weeding in her garden. She tips the brim of her straw hat until her black eyes are visible. She shakes the dirt off her brown hands and waddles out to the front gate. Dylan asks me to wait until he can come around and help me. Here we go.

"*Nieta?* What is wrong with my *nieta?*" Gramma never uses my name. She just calls me *granddaughter.* "The sun is too bright. Bring her inside."

"I'm fine, Gramma. I just have a headache."

She puts her hand on my forehead. "You are hot. Tell your man to get you a cup of water."

Gramma never speaks directly to Dylan. She says she will only acknowledge him if we get married. Another one of her odd behaviors. She once read his future for him, but neither of them will tell me.

Dylan runs the tap in the kitchen as I sit on the shabby, patchwork couch. A moment later he comes through the beaded curtain doorway holding the glass. Gramma takes it from him and gives it to me.

I take a small sip. All the while Gramma is staring at me with her small, black eyes. The skin around them is so wrinkled her eyelids nearly fall over and cover them up. I'm amazed she can still see through them.

"Have you done something to offend God?" she asks, gesturing her head toward Dylan.

"What? No, Gramma!" I don't dare look at Dylan in case he's laughing. "What has that got to do with my headache?"

"I am seeing if you are cursed. When I was your age, I was getting married, not skipping off to university. It is possible God is teaching you a lesson for being disobedient. So what have you done?"

"Nothing. I stole some cookies from work—"

"No, that is not it."

Dylan puts his hands on his hips, waiting for me to give a proper explanation. I rub my temples. "Gramma, I'm having visions of things from the past. Things that I think happened in Grandpa's family."

"Rest his soul." She crosses herself, making me roll my eyes. She slaps my shoulder, "Smarten up, *nieta*. Do not disrespect the old ways. You will need healing to purge your mind of these lost malevolent spirits. Lie down and tell me these dreams."

I look to Dylan. He nods. I put my feet up over the arm of the old couch.

I'm with the tall man, the reporter. His accent is so intriguing. He talks about the war, the heroes, and the casualties. The baby in my arms is sleeping. His eyelashes brush against his dumpling cheeks like butterfly wings. The hum of the car, the man's voice, and the breathing child put me to sleep.

"Take me with you," I say in my sleep.

"The Dock is jammed," he says. "There's no way out unless... Well, I know a way to make emigration a whole lot less messy. Of course, I'd never take advantage of such a pretty little thing like you."

"Of course you wouldn't." I sigh. "But the baby..."

"Lenora, what is the baby's name?" Gramma Hansen asks me.

"Basil."

"*Merced de Dios*. It is *mal de ojo*." Gramma crosses herself again. "Someone powerful from beyond the grave has looked upon your innocence with envy. Lenora, my dear child, you have been given the evil eye."

"I don't believe in this stuff, Gramma." I try to sit up, but she presses my shoulders back into the cushions.

"But I do. You have the fever, headache, and weeping. Next will come the blindness and then the madness. You must be healed. Have your man bring me an egg."

I don't have to tell Dylan. He gets up and goes back through the bead curtain. Gramma closes her eyes and begins whispering. When Dylan brings her the egg, she holds out her hand, keeping her eyes closed, and takes it without looking. She rolls the egg slowly from my forehead down to my stomach. I can't tell what she is saying. It's not English. It doesn't even sound Spanish. She rolls the egg again. She takes my glass of water and cracks the egg into it with one hand. She puts the glass under the couch.

Finally she opens her eyes, "You must call one of these dreams to you. Close your eyes."

I want the dream to come. I welcome it.

I am in a church, standing before a priest in a white robe. It reminds me of the white dresses of my sisters, and I wish I knew where they were. I sent them to bury Mary Anne's body. I was supposed to find Garret, but he disappeared the night of the bombing. I wish my sisters were here with me, although they probably wouldn't be happy with what I am doing. They would tell me I am foolish. They would try to stop me. Mary Anne is already gone. The others are missing. I might be the last. The youngest and last of the Dole daughters. My heart hits my sternum like a punch in the chest. This is not foolish. Waiting for Garret was foolish. He never came to claim his son.

I write my name on the legal certificate. Dole. I envision my hand scraping the name in dirt, like the last effort of my dead sister.

When I wake up, I'm crying. Dylan is stroking my hair. Gramma is studying the egg in the glass of water. She swirls it with her finger. I sure hope she doesn't make me drink it.

"You need the touch of the *curandera*—a healer—to guard against the ancestor who holds this jealousy of you."

"Can't you do it, Gramma?"

"I am not the one. It is not my blood, but your grandfather's. Rest his soul." She crosses herself.

"Can Dad?"

"If he had the touch, it would have worked long ago. No, a *curandera* must be a woman."

I have no aunts, no sisters, and no female cousins. Gramma Hansen knows this. "You must seek her out." She whispers to herself as she waddles over to her pedal sewing machine. She opens the top drawer and pulls out a red ribbon. "Tie this around your neck to avert the *curandera's* jealousy." She pats my cheek. "Now go. Tell your man to take you to her."

"But, Gramma, where is she?"

Gramma smiles until her eyes are hidden within layers of brown skin. "She is in your papa's book."

Annie Horseberg is the only Hansen girl on the open page

of the family Bible. Sarah's daughter. She is the one. There is no date of death, but how accurate is the book? Does my father keep it current? Does he even write in it at all? The black ink on the parchment is all in the same cursive hand, written with the same fountain pen. It's old—too old to be true. Annie has no daughters, unless they are written on the next page. I fiddle with the lock.

"Dad, can you please tell me where the key to the display case is?" My hand holding the phone is sweating. I have never asked for the key before.

He sighs. "Can it wait until I get home? Then I can help you."

He knows I am responsible enough, but I give up. I don't want to push him.

I try a different strategy. "Do you know if your great aunt is still alive?"

"Great Aunt Annie? Oh sure. She must be ninety by now. She lives with her son Basil down in, uh, Lubbock. We send her a postcard every Christmas."

"Basil?" my hand shakes. My vision blurs.

"Yeah, he was named after her brother. His address is in my desk at home."

"Thanks, Dad." I hang up the phone before I fade out of reality.

Thirty years have passed since I was in England. When they found out where I was, my two surviving sisters begged me to return Basil to his father, but money was so scarce, and I couldn't bear to give him up. Years later, after I learned Garret had been killed during D-Day, I burned all of his letters. I could never tell Basil I'd taken him away from his rightful father.

"Sarah, you are simply spiteful, not coming until now." The two old women sitting with me, teacups in hand, lace kerchiefs over

thinning hair, remind me of Mother.

"And this must be young Annie. We have only seen you in photographs. How beautiful you are."

"I am engaged." Annie beams and shows yet another photograph for the aunts to admire.

They titter. "Ooo, how handsome." And, "Such a lucky lad to win our Annie."

"And what about Basil? Why is he not here with you?"

"I've already explained. He couldn't shake his commitments with work. He sends his love."

My sisters are quiet for a moment. They sip their tea. "Does he know?" they ask.

"No, and he is never to know."

"Know what mother?" Annie asks.

Sarah's memories are frying my brain. I no longer know what's real.

I hold the phone in my hands again. "I can't just phone Lubbock. I have to go there."

"Why, Lenora?" My mother's voice over the line is thin and distorted.

"Because Gramma Hansen said I had to."

"Your Gramma Hansen is crazy."

I bet she's wanted to say that for years.

"I'm moving in a week, and I might not get the chance. She's ninety years old, she could die any day."

"Honey, you met Aunt Annie when you were little. Don't you remember?"

"I have? When?"

"When she had her first stroke. We thought she was going to die. We visited her in the hospital."

I faintly remember an old woman slumped in a wheelchair with the sun streaming through the atrium windows. "Did she touch me?"

"What do you mean?"

"Has she ever touched me?"

"Now that I think about it, I don't think she has. She wasn't really coherent last time. Why would that matter?"

Annie Horseberg must be the *curandera*. I need to go to her.

"Dylan said he would drive me."

"Lenora..."

"Don't lecture me, Mom. I'm moving out soon. I'll be living on my own. I can handle a little road trip."

She was quiet on the other end. She wouldn't argue with me the last week before she became an empty-nester. Besides, this problem wasn't hers to fix.

"OK," she said. "Be careful."

Be careful? How exactly do I do that?

"Can you control it? Make it turn on and off?" Dylan's fingers are wrapped around my hand.

The sun is low on the western horizon. We should have waited to leave in the morning, but I wanted to get packed and out of the house before my folks came home from work. I left them a note. I turn off my phone so they can't bug me.

"Not really. I can invite it, but I can't make it stop." I stare out my window, watching fields of rich, golden wheat rolling by. I don't want to look at Dylan. I feel like I'm using him, making him take me on this fantastical journey to settle the spirits of my dead ancestors, and when we get back, I'm going to dump him. The fact that I'm even holding his hand is giving him the wrong impression. I'm leading him on. I should stop, but I just can't let go. A tear falls from the corner of my eye.

Dylan sees it. "Everything OK?"

"Not really."

"'Nora, we need to talk about this whole—"

"Not right now. Not yet."

We watch the sun set in silence.

We find a roadside turn out and pull up the camper top. Crickets are singing under our feet. Stars are falling on our heads. I absorb Dylan like this is the last night of our lives. I can't help it. He's beautiful. He lays out the bedrolls head to foot.

"Don't kick me in the face when the dreams come." He smiles as if it's a joke.

I do kick him in the face. He pins down my legs before I remember where I am.

"What happened?" he asks.

"H-her b-body! I know where they t-took it!" I shiver with fear and cold. "It's raining!"

He hugs me to stop the shaking. "No, it's not. It's just the crickets."

I plug my ears. "The w-water is dripping on h-her. I c-can't see. There is n-no light. The mine. They threw her body down the mineshaft!"

Dylan doesn't let go. He falls asleep with his arms still around me.

"Mary Anne, is that you?"

We are standing in the doorway of room 207 in the extended care unit in the St. Rose Hospital in Lubbock. It has taken us all morning to find her.

"No, Mrs. Horseberg. I'm your nurse. I've brought some people to visit you." The nurse pushes back the flimsy curtain to reveal a tiny woman enveloped in quilts. She motions for the nurse to get her glasses from the bedside table.

"Oh, you're not Mary Anne. Your hair is too dark."

"My name is Lenora Hansen. I met you once when I was seven. I'm your nephew's daughter."

I wait for recognition to spread across her face, but it doesn't. She strains at the quilt under her chin, even though she doesn't have the strength to lift it. It's already as high as it will go before it covers her face.

The nurse whispers *Good luck* under her breath before she leaves.

"That's a lovely ribbon you have around your neck." The old woman sighs. "My brother married a Mexican woman who wore one of those."

I sit down beside her. "Your brother, Basil Hansen, was my great-grandfather."

Her eyes widen. "He is not a Hansen—not my brother."

I look to Dylan for help. He motions to hold her hand. The second my skin contacts hers, the room falls into darkness.

"Give me more rope," Annie calls up to the circle of light above her head.

If Mother knew what she was doing, she'd have a conniption. Annie looks down at the rope tied around the hips of her jeans. The light from her headlamp catches spatters of white water as it drips from the rocks. Curiosity killed the cat. So why was she doing this?

It's the hair. Basil always had the most beautiful hair. It grew in bouncy blond curls as bright as sunflowers, but hers was dull and straight like her father's. She had coveted his hair her whole life. Now he was married to that beautiful girl from Mexico, and their twins were dark like her and had curly hair like him. It's just not fair, especially on boys.

That was why she always wondered about Basil's parentage; otherwise she might not have believed what the aunts told her when they sneaked her into the cellar.

"Have you ever compared the dates of Basil's birth and your parent's marriage?" they ask.

"What is this all about?" Annie felt a bit claustrophobic in there with unfamiliar relatives and shelves of peach preserves.

"He is not hers. She stole him. Took him across the sea when she ran off with that reporter. We have never seen him since. Sarah was too afraid to bring him back here in case he learned the truth."

"Such a scandal," one says.

"We will never forgive ourselves for what we did." They begin blubbering like babies. The hankies come out, and they blow their noses like horns.

"Promise not to tell your mother."

Annie is skeptical. She doesn't believe their story, so she has to find out for herself. She never would have found the old shaft if it weren't for their detailed instructions. She gropes along the steep passage, securing her footing with each step.

"That's far enough," someone yells down. "We're bringing you back up."

"Just a few more feet," she shouts. "I can see the end." Her voice echoes through the hollow earth, melding with the drip-drip of water.

Her dim light focuses on something other than black rocks. Something pink. A tattered, faded ribbon. Her breath shakes, and she loses her footing, slipping a few inches over the pebbles. The stones roll down the slope and join the growing pile below. The tunnel has collapsed where the rail track disappears into a wall of rocks. She reaches for the nearest boulder and tips it over to reveal a scrap of gray lace covered in mildew. She heaves the next boulder out of the way and stifles a scream. An arm, a skeleton arm, hard and blackened with ninety years of rot. She cups her trembling hands over her mouth. One more rock pushed aside reveals the skull. Shreds of ribbon are still tied around a disintegrating, blonde curl. A blonde curl like Basil's.

"Pull me up!" Annie hides her panic. She promised the aunts not to tell. They can live with their shame.

"Find anything?" a voice asks.

"No, there's nothing."

I gasp. Dylan has pulled our hands apart. Annie is looking at me with tears in her eyes.

"You saw my memory." She weeps.

"Your aunts threw Mary Anne's body down the mineshaft."

"They had no money and no other way to bury her. They lied to Garret and told him she was in an unmarked grave in the Folkestone cemetery. Even when he saved up for a headstone, they remained silent. My whole life I have kept their secret. They made me promise never to tell anyone." She sniffed.

"You've been carrying this burden for so long."

"I'll carry it until I am released." Her frail hands poke out from the mass of blankets on her bed. Has she been hanging onto life until I found her? I close my eyes and try to summon the ghosts. They do not come. They have gone to their rest.

"Thank you, Aunt Annie. You have healed me."

"No child, you have healed me." Her smile fills my heart.

I hug her gently. She touches the red ribbon. I take it off and give it to her. She gives me one of her handmade quilts. I thank the nurse on our way out.

As we drive out of the city Dylan blurts out, "My brother helped me find a journeyman in Tallahassee who would honor all of my apprenticeship hours. I can get a transfer by next month."

I stare at his white knuckles and flushed face. He gulps, waiting for my reaction.

"Uh, what did you say?"

He pulls the truck over. "I got a job so I can come to Florida

with you."

I've never seen him so nervous. He takes my face in his hands. "Do you want me to?"

"Why didn't you tell me?"

He thinks I am angry. "Well, we never talked about it. You never said anything. I wasn't sure. I didn't know what you wanted."

I reach over and kiss him. "I love you." I surprise us both.

"I love you too."

I lean back and cover my smile with Annie's quilt. He gives a shaky sigh and pulls back onto the road. The wheat fields are neon bright in the August sun.

A couple of hours later I turn my cell phone back on. Dad calls within minutes.

"Lenora, have you been in to see Annie?"

"Yeah, we saw her around noon."

"Oh, honey, I'm so glad you did. Basil just called. Annie passed away about an hour ago. I'm sorry."

Tears fill my eyes. "It's OK. She was just waiting for me."

"What did she tell you?"

"We aren't Hansens, at least not by blood. We're Doles. There was a mix up in the aftermath of the war..."

Dylan takes my hand. I don't let go. Instead of stopping to sleep along the roadside, we decide to drive all night.

Tomorrow I'll start packing.

Phantom
of the
PROM

Psychic Sabine Rose from THE SEER series has
solved mysteries of tragic ghosts, toxic spirits and
malevolent magicians. But now she's faced with new
challenges—convincing her boyfriend Dominic to
take her to the prom and banishing an angry ghost
from a castle. With the help of good friends and her
spirit guide, Opal, she enters a creepy castle in search
of answers—and the ghost of a killer.

◆◆◆

Although Linda Joy Singleton can't magically
summon spirits, she can make characters and stories
appear with the touch of her fingers to her computer
keyboard. That, in her opinion, is the very best magic
of all.

Linda Joy Singleton

When I volunteered to help decorate the infamous Wilshire Castle for the prom, I hadn't talked to Dominic. I didn't know that to him "prom" was a four-letter word. The guy I love to the depths of my heart refused to take me.

It's just a dance, I tell myself as I slip into jeans and a baggy tee. I'll go anyway as an unpaid and underappreciated volunteer. Manny, my editor and friend, might even pity-dance with me. Dominic won't be there, but most of my friends will, and I *will* have fun. Without. Him.

No shock when Penny-Love—full name Penelope Lovell, my bestie and the royal highness of Sheridan High's social scene—drives up twenty-three minutes late. No apologies, just the question I hoped she wouldn't ask. "Where's Dominic?"

"Proms aren't his thing." I shrug as if it doesn't matter and slip into her car.

"But you've been going out forever. He has to take you."

"Not going to happen. But don't stress, I'll still go and help out."

"I was counting on his muscles today." Penny-Love taps her

223

finger on the steering wheel, frowning. "Sabine, how will we ever get that drafty, dusty castle ready by tomorrow without him? This is a disaster."

"Tsunamis, tornados, and earthquakes—those are disasters. A school prom doesn't even rate a number four on the disaster scale."

"It will if we don't get another strong guy." Penny-Love twists one of her copper curls. "Ransom can do most of the heavy lifting, but he needs help setting up the turrets. The tallest tower is twelve feet high and made of corrugated metal. Can't you persuade Dominic to change his mind? I thought he'd do anything for you."

I'd thought so too. Things had changed between us since his business had taken off. I hardly ever saw him anymore. Between tending to Nona's livestock in the morning and working late for his clients, he seemed to have time for everyone—except *me*.

P-L glances over from the driver's seat. "Do I detect trouble in hot-and-sizzling romance-land?"

"No. We're fine. But—" I shake my head. "Nothing. We're great."

She doesn't believe me, of course, and what's worse is I don't believe me either. But I shove doubts aside as we arrive at Wilshire Castle.

This year's prom theme is Castle Dreams. When the Wilshire estate offered us the castle ballroom for FREE (best four-letter word ever), the prom committee back-flipped for joy—most of them are cheerleaders. Not me. I'm more of a mascot.

Prom is tomorrow night. Cleaning and decorating will be a huge job.

A job I'd expected to share with Dominic.

But I guess not.

I've only seen Wilshire Castle from a distance, so I'm surprised how sorrowful it looks up close—a graying shade of forgotten. It's supposed to be haunted. I reach up to touch the patch of dark in

my blonde hair: the mark of a Seer. I've been able to see ghosts since I was a little girl, but I don't expect to see any today. Wilshire Castle is only a few decades old. A reproduction of a castle, not the real thing. Still, when we drive through the wrought-iron gates, I shiver.

Open your senses beyond the expected to see more than is visible, a familiar voice speaks inside my head.

"Not now, Opal," I mind-talk to my spirit guide. I'm the only one who can see her, so I have to be careful not to talk to her in public. She's bossy and has so much attitude you'd think when she lived more than three hundred years ago, she was a Mayan princess instead of a sacrificial peasant girl.

Disturbing vibrations imperil your aura, Opal warns. *Best heed my words or suffer a pyramid's weight of regret. Darkness looms ahead if you stray from silver threads of friendships.*

"Huh? Stray what?"

Beside me, Penny-Love unclips her seatbelt. "Did you say something?" she asks.

Did I? *Oops.*

"Opal, not now." I use my sternest mind-voice. "Pen doesn't believe in ghosts, but she does believe in crazy people, and I don't want her to think I'm flipping out."

What means this "flipping out?" Your language lacks a logical foundation.

I cover my mouth so I won't laugh. I'm the one who usually needs a dictionary to decipher our conversations. For once I've confused Opal, and it feels good. I know she means well, but my shivers are gone, and I have no sense of danger. I tell Opal to leave, promising to be careful.

Because really, what can be dangerous about decorating for a prom?

Penny-Love's new boyfriend Ransom is a nice guy. I'm surprised because she usually picks bad dudes wrapped in Trouble. Don't even ask about her last boyfriend. But this guy is…well… sweet. Ransom is a polite Southern boy—opening doors, offering to carry things, and gazing at Penny-Love as if she's the queen of his world. It makes me a little sad because Dominic's sweet to me too. And I miss him.

We get to work right away. And, man, is there work. It's like Wilshire Castle has been vacant for centuries, although Pen tells me it's only been a decade. "Since the tragedy," she says in a hushed tone as she hands me a broom.

"What tragedy?" My sixth sense must be off, because I'm not picking up any otherworldly vibes. Only dust, which makes me sneeze.

"I can't believe you don't know."

"All I heard is it might be haunted."

"Ignore those ridiculous rumors," Penny-Love scoffs. "Ghosts aren't real."

I could prove otherwise, but why shock her with reality? Most people are content to live their earth lives without ever seeing a ghost. Not me. Spirits are my normal, and even though I complain sometimes, I love my special connection to the other side.

"So what was the tragedy?" I ask.

"The dude who built this castle, Jeremiah Wilshire, murdered his wife. Everyone knows he buried her on this property, but no one's ever found the grave, so he wasn't even arrested. He lived alone for years until he fell down the stairs and died here."

My shivers return. Dizzy, I lean on the broom for balance. Darkness sweeps me somewhere else, back to another time in this ballroom, only the walls are newer with gilded-framed paintings, and high above the center of the ballroom, a chandelier glitters like cascading diamonds. A young bearded guy in a tux holds hands with a freckled red-headed girl wearing a lacy white gown. Bride and groom, I realize, warmed by the honey-sweetness of their love for each other. The groom draws his bride close, and she leans her head against his shoulder. They dance beneath the silvery shine of the chandelier.

"Sabine!"

The broom slips from my fingers at the snap of Ransom's voice.

"Are you all right?" he asks with a frown. "You didn't answer when I called you, and you look awfully pale."

"It's nothing. I'm fine."

"Are you sure? Can I get you some water?"

I shake my head, even more impressed with Penny-Love's boyfriend. I just hope he isn't too nice for her. Being around P-L is like climbing aboard a thrill ride—lots of fun, but you'd better buckle up securely and hold on tight.

Penny-Love calls Ransom back to a stack of metallic towers lying on the floor. This must be the heavy lifting P-L needed Dominic for, and this thought stabs me with sadness. I consider texting him, but I won't beg for his time. Besides, Ransom seems strong enough. He lifts the first metallic tower as if it's made of paper. The second goes up fast, too. But as he bends for the tallest and heaviest tower, I get a bad feeling. A vision flashes in my mind of the tower lurching sideways, tumbling down, and crashing onto Ransom.

I open my mouth to shout a warning. But it's too late.

Screams echo around the ballroom. Another sound bounces off the walls, too—gruff, mocking laughter.

When I turn toward the laughter, a strange man is standing so close to a wall mirror that he seems to be inside the glass. He

has short dark-brown hair, a trim brown beard, and narrowed demonic eyes. I recognize him from my vision, although he's older and deader. The ghost of Jeremiah Wilshire.

Even worse—he's staring back at me.

Good news: Ransom survives with only bruises and a nasty bump on his head.

Bad news: The ghost will strike again.

Jeremiah is one angry dead dude. Although he vanished without giving any hint of what he plans to do, his aura burned like lava, so he'll be back with vengeance. Wasn't killing his wife enough? You'd think dying would have cured him of being psycho. Guess not.

But why attack Ransom? Was it random or deliberate? Either way, a psycho ghost at the prom equals trouble. I wish I could warn Penny-Love, but I've worked hard to hide my psychic secret from her and don't want to be labeled a freak at school. Besides, she'd never believe me. Not even if a ghost spit in her face.

We work another hour, until the ballroom shines with cleanliness. Silver and purple streamers twist like royal vines along the walls and a giant banner "Castle Dreams Come True" sways high across the stage. All that's left to do is stock the kitchen with refreshments and put up the fallen turret. Penny-Love says she'll bring one of her brothers to help, and we agree to meet in the morning.

On the drive home, Pen raves about her prom dress, the hot new stylist who'll beautify her hair, and the limo Ransom hired to take us to the prom. But I'm hardly listening. I need to get rid of the psycho ghost before he does something worse than knock over a tower. Next time he might really hurt—even kill—someone.

"Who's doing your hair?" Penny-Love stops for a red light.

"Huh? Oh… for the prom?"

"Well, duh."

I shrug. "I haven't thought about it."

"That's because all you're thinking about is Dominic. You can't hide your feelings from me, Sabine. It sucks he won't take you to the prom."

"Well…" I let her think what she wants. "His work is important to him, especially starting a business in this economy. He's not in high school anymore, so I can't expect him to get excited about a school dance. Still—" I sigh. "I found an amazing prom dress, and now he won't even see me in it."

"Know what you should do?" P-L says with a wicked grin as the red light changes to green and she stomps the accelerator.

"I'm afraid to ask."

"Tell Dominic that if he doesn't take you to the prom, you'll dance with other guys. I'll bet Josh will be there. Nothing stirs up the jealousy juices better than an old boyfriend."

I shake my head. "Dominic and I don't play jealousy games. We trust each other."

"Sweet but bor-ring." Penny-Love purses her lips as if thinking deeply. "You know what puzzles me? Dominic's anti-prom attitude. Sure he's an outdoorsy guy, but he's not a coward. I can't see him letting you down like this without a good reason."

"His good reason is his work," I say with a weary sigh.

"Maybe," she says, but she doesn't sound convinced.

It hurts too much to think of my strapless chiffon prom dress with the tiny sequins trailing like stars in a golden sky. I found the perfect gold strappy heels, too, and planned to wear a gold chain with an oval diamond that my grandmother had given me for my seventeenth birthday. I'd been so sure Dominic would go with me that I bought the tickets without actually asking him. Until yesterday.

His refusal. My silent agony. I didn't cry then, but I might lose it if the prom topic comes up again. Unless we talk about prom for a non-personal reason. Like a psycho ghost.

Dominic has intuitive skills that could help with ghost-busting. He doesn't see ghosts, but he's tuned in to the other side and can communicate with animals. I smile as I imagine us driving to Wilshire Castle and taking down the ghost. Together.

When Penny-Love drops me off, Dominic's pickup truck is parked in its usual spot by the barn. Instead of going into the main house where I live with my grandmother, I head for Dominic's loft studio. I tap on the door, but get no answer. It isn't locked, so I enter. The combo living room-kitchenette shows evidence of Dominic—dirty dishes in the sink, a loaf of bread on the counter, and western boots by the couch. Biggest evidence is the lump underneath a blanket on the couch. Dominic.

He's curled on his side, his tanned rugged face softened by sleep. My feelings soften, too, as I gaze down at him. I reach down to gently push aside a curl of sandy-brown hair from his face. I feel such an overwhelming love for him that I can hardly breathe. I long to curl up beside him and hold him so tightly that he never leaves.

His eyelashes flutter. "Sabine?" he murmurs with a smile.

"Hey," I say. "How come you're sleeping on the couch?"

"Was I asleep?" He sits up, yawning. His blanket slips, and he's shirtless, wearing only his jeans. Blond chest hairs trail down to a rock-hard six-pack. Be still my lustful heart. Delicious naked images dance in my head.

"Want to crawl under my blanket?" Dominic invites.

My body begs me to answer *yes*, so I'm surprised when I say, "No. I have something important to discuss."

"Your loss," he teases.

"Don't tempt me." I sit beside him and squeeze his hand. "We

need to talk."

He frowns. "If it's about the prom, I'm really sorry, but I just can't go."

"I know." I bite my lip, trying hard to be understanding. "This *is* about the prom, but not about us. It's about the prom ghost." I tell him what happened at Wilshire Castle.

He shows no doubt when I describe the ghost. He believes me.

"If I can just talk to the ghost alone, I'm sure I can get rid of him," I explain.

"Do *not* go near that ghost again."

"We're decorating in the morning, so I have to be there. That's why I need to deal with this tonight. If I convince Jeremiah to go into the light, he'll be gone by morning. The prom can go on without any danger."

Dominic shakes his head. "No way. You're not going to a deserted castle alone."

"I don't plan to." I look into his blue eyes. "I want you to come with me tonight. Will you?"

He frowns. "I have a 6:00 a.m. job with a new client who owns three boarding stables. If this client likes what I do, it'll mean steady work, so I can afford to take more time off to be with you. But I have to get my gear ready. Sorry, Sabine. But I can't go."

"Can't or won't?" I turn away from him.

"Can't." He lightly touches my chin, turning me back toward him. "Sabine, you know I love you, and I'm working hard so we can have a good life together. I'm sorry if I can't be with you much right now. But it will get better. I promise. If I can get away for a few hours between jobs tomorrow, I'll help with the ghost and even prom decorating if you still need me."

"I always need you," I say with an ache of longing.

"Will you promise not to go out alone tonight?"

He'll stop me if I don't promise, so I nod. "Good." He smiles.

But if he could read my mind, he wouldn't look so relieved, because I'm still going to Wilshire Castle tonight.

Just not alone.

I wait till after dinner when Dominic is busy in the barn and my grandmother is working in her home office before hiking down my rural driveway.

"You're the best," I tell my partner-in-scheming and school newspaper editor, Manny DeVries, when his car pulls up beside me.

"That's what all the girls say," he teases.

I laugh. He's so full of himself, but not lying either. Girls are really into his confidence and dark handsome looks. We've never been romantic, just good friends, and he's one of the few people at Sheridan High I trust with my psychic secret.

"How could I resist a secret rendezvous at a castle?" Manny's dreadlocks woven with beads rattle as he gestures for me to climb into his Chevy. He points to a stack of printouts between our seats. "Want to hear what I found out about your ghost?"

I nod, fastening my seatbelt. Manny isn't only helping with transportation; he's got mad hacker skills.

"Jeremiah Wilshire married Hannah McDermish sixteen years ago, and they appeared happy except they couldn't have children. Hannah loved to collect princess figurines, so Jeremiah built her a fairytale castle fit for a princess. But after a few years, rumors spread about violent arguments. When Hannah vanished, her sister Beverly told the police she'd seen Jeremiah with a shovel. They searched the property, but the body was never found. Beverly accused Jeremiah of killing Hannah in a jealous rage. But he's dead now too—from a freak fall down the ballroom stairs—so no one knows what really happened."

"Except his ghost," I say.

"Murderous ghosts aren't the most reliable sources," Manny says. "Are you sure you want to confront him?"

"Ghosts don't scare me. I'm sure Jeremiah regrets what he did to his wife. That's why he's so angry. I'll convince him that his wife is waiting for him on the other side and he needs to cross over to tell her he's sorry."

"You think he's really sorry? Or a sick twisted killer?"

"Most ghosts aren't dangerous, just confused." I hope I'm right. Not only will I help Jeremiah, but I'll save the prom too.

When we reach Wilshire Castle, I ask Manny to wait in his car, but he pulls a macho act, insisting on protecting me. Like I'm the one who needs a bodyguard? I remind him that I can see ghosts and he can't. "I'll call you if I need help," I say, waving my cell phone.

I leave before he can argue and then retrieve the key I'd watched Penny-Love hide inside a faux rock. The castle foyer is dark, and I don't want to attract attention by flipping on the lights, so I pull out my flashlight. But the faint glow isn't bright enough to cut through the gloominess. I sense my spirit guide nearby, hovering silently.

Are my warnings no more than empty air to you? Opal scolds.

"I know what I'm doing," I assure her.

The knowledge of those attached to earth is diminutive.

"If you don't approve, then leave."

Unfortunately she takes me at my word. After she's gone, it's like the light in my aura has faded, and I'm alone in a dark, creepy castle.

Maybe not so alone, I realize when I push open the door to the ballroom and shivers prickle my skin. Across the dance floor on the staircase leading up to the second floor, a wispy outline of a man beckons to me.

Jeremiah Wilshire.

I get an urge to flee to the safety of Manny's car, but I came here to talk to Jeremiah, and I'm not wimping out. He's only a ghost, and most ghosts have no more strength than a gust of wind. Still he did manage to topple a tower, so maybe he's stronger than most ghosts. Rage can be a powerful fuel.

When I'm near the staircase, I stop to face him.

"Hi, Jeremiah," I say in my calmest tone. I even manage a smile.

"Who are you?" His harsh voice seems to come from a long distance, although he's only an arm's reach from me. His black eyes narrow under dark brows.

"I'm Sabine Rose."

"You aren't dead, so how can you see me?"

"I've always been able to see ghosts." His burning anger drains some of my courage. "I-I came here to help you."

He snorts. "A little girl like you is going to help *me?* Fat chance."

I think back to my vision of him dancing with his wife. "I know about you…how much you loved your wife. You used to dance with her underneath the sparkling lights." I point up to the chandelier. "I know you never meant to hurt her."

"She's the one who hurt me!" He swirls down a step, and I stumble backwards. "Yeah, I loved her and gave her everything she wanted—but it wasn't enough. I warned her I'd kill her if she ever tried to leave me."

"Whatever happened… Well, it was a long time ago. You must let go of the past if you want to see your wife again."

"I've already seen her. She was here with you."

I gasp. "Impossible! I would have seen her like I'm seeing you."

"She's changed; she's younger and her voice is different, but her hair and freckles are the same."

"Where exactly did you see her?" I ask.

"Here—in the ballroom. But she ignored me, because she was with *him.*"

"Who?"

"The man who stole her from me."

"There weren't any other ghosts—only you."

"When I see that wife-stealer again, I'll do more than drop a tower on him." Jeremiah's aura swirls blood red. "He won't get off so lucky next time."

I stare at Jeremiah. "You pushed the tower on Ransom because you think he stole your wife?"

"I didn't push hard enough. He has no right to her."

"But she's dead."

"Liar! You held the ladder for her while she put up that banner." He points to the silver and purple "Castle Dreams" banner high over the stage.

"You can't possibly…that's crazy…you think Penny-Love is your wife?"

"Don't call her that silly name. Hannah is my wife, and I'll kill anyone who tries to keep her away from me."

He really is psycho, I think, glancing around and ready to run.

"She's not your wife. She doesn't even look like her except for the same color hair and freckles." I'm trying to sound calm, but my voice rises. "Her name is Penny Lovell, and Ransom is her boyfriend. They were just little kids when you died. Your wife would be much older than you if she was still alive."

"My. Wife. Is. Alive!" he roars, swirling down the stairs. His cold fingers clamp around my neck.

"Let go!" His grasp isn't solid like flesh, but his energy grips me until I pull away from him.

I spin around to run, but he blocks my way. "She couldn't see me, but you can."

"She'll be able to see you if you let go of your anger and go to the light," I say. "She's there waiting, and she'll forgive you if you tell her you're sorry."

"I'm not sorry. I'm going to kill the guy who took her from me."

"Ransom doesn't know your wife. You have to believe me. Don't hurt him—please!"

"Maybe I won't." A sly look crosses his misty face. "If you do what I ask."

I tense. "What?"

"Bring my wife to me."

"But I—"

"Tomorrow." His gaze holds mine. "Or the boy dies."

What am I going to do? I can't hand Penny-Love over to a vengeful ghost. She can't see ghosts anyway, so the whole idea is ridiculous. Jeremiah isn't only dead—he's delusional. How can Jeremiah think my friend is his dead wife? Doesn't he remember killing and burying Hannah? If only I could ask Hannah what happened. But she's probably already crossed over, and I've never been good at summoning spirits. I call out for Opal's help, only she's not listening. If I could find Hannah's grave, that might give me a strong connection to her soul. Yet if no one else could find her grave in more than a decade, how can I find it before Penny-Love returns in the morning? Besides, I can't stay any longer. I need to get back before I'm missed. Grave hunting will have to wait till tomorrow.

I join Manny in his car, and on the drive back, we try to come up with a plan. But it's a total plan fail. No ideas.

236

No surprise, I can't sleep. So I flip through the printouts Manny left with me. Names, dates, newspaper articles, financial information, and photos. Studying a photo of Jeremiah and Hannah on their wedding day, I can't understand how he can mistake this round-faced, dimpled girl-next-door type with dramatic, trendsetter Penny-Love. The only thing they have in common is hair color.

Sighing, I twist my long blonde hair into a braid and climb into bed, then jolt up when an idea hits me. I can't keep Penny-Love away from Wilshire Castle, but I *can* keep the ghost away from her with the right distraction.

It's a crazy idea, but when dealing with a psycho ghost, "crazy" might just work.

Ridiculously early the next morning, I dig through my closet, dresser drawers, and even under my bed—which is where I finally find it. The red wig I wore once to impersonate my half-sister Jade. It's not Hannah's shade, more crimson than copper, but in dim light it might do the trick. All I want to do is lure Jeremiah away from the ballroom for a while. It won't take long for Penny-Love and the other volunteers to finish.

I skip breakfast and hurry outside, hoping to show Dominic the printouts before he leaves for his first horseshoeing job. But his truck is already gone. When I hear Penny-Love's car rattling down the driveway, I glance at the papers in my hand. I don't want her to see them, so I hurry into the barn and leave them in the loft for Dominic. I send him a text saying I hope to see him later at the castle.

We have a smaller decorating crew, only Penny-Love, her oldest brother, Ransom, and me. While they work to make the towers secure, I say I'm going to organize the kitchen. Instead, I

search for the ghost.

"Jeremiah," I whisper as I peer into room after room.

I'm wearing the red wig, my head bent low, so the hair falls like a mask hiding my face. I look even less like Hannah than Penny-Love does, but I only need to confuse Jeremiah to (a) keep him away from the ballroom, and (b) persuade him to cross into the light.

Only I can't find the ghost. When I search through the castle, my skin remains goose bump free. Closing my eyes, I concentrate on Jeremiah. A vision slowly forms of a filmy figure kneeling on the ground, tracing his fingers on a smooth oblong rock. Not a rock, I realize as my inner-vision clarifies. A gravestone engraved: H-A-N-N-A-H.

I follow my intuitive GPS outside. Wilshire Castle is surrounded by thick woods and rolling hills dense with weeds. I take a path with a faint trail of gravel. I keep walking as if being pulled by an invisible rope, through shadows of oaks and around rocky outcroppings until I reach a meadow of yellow flowers. No weeds. And in the center of the meadow, Jeremiah huddles over the ground.

His ghostly shoulders shake as if he's crying.

"Jeremiah," I call out in a soft whisper, leaning forward so the red hair waves over my face.

He whirls around, his feet hovering over the ground. Anger shifts to a pale fog of shock. "You… You're here? Hannah?"

This is too easy, I think. Whatever. I go with it. "Yes. I'm worried about you."

When he moves closer, I hold up my hand. "Don't come any closer. Just listen."

His translucent form wavers to a stop. "I've missed you so much, Hanny. Why did you leave me?"

"You know what happened." I point to the grave just beyond

him.

"I didn't mean to hurt you."

"I know," I say in a forgiving voice.

"You hurt me more." A tear slips down his ghostly cheek. "I'm sorry my job kept me away so much. I tried so hard to make you happy. I bought you those princess statues and pretty clothes and everything you wanted. But it wasn't enough. Why did you cheat on me, Hannah?"

"I-I did?" My wig slips, but I hold it in place.

"I'll never forget coming home early to surprise you with flowers and reservations at your favorite restaurant—only I was the one surprised. You were putting your bags in *his* car." He aims a ghostly finger at me. "Leaving me after everything I did for you."

"That's terrible, but no excuse for what you did," I accuse.

"You killed me, Hannah." His voice breaks. "But I never stopped loving you. Then your sister told people I killed you. I wouldn't hurt you…not ever."

"How do you explain that?" I point to the grave.

"Revenge. I took away what you loved most."

Life, I think. He took away her life.

He's staring at me, frowning as if puzzled. "You're not Hannah. You're that psychic girl."

"You're right." Glad to end this horrible charade, I pull off the wig.

His face darkens. "You promised to bring Hannah to me."

"I can't do that. You're the only one who can find her, but you have to let go of all of this." I gesture toward the castle and then to the grave. "She's not in there anymore. She's in the light, waiting for you."

"You're lying!" His roar gusts into a wind that rips the wig from my hands and sends it flying across the meadow. "You let me think she was back."

239

"I had to stop you from killing anyone else," I say, backing away.

"I never killed anyone!" Another branch snaps and is swept up in his twisting fury. "I didn't mean to push that tower on your friend. It just happened when I got angry. When I was alive, I could control my temper. I didn't even yell when Hannah drove away with another man. I died inside, watching my love leave me. I stopped caring about anything when friends turned against me—accusing me of killing her."

I'm stunned by the realness of his words. "You didn't do it?"

"I would never harm my Hanny. But everyone believed her sister. No one believed me."

In my gut, I know he's telling the truth. "If you didn't kill her, what really happened? Where is Hannah?"

"I can answer that," a voice rings out.

When I whirl around, a middle-aged woman with reddish-silver hair is striding toward me. Her thin face is shadowed with circles beneath her sad eyes. At first I think she's the ghost of Hannah, but she's not the same woman from my vision. Besides, she's solid, not see-through, and very much alive. She's not alone, either.

My gaze shifts to the guy behind her.

Dominic.

The following conversation is beyond weird. As the only ghost-interpreter, I have to repeat everything Jeremiah says. Mostly, though, we listen to Beverly—not Hannah, but her sister.

"I thought you killed her," she says to Jeremiah, looking around uncertainly because she can't see him. "She showed me bruises and said you were abusing her. Then she disappeared, and I saw you carrying a shovel. A year after your death, she showed

up and confessed that it was her boyfriend who hit her. She said she'd made a horrible mistake by leaving you. She wanted me to go with her to see you, so she could tell you she was sorry. Instead I told her you'd died. She was heartbroken."

Only I can hear Jeremiah's low sobs. My heart breaks a little too.

Beverly explains that Hannah was already ill with cancer. She didn't have much time left and wanted to die quietly. "I visited her every day in the care home…but today was the last day." Beverly wipes away a tear. "She… She's gone."

She chokes up, so Dominic takes over. He says he read through Manny's printouts and realized Beverly's address was near the area he was working. He had a "feeling" she knew more about Hannah. But by the time he found her, Hannah had died.

"Beverly had no reason to keep Hannah's secret anymore," Dominic adds. "After she told me everything, I told her what I knew. Fortunately she believes in ghosts. She insisted on coming here when I told her about Jeremiah's ghost. But we got here and couldn't find you—until I heard a voice in my head telling me to following the gravel path in the woods."

"A voice?" I ask.

"A spirit woman," he answers with a knowing look at me. "She had a Spanish accent and spoke in a formal way like she was born a hundred years ago."

Three hundred years, I think, smiling. Opal is still watching out for me.

Jeremiah glides next to me. "Thank you for everything," he says, tears still shining through his ghostly form. "No use waiting around this old castle anymore. Hannah isn't coming back."

"One last question," I say as a bright light bursts around him. "Hannah isn't buried here. So who's in that grave?"

"Not who, but what." Jeremiah chuckles. "Hannah's princess

statues. The whole danged collection."

The ghost is gone, but there's still work to be done in Wilshire Castle.

Dominic comes inside to see if the guys need his help, but the towers are upright and gorgeous. I head for the kitchen to finish my duties, and Dominic says he has to return to work. I don't pressure him about going to the prom. We can't always be together, but that doesn't mean he loves me any less. Before he leaves, though, Penny-Love takes him aside for a private talk, and they won't tell me what it was about. Frustrating. When I ask Pen, she only flashes a wicked grin.

I'm exhausted when I finally go home. But there's no time for napping. My grandmother fixes my hair so it tumbles down my back in soft curls. She zips up my dress and tells me I'm beautiful. I smile, but inside I'm wishing Dominic were saying those words. He's still at work, though, and I'm okay with that.

Penny-Love and Ransom pick me up in a sleek white limo. My grandmother snaps a million photos, and I swear she's crying as she watches us drive away.

Wilshire Castle sparkles with lights and banners and is so beautiful no one will believe it was ever haunted. I go straight to the kitchen, planning to help there most of the night. Manny finds me and makes me promise to save him a dance.

"Sure," I say with a laugh. "If you're not too busy."

"Never too busy for you, Beany."

"Don't call her that," a voice interrupts. "Sabine doesn't like that nickname."

I turn, and there's Dominic, looking oh-so-handsome in a western suit—black cowboy hat, black vest over white dress shirt, and sexy tight black denim jeans.

"No prob, Nick." Manny chuckles as he leaves the room.

Left alone with Dominic, I smile up at him. "So…you're here."

"Wasn't easy, but well worth it." He grasps my hands. "You look beautiful."

My heart swells. "You look amazing yourself."

"Thanks to Penny-Love. I have a confession to make." He bites his lip. "My work isn't the only reason I said *no* to the prom. I'm an outdoor guy, not the type to wear a fancy tux and strangling tie. It seemed easier to skip the whole prom thing. Still I wanted to do it for you. When Pen demanded to know why I wasn't taking you, I told her. And she pulled out her phone. She found a place where I could rent a western suit. No tie or tux. I still had to juggle my work schedule. But I did. And here I am."

"Here you are." I smile into his face.

He tugs on my hand. "Sabine, would you like to dance?"

"I'd love it."

We move out of the kitchen into the ballroom, where we join other couples swaying to a slow song. I lean against Dominic's chest and have a vision of us dancing at our future anniversary party, even more in love.

Across the ballroom, another couple dances beneath the glittering chandelier to a beat of their own. Their feet don't touch the ground. But no one notices them. The only person in the ballroom able to see them has her eyes closed.

"Welcome home, Princess," the man whispers.

And they dance.

FUTURE

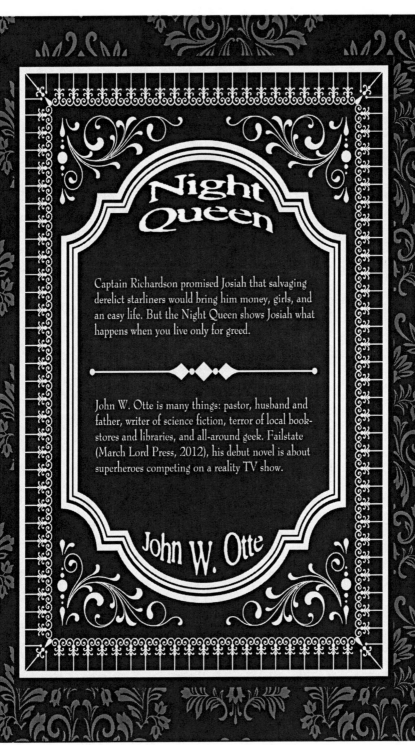

Night Queen

Captain Richardson promised Josiah that salvaging
derelict starliners would bring him money, girls, and
an easy life. But the Night Queen shows Josiah what
happens when you live only for greed.

Josiah W. Otte is many things: pastor, husband and
father, writer of science fiction, terror of local book-
stores and libraries, and all-around geek. Failstate
(March Lord Press, 2012), his debut novel is about
superheroes competing on a reality TV show.

John W. Otte

"Don't botch this up, kid." Captain Richardson's hot breath stung Josiah's ear. "You want to earn your share? Make sure your readings are solid, got it?"

Josiah tried to ignore the captain's looming presence. The man's breath alone was overpowering, a sickly mix of eggs and coleslaw. His constant need to badger Josiah didn't help. For a fleeting moment, Josiah wished he could elbow the old man in the gut to get him to back off.

"C'mon, Cap, ease up. You keep ridin' him that hard, he's liable to piss himself." Thompson, the demolitions expert, didn't look up from sharpening a knife that stretched the length of his forearm.

"We don't have room for error on this." Richardson smacked the back of Josiah's chair. "Do you know how much I paid to get this lead? We won't have an opportunity like this again. That's for certain."

Thompson snorted. "We ain't got much of an opportunity now. Right, kid?"

Josiah swallowed a groan and squeezed the bridge of his nose. He had never imagined a salvage run would be like this. The tri-vids at home had made it seem so glamorous: find derelict spacecraft, strip them for valuables, and sell to the highest bidder. Money, girls, adventure—everything Josiah had ever wanted— would finally be in his grasp. It'd be better than working at the family aquaponic farm the way Dad wanted him to. There'd be more money in wrecked ships than tilapia. So he'd gone to the nearest port, lied about his age, and shipped with the first captain to sign him. Now he was trapped in a contract with an abusive jerk. Josiah wished he could go back in time two months and slap some sense into his younger self.

Apparently Richardson wanted to help with the slapping part. Sharp pain flashed through the back of Josiah's skull. "Keep your eyes on the sensors, boy. I'm not paying you to daydream."

As if the captain would pay him. So far Josiah had helped salvage two tugs and an empty freighter, but Richardson had claimed Josiah's share as "training and boarding expenses." Josiah would probably wind up in debt to the captain by the time his contract was up.

"As ordered." Josiah forced the words through his clenched teeth. "What am I looking for again?"

"You'll know it when you see it." Richardson stomped over to the astrogation panel. "Arrival in five seconds. Look sharp, Thompson."

Thompson tossed his knife end over end and then snatched it out of the air. "Always, Cap."

A tremor wormed through the deck beneath Josiah, and the constant droning of the engines grew quiet, more sedate. Josiah leaned over the sensor readouts.

Once again, Richardson loomed behind him. "Well? What do you see?"

Josiah bit his lip, not wanting to answer honestly. The captain sounded so eager, so sure of himself, that Josiah wished he could say he saw something of interest. But no, all that was out there was a gas giant, with a small flock of three dozen orbiting moons, and—

Wait? What was that?

At first it looked like nothing more than a sensor ghost in the planet's rings. But once Josiah focused on the object, more details emerged. A large mass of heavy metals, much larger than the salvage vessel. What's more, the sensors detected the intermittent signal of an engine core, erratic but functional. A ship? If so, it was huge, large enough to carry thousands of people.

Josiah shook his head. Best not to keep the captain waiting. "I've got something."

Richardson sucked in a sharp breath. "ID?"

"Working on it." Josiah's slender fingers danced over the sensor controls. An image of the other vessel appeared on screen, a stately and sleek starliner with wide, glassed-in viewing galleries. Six engine bells flared from the stern.

Josiah frowned. He had seen images of this ship before but couldn't quite place it. He focused the visual sensors on the bow. Brilliant red letters stood out against the pristine white hull.

Ice sluiced through Josiah's veins. No way. It couldn't be.

"Yes?" Richardson's voice had dropped to a bare hiss.

"It's the *Night Queen*."

Thompson's knife clattered to the deck. Josiah couldn't blame him. Even though it had disappeared thirty-five years earlier, long before Josiah had been born, he knew the details. Launched from the Orion colonies, the *Night Queen* had carried 4,000 passengers, some of the wealthiest people in the galaxy, on a maiden voyage that ended when the ship vanished. He never imagined he'd be the one to find the lost starliner. Suddenly his dreams of quick wealth seemed like a distinct possibility.

"Excellent." Richardson's voice brimmed with excitement.

Thompson retrieved his knife from the floor and slipped it into a sheath at his hip. "Forgive me for saying it, Cap, but you don't seem all that surprised. You knew she was out here?"

"A Federate survey mission passed through here a month ago. One of the techs spotted the wreck but didn't get a good reading. He sold me the data, and it looked right. I figured it was worth a shot."

Thompson's expression soured. "If the Federates know about this…"

Richardson shook his head. "Let's just say I made sure the tech is willing to remain discreet. We've got a week before he'll report his findings, more than enough time to strip her to the hull."

Thompson's lips peeled back into a predatory grin.

Josiah shifted in his seat, glancing at the readings again. "Don't you think the passengers' families deserve to know what happened to their loved ones?"

The captain shrugged. "We'll inform them, but only after we've seen what's on board. Keep scanning. Leave the details to us."

Josiah turned back to the sensors, stung. He tried to focus on the data spooling by on the readout. And yet he couldn't stop thinking about the dead on board and those mourning them.

Three hours later, Josiah had scanned the entirety of the *Night Queen*, leaving him with too many unanswered questions.

"You done yet, boy?" Richardson asked.

The answer caught in Josiah's throat. He didn't want to share what he had found: that the *Night Queen* was in pristine condition.

No hull breaches, the engines hadn't overloaded, and all of the escape pods seemed to be in place. The paint hadn't even been chipped by micrometeorite collisions. The *Night Queen* appeared as if she had just left dry dock brand new. Even the engines were still on-line, powering the ship.

It made no sense. If everything was intact, why had she disappeared? More puzzling, if she had been orbiting this gas giant for the last three decades, why hadn't she sustained any damage? Needles of ice danced over his skin as he tried to decipher the mystery.

Captain Richardson, however, wasn't willing to wait. He shoved Josiah out of the way and leaned over the sensors. He hooted and pounded the console with his fist. "Excellent! If the interior is intact as well, we should get a good haul." The captain dropped into the pilot's seat, and his stubby fingers stabbed at the controls. "Let's dock and see what we can find."

A slight tremor in the deckplates tickled Josiah's feet. He frowned. Something felt off. Yes, the engines tended to rattle the ship, but that faded quickly. This time, the tremor turned to a shudder, then to shaking, then to a rocking that nearly pitched Josiah out of his seat.

"What's going on?" Richardson demanded. His fingers clawed at the piloting station, his knuckles white.

Josiah couldn't answer. His teeth ground together as the violent bucking intensified. The entire ship howled around him, starting as a low moaning that pitched higher and higher until a deafening shriek swirled through the bridge.

And then a voice, low and grating, the sound of massive rocks grinding together deep within a planetary core, spoke: "Leave us. You are not welcome."

"Says who?" Richardson shouted.

The voice repeated its message, so loudly that Josiah clapped

his hands over his ears. If this kept up, the ship would shake itself to pieces. In mere seconds, he would be sucked out into the vacuum, taking up orbit with the *Night Queen* around the planet. He laughed, a mirthless bark. He didn't even know the gas giant's name.

Silence sliced through the cacophony. The violent shimmy stopped. Josiah clung to the edge of his chair, expecting it to start again.

After a few moments of tense peace, Richardson hauled himself out of the pilot's chair. He turned to Thompson and jabbed a finger at him. "Go check the ship, make sure we're not venting atmosphere or anything." As soon as Thompson disappeared from the bridge, the captain whirled on Josiah. "What did you miss?"

Josiah glanced between the sensor console and the captain. "Nothing! There were some anomalies, sure, but there was nothing that would—"

Richardson yanked Josiah out of his chair and leaned over the sensor console. He scowled at the data readout for a few moments before snorting. "Thought so. What's that, genius?"

Josiah peeked over the captain's shoulder. A faint ion trail, probably caused by the engines of another ship, twisted through the system, heading for the *Night Queen*.

"From a Federate ship?" A guess, but Josiah hoped he was right.

Richardson shook his head. "No way. The fuel mix is all wrong for the Federates. No, I've seen this signature before. It's…" The captain's eyes narrowed to dangerous slits. "Sanchez."

Josiah's eyes widened. He had never met Sanchez, but the captain had spoken of her often enough. Richardson's former partner, she'd stabbed him in the back six years ago, cutting him out of the best salvage operation they'd ever run. Since then, she was always one step ahead of Richardson, claiming the best salvage and leaving him the crumbs.

The big man's hands spasmed into fists. "Thompson! We gotta move! If she thinks a little shake and shimmy is going to scare me off…"

"You think she did that?" The question escaped Josiah before he could think about it.

"Isn't it obvious? She hasn't been able to start her salvage operation yet. So she set up something to scare off the competition. We have to move fast, get in there and claim the wreck before she can return. Thompson!"

"Way ahead of you, Cap." Thompson handed Richardson a holstered weapon. "Ship is good. Whatever that was knocked some cans out of the galley cupboards. That's about all."

"Good." Richardson strapped on the gunbelt. "Let's get what's ours."

Josiah eyed the captain's gunbelt. Shouldn't he be armed too?

Thompson patted him on the shoulder. "Don't worry, kid. If you get scared, you can always hide behind me. I'll protect you."

Somehow Josiah didn't find that reassuring.

A rhythmic clanking echoed through the ship as the salvage vessel docked with the *Night Queen*. Josiah jumped at the sound, the muscles in his arms twisting painfully tight. Would they hear another angry command, ordering them to leave? When nothing happened, he relaxed, but only a little. His stomach tumbled at the thought of boarding the derelict.

Richardson slapped the back of Josiah's head again. "No daydreaming, boy. Get on the probe controls and see what we have."

Josiah rubbed his head to massage away the sharp sting. Ever since he'd discovered the ion trail, Richardson had been a coiled

spring. If they didn't board the *Night Queen* soon, Josiah worried the captain would snap.

Josiah slipped through the salvage vessel's narrow corridor and into the expansive cargo bay. He hesitated in the doorway for a moment, the deep shadows pressing down around him. A chill shimmied up his spine, radiating out through his arms. But he couldn't keep the captain waiting. A quick jog through the emptiness took him to the airlock hatch.

The probe, little more than a box on wheels, squatted next to the hatch. Josiah pulled on the virtual reality helmet and slipped on the control gloves. After he switched on the system, a hologram sprang to life inside the helmet, hovering before his face, an image of what the probe could "see" through its sensor. The airlock hatch towered over him, his own dark shadow looming across the pitted metal. Weaving his hand through the proper motions, Josiah ordered the hatch open, and the probe rolled through.

"We haven't got all day, boy. What are you waiting for?" Richardson's voice, though tinny through the helmet speakers, still carried enough venom to cause Josiah to wince.

"Equalizing pressure now," Josiah reported.

A hiss shot past the probe, and the doors to the *Night Queen* ground open. Josiah swallowed as a well-lit but empty hallway appeared before him. He ordered the probe forward, but it hesitated, as if it didn't want to enter the derelict alone. Josiah revved its engine, and finally it darted forward.

The probe skittered down the starliner's corridor, and Josiah swiveled its sensors left and right. The interior matched the exterior: the walls gleamed, the carpet looked untouched, and according to the atmospheric readings, the life support systems were still working. But beneath the virtual reality helmet, Josiah frowned. It all looked too perfect. Where had the passengers gone? The probe rolled by a corner lounge, the furniture, the decor, all in place, as if waiting for human occupancy.

Five minutes crept by, and the probe moved deeper into the *Night Queen*. By Josiah's count, the probe had passed sixteen cabins and an entrance to a promenade, but he still hadn't found any indication the *Night Queen* had ever been occupied. Had the passengers abandoned this part of the ship after the disaster? But if that were the case, why would they have cleaned up after themselves so thoroughly?

The probe rolled past a bank of escape pods, still in their berths. So the passengers hadn't abandoned ship. Josiah grunted. That would have explained a lot, but—

Josiah paused the probe to get a better look at the control bank. The whir of the probe's engines died, only to be replaced by the sound of footsteps behind him.

Josiah turned, lifting the helmet up to peek into the shadowed cargo bay. Nothing. And yet, he could still hear the footfalls, coming closer…

No, wait. *He* wasn't hearing footsteps. The probe was!

He tugged the helmet in place and frantically signaled for the probe to turn around. The wheels dug into the carpet, and the probe spun in place, even as the footsteps sounded louder and louder in the helmet. Josiah trained the sensors on the hallway behind the probe.

Nothing.

Josiah's breath thundered in his ears, filling the helmet. His heart ricocheted off his ribs. He squinted at the holographic images. Tense minutes unraveled until Josiah calmed himself. He shook his head. He must have imagined the whole thing. Taking several deep breaths to steady himself, Josiah ordered the probe to turn back around. The wheels hummed, and the images inside the helmet spun…

Only to come to rest on a small boy staring at the probe with wide eyes.

Josiah gasped. Whoever the boy was, he looked horrible. His clothing was little more than rags, his blond hair ratty and matted. His eyes, blue pools, shone in the bright light, his lower lip trembling. He spun and dashed down the corridor, disappearing around a corner.

"Hey, wait," Josiah cried, then snarled at his own stupidity. The boy couldn't hear him. He ordered the probe forward. It careened down the hall, almost tipping over as it shot around the corner—

A brilliant flash of light sliced through Josiah's eyes, accompanied by a loud shriek. He ripped off the helmet and tossed it onto the floor. He stared at it for a few moments, then cautiously picked it up and peeked inside. The holographic interface had gone dark, the signal from the probe lost. He looked up at the sealed airlock door, his breath ragged.

"What's going on down here?" Richardson stomped through the cargo bay, Thompson in his wake.

Josiah glanced down at the helmet, then up at the captain. "I think…I think something destroyed the probe."

Richardson's face screwed up into a scowl. "What did you do?"

"Nothing! The probe picked up footsteps, and then there was this little kid, but when I tried to catch up with him, a light flashed and—"

The captain glanced at Thompson, who rolled his eyes with a chuckle.

"Kid's just jumpy is all, Cap. Cut him some slack."

Heat flashed through Josiah. "I am not."

Richardson slammed into Josiah, driving him up against the bulkhead. Josiah squirmed under the captain's iron grip, but Richardson pressed a forearm against Josiah's throat.

"Do you know what's on that ship? Rare art by the Geoshan master Kirkwall. Uncut Orion gems. Twenty crates of six-hundred-year-old brandy from Earth Prime. And that's just in the cargo holds. No telling how much wealth is waiting for us just beyond that airlock. I'm not gonna let some vac-head, waste-of-atmosphere like you ruin this for me, got it? Now suck it up and let's get going."

"But the probe—"

"It's Sanchez! She must have rigged a trap, and you rolled the probe right into it."

"But—"

"Shut up! You'd better keep it together, got it?"

Josiah didn't meet the captain's wild gaze. Richardson snarled and pressed harder. Josiah winced but nodded. Richardson stepped back, allowing him to slide to the deck.

"I'm docking the cost of that probe from your cut."

Richardson stepped over him into the airlock. Thompson started to follow, but he paused, stretching out his hand to help Josiah up. Josiah grabbed hold and started to pull himself up, but Thompson let go. Josiah fell with a thud.

The demolitions expert laughed. "Keep up, kid. Wouldn't want the spooks to get you."

Thompson disappeared into the airlock. Josiah followed rubbing his rear. As soon as he got his cut, no matter how big it was, he was out of here. He just hoped he survived long enough to collect it.

"Deploying lock-pick." Thompson pressed a small lump of explosives against the cabin door, jammed a detonator into the gray goo, and took a step back.

Josiah rolled his eyes. Was Thompson going to make that dumb joke for every cabin?

With a muffled *whump*, the explosive blew a hole in the door. Thompson stuck his hand into the opening and forced the doors open. Richardson brushed past him into the cabin beyond. Thompson glanced at Josiah and made a grand, sweeping gesture with his arms as if welcoming him to high tea.

Richardson wasted no time. Once again he pulled the drawers from their slots and dumped them on the floor. He ripped the sheets from the bed and looked underneath. With a roar, he tipped over a bedside stand and kicked it across the room.

"Where is everything? Every cabin, empty."

Josiah looked away, not wanting to anger the captain further. By his count, they had ransacked a dozen cabins and found nothing. The beds were made, the lights on. They looked like images from an advertising brochure. But they hadn't found any luggage or any indication anyone had ever been in them.

Thompson leaned against the open doorframe, idly picking at his fingernails. "Maybe this part of the ship wasn't used?"

Richardson shook his head. "According to the records, the ship was booked full. No empty rooms. I don't get it."

Josiah glanced over Thompson's shoulder to the corridor beyond. He wanted nothing more than to leave the *Night Queen*, the planet, the entire system behind and look for something else.

"Let's move on. Next cabin." Richardson dusted off his hands.

Thompson saluted, smirking. "Got it, Cap."

Josiah sighed, nudging one of the overturned drawers with his toe.

"You have something to say, boy?"

He didn't meet the captain's gaze. "No, sir."

"I think you do. You've done nothing but sulk since we came on board. If you have an opinion, some insight into what we should be doing, now's the time to share it."

Josiah shrugged. "No, it's nothing. I just—"

Thompson bellowed from the hallway, an indistinct shout that suddenly bled into a blood-curdling scream. Richardson shoved past Josiah into the corridor. Josiah hesitated for a moment, casting one last look around the trashed cabin, and then followed the captain into the hall.

Richardson stood in front of a cabin door, staring at the explosives packed along the lock. But Thompson was nowhere to be seen. Instead, a detonator and his knife lay on the deck as if dropped. Josiah turned a full circle, looking for some sign of struggle, maybe scuff marks on the carpet. Nothing. The demolitions expert had simply vanished.

The captain picked up the knife and stared at the blade. Large chunks of the black metal were gone, as if melted away. Wisps of smoke curled from the blade. Richardson glanced at Josiah. Richardson's eyes grew wide, and he ripped the gun from his holster, aiming the weapon at Josiah.

Josiah threw up his hands. "What are you doing?"

"Behind you."

Josiah whirled and found the young boy staring up at him with wide eyes. How had the kid snuck up on them like that? Did he have something to do with Thompson's disappearance?

Richardson stomped forward, his eyes alight with fury. "Where's Thompson? What did you do to him?"

The boy took a step backward, as if getting ready to run. A crimson laser blast burned through the carpet at his feet.

"Don't move," Richardson roared. "You're not going anywhere until I find out—"

Josiah stepped between the captain and the boy, knocking the gun away. "What's the matter with you?"

Richardson snarled and tried to sidestep him. Josiah moved, spreading his arms to block the captain's way.

"I'm not going to let you hurt him," Josiah said. "Dock my

part of the haul if you have to, but can't you see that he's scared? He's only a kid."

For a moment, Richardson's features softened. He looked down at the gun, which dipped lower.

"I'm worried about Thompson too." Josiah wasn't lying, not really. "But this isn't the way."

Richardson nodded. He holstered his gun and slowly stepped around Josiah. "Sorry, kid. I'm just worried about my partner, and—"

Josiah turned. The boy had vanished once again. Richardson stared at the carpet. Even the burn mark from the laser had disappeared.

"Sanchez!" The captain spit the word like a curse. With an inarticulate roar, he stabbed the knife into the wall. The blade ricocheted off and clattered to the floor. "Where are you?"

The captain stormed off. Josiah jogged after him, not sure why he was following Richardson but not wanting to be left alone either.

They ran deeper into the ship, past closed cabin doors, a pristine dining room, the still-full swimming pool. Josiah catalogued it all as he ran. He didn't like it. They still hadn't found a single sign of the original passengers, the probe, the little boy, or Thompson. Worse, a heavy dread pressed down on him, as if the corridor walls were collapsing.

Richardson bellowed Sanchez's name, pausing only long enough to look in open rooms for his nemesis. He skidded to a halt in an open atrium.

A massive tree filled the open space, branches straining toward a clear dome. Beyond the dome, the swirling clouds of the gas giant danced. Several decks opened onto the room, each one brightly lit and seemingly empty. If Richardson noticed any of this, he didn't let on. He focused on the person standing at the base of the tree.

The woman had long black hair pulled back into a frayed ponytail. She wore a gray jumpsuit, tattered and soiled at the elbows and knees. Her face looked gaunt, her eyes shadowed, but they shone with a fierce fire. Josiah had never met her, but this had to be Sanchez.

"It's about time you showed up." Her voice was a low growl, with enough fire to burn Josiah. "What did you do to my ship?"

"What are you talking about?" Richardson stomped toward her.

"Don't play dumb with me, Bruce. I know what you did here, setting all those traps. What did you do with my crew and ship?"

Richardson sputtered. Josiah stepped to one side, hoping to remain unnoticed. Overhead, the lights on one level flickered and went out.

"I didn't do anything." Richardson's voice thundered through the atrium.

"Don't give me that. I don't know how you did it, that spooky voice that rattled my ship, the way my crew disappeared one by one, my ship vanishing too." Her gaze raked over the captain, her disgust palpable. "I always knew you were petty, but this—"

"Petty? You want to talk about petty?" Richardson stomped forward. "Who bribed that Federate patrol to impound my ship to get to the *Hemes Ascendant* first?"

Sanchez snorted. "All's fair, remember? Isn't that your motto?"

Josiah frowned up at the balconies overlooking the atrium. Another light had winked out.

"You learned well enough. You're always stealing my claims."

"Not my fault if you've slowed down, old man."

Yet another light went out. Now darkness ringed the upper decks overhead. Josiah took a step back. "Uh, Captain?"

"This isn't about speed. You're not stealing the *Night Queen*

263

from me. Get out!"

"Love to. Give me my ship back."

"I don't have your ship."

Sanchez blinked, surprise painted across her face. "You don't?"

"No!"

The shadows overhead boiled, swirling like smoke. Josiah gagged on a bitter taste that suddenly flooded his mouth. He wanted to run, but his feet felt bolted to the deck. "Captain…"

"Then I got here first." Sanchez jammed her fists on her hips. "This wreck is mine."

Richardson's head snapped back as if struck. "Now wait just a moment. I paid a lot to a Federate tech crew to find this wreck, and I'm—"

"The crew of the *Farseer*? Technician Isaac Parker?" Sanchez laughed. She crossed her arms over her chest. "I bet I gave him three times as much."

"You—" The captain's face purpled, and his hands clenched.

The darkness had woven together, obscuring the dome. Josiah bumped into the wall behind him. The entire mass swirled and writhed, tendrils of shadow dropping lower, swiping at the air over the bickering salvagers' heads.

"You're not stealing this from me. The *Night Queen* is mine." Richardson yanked his weapon from its holster and leveled it at Sanchez. "I should have done this a long time ago."

Sanchez laughed. "You don't have the guts, old man. Never have, never—"

A crimson laser bolt flashed past her cheek. The shadows rumbled overhead. Sanchez spun around the tree, emerging with a weapon of her own. Richardson dove for cover as she unleashed a few shots.

"Captain…" Josiah edged for the door, keeping one eye on the darkness overhead.

Richardson ignored him and leaped from his hiding place. Sanchez responded with a war cry of her own.

Then the darkness shattered, pouring down like water over the tree and the two salvagers. Richardson and Sanchez were knocked from their feet, swallowed up by shadows. Richardson shouted something at Josiah, but his words were overwhelmed by the roar of gale winds that practically ripped the tree from its perch.

Josiah froze, unable to move, as waves of shadow swirled through the room, coalescing into a towering pillar. And then Josiah felt it, unseen eyes boring through him. The phantasm bent low, tendrils snaking from its body, grasping for him.

A hunger rose up inside Josiah, a primal desire for more. More money, more respect, more of everything he deserved. A gasp burst from his mouth, and he closed his eyes. He wanted the *Night Queen*. She was his, as she should be. He could strip her to the hull, sell everything he could find, and be rich beyond his wildest—

He shook his head and opened his eyes. The darkness hovered mere centimeters in front of his face, hot breath washing over him. Josiah fell back a step, searching for a way out.

There! The little boy beckoned to Josiah from an open passageway. Josiah dove for the door, scooping up the child as he passed. The boy wrapped his arms around Josiah's neck and squeezed.

"It's going to be all right." Josiah hoped that wasn't a lie. He peeked over his shoulder. The shadow gobbled up the corridor. Rage, pure anger, screamed after them.

Josiah sprinted past doors that had been restored to their original condition, as if Thompson had never blown them open. Josiah wished he could stop to take a closer look, to make sure his eyes weren't tricking him. But the darkness wasn't slowing. Its pressure nipped at his heels, cold clawed at his back and neck.

 265

Josiah perked up when he saw the airlock. Just another twenty meters, and they'd be safe.

A wall of shadow burst from a nearby cabin, cutting off their escape route. Josiah dug in his heels and whirled, ready to run back, only to see the billowing column of darkness behind them.

Terror churned through his gut. This was it, then. He was surrounded, cut off completely. The darkness would devour him as it had Richardson and Sanchez. Probably Thompson and Sanchez's crew too. Worse, Josiah deserved it. He was no better than the others, even if he didn't want to believe it. He'd been just as greedy. In spite of his misgivings, he too had hoped to find riches on board. The only one innocent of all of this was the boy in his arms.

He scowled at the roiling darkness in front of him. "You can have me. But you can't have him. I won't let you."

A shadowy tentacle unwound, inching toward the boy.

"No, I said you can't have him!"

With a loud screech, the tendril disappeared into the darkness, which opened like a curtain, revealing an open corridor. Josiah stared down the hall. The path the probe had taken to the escape pods. Should he risk it?

He looked down at the boy. Yes, he should.

Josiah slunk down the hall, the darkness creeping along the wall on either side of him. Tiny wisps of shadow snaked out at them but didn't touch him or the boy. Josiah passed the spot where the probe had been destroyed. Not a shard remained.

His strength bled through his legs with every step. By the time he made it to the escape pods, he was ready to collapse. He set the boy inside the nearest one and turned to face the darkness. It snapped and flared, its rage washing over Josiah. Once again, its siren call wafted through his mind. Josiah groaned as images of wealth and power flitted through him. All he had to do was stay.

All he had to do was stay. All he had to do was...

His legs buckled beneath him, and he toppled backward into the escape pod. His head bounced off the cold metal floor, clearing his thoughts. He lunged for the large red button next to the door and mashed it with his fist.

The hatch sealed, and with a muffled boom, the escape pod rocketed away from the *Night Queen*. The sudden acceleration tossed Josiah into one of the padded couches. He struggled against the g-forces to drag himself to a porthole and peek outside.

Light erupted across the *Night Queen*'s hull, so bright Josiah had to shield his eyes with his hand. Then, an instant later, the light faded. When Josiah's vision cleared, the *Night Queen* had vanished along with the salvage vessel. Had the *Night Queen*'s engines propelled the ship out of orbit? Or maybe the shadow had consumed both vessels. Either way, he breathed a sigh of relief and leaned back on the bench.

"So, do you have a name?" He turned to look at his companion, only to discover that the little boy had disappeared too.

Josiah stared at the empty bench. What the—? His mind churned with half-formed explanations as to where the boy had gone, but Josiah didn't want to consider any of them. He wrapped his arms around himself, leaned against the wall, and settled in for what could be a long wait.

Josiah lost count of how long he was in the escape pod. At first he thought he'd have plenty to eat. The pod was designed to hold twelve and was stocked with enough food for that many passengers. But within hours, the food rotted away, crumbling to dust in Josiah's hands. What little remained smelled so horrible Josiah didn't even want to touch it.

His stomach had turned into a painful knot by the time the

Federate survey vessel arrived to investigate Technician Parker's readings. The officers dutifully listened to his story, but Josiah could tell that they didn't believe him. Truth be told, he didn't really believe the story himself.

They brought him back to the nearest port, dropping both him and the escape pod in an empty cargo berth. When he asked, they explained that the pod was his rightful salvage.

Josiah was standing next to the pod, wondering what to do with it, when a dapper looking older man in a gray suit approached him.

"Are you the boy who claims he found the *Night Queen*?" the man asked.

Josiah frowned. "I just got here. How did you hear about that?"

"Gossip travels faster than the speed of light in ports like this, especially when the news pertains to the *Night Queen*. My name is Erik Chandler." He produced a business card. "I represent a man who is interested in all things related to the doomed starliner. When he heard you were in possession of a life pod, he demanded I make an offer immediately. Providing, of course, that the pod is genuine."

"See for yourself." Josiah waved at the pod.

Chandler crawled over every square centimeter of the pod. At first, he wore his skepticism openly, but as his examination continued, his demeanor changed. By the end, sweat beaded his forehead, and his hands trembled as he took notes on a personal data recorder.

"It would…it would appear that this is indeed what you claim." Chandler mopped his brow with a white handkerchief. "I am authorized to negotiate on behalf of my client. I'm sure that we can come to an equitable—"

Josiah held up a hand, cutting him off. "Name a price."

Chandler scribbled a number on a scrap of paper and handed it to him.

"Done." Josiah tucked it into his pocket.

"Don't you even want to see what the offer is?"

Josiah shrugged. "I'm sure it's more than I'd ask for. Nice doing business with you."

Chandler smiled, glancing at the escape pod. "So what's next for you? Going out on another salvage run?"

"No way. I'm done with salvage runs. And if I were your client, I wouldn't go looking for the *Night Queen*. That kind of greed only consumes you. Believe me, I know." Josiah turned and walked out of the bay. "Me, I'm going to buy the one thing I want most: a ticket home."

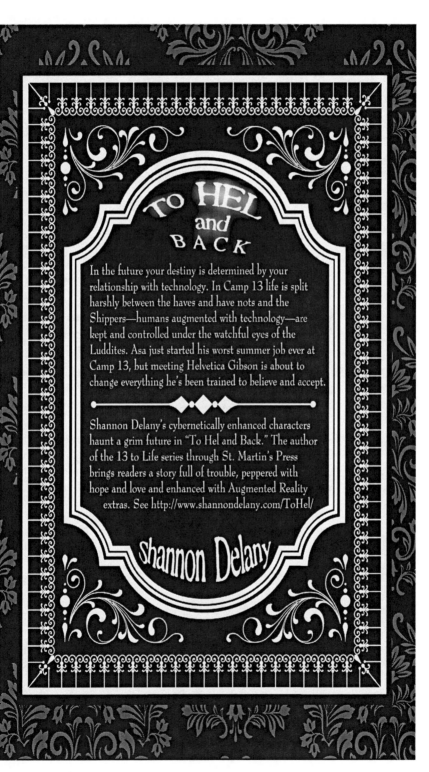

To HEL and BACK

In the future your destiny is determined by your relationship with technology. In Camp 13 life is split harshly between the haves and have nots and the Shippers—humans augmented with technology—are kept and controlled under the watchful eyes of the Luddites. Asa just started his worst summer job ever at Camp 13, but meeting Helvetica Gibson is about to change everything he's been trained to believe and accept.

Shannon Delany's cybernetically enhanced characters haunt a grim future in "To Hel and Back." The author of the 13 to Life series through St. Martin's Press brings readers a story full of trouble, peppered with hope and love and enhanced with Augmented Reality extras. See http://www.shannondelany.com/ToHel/

Shannon Delany

This story is embedded with Augmented Reality (AR) markers. Go to http://www.ShannonDelany.com/ToHel on a computer with an Internet connection and a webcam and click "Interact" to augment your reading experience. *Thanks to Karl Gee for creating this 3-D experience.*

In the blockhouse office, the camera on the X3 monitor switched from a wide shot of space, dark as diesel and spattered with lights, like the blinking bugs people wrongly called fireflies, to inside the ship readying to burn the space bridge.

I stumbled back from the counter at the sight of the Shipper in his dimly lit metal cradle. More machine than man, he was wired into his ship—chained like a dog through a cable at the base of his brain. My parents said that once he was a rock star, but they didn't mean he made music.

Once, he'd had it all.

Women, wine… *whatever.*

That was before the Luddites.

And the Camps.

The camera zoomed in on his scarred face, indigo light flickered across his features, painting an image straight from Hell. No spirit ghosted behind his eyes. The best pilot we had, and he might as well be dead.

A whirring noise broke my concentration. I blinked at a Shipper standing on the other side of the counter. Nearly as bad as the one on the screen, almost half metal. I forced my gaze beyond it and to the X3. "Light it up," I urged the ship. "Burn, baby, burn…"

Beside me Jared groused over the counter, "I can't give a key to *you*. Shippers can't carry keys. It's in the regs." He pointed at the book of laws that guides camps and all interactions with the Shippers.

The hum of mechanical parts increased. The Shipper leaned in. "I need the key."

"Then you *need* an escort." Jared elbowed me. "Take a key to Blockhouse 7."

"Now? But—" I pointed to the screen.

He thrust the iron key into my hand. "Magnetizing," he warned, waving an electronic wand over the key. "It's like you have a job, man."

I shoved the door open, and the Shipper's metal shoulder scraped the frame.

Lights blinked, the monitor screen fuzzed with static, and behind me the blockhouse filled with cursing.

"I'm missing the burning of Bridge Four-Two-Two, thanks to you," I told it—well, *her*, if face and boobs were any indication. She clumped along behind me, her human foot booted and soft-sounding compared to the hiss and drag of her mechanical one.

I wished we'd let them keep their full skins. I didn't need to see so much of them.

"If they kept them, how would we tell them from *us?*" Mother once asked, repressing a shiver.

Blockhouse 7 wasn't far. I might still have the satisfaction of seeing the bridge burn and know my parents' stocks were rising because an Einstein-Rosen bridge to a resource-rich system had been burned out. The burning, the last possible trip across the bridge, forced Shippers to use another space bridge—the one where my parents' claims sat. This was huge for my family. "Speed up."

A group of Shippers sputtered past, jerky and awkward, dust grinding in their gears. They didn't acknowledge me, or even her, in their zombie-like progress. Soulless. Without a spark of life.

"Apologies." The fiber-optic filaments, like short hair shrouding half her head, shimmered, running from white to purple as she pushed to keep up.

"Hurry, poppet."

Her head snapped up, her eyes glittering. Correction. Her *eye* glittering. The replacement fixture that took up most of one side of her face couldn't be considered an eye, could it? A spinning scope mounted in a mess of metal and mech, it glittered too, but in that creepy alien way Shippers had.

Although Shippers were anything *but* alien.

Still—creepy. This officially was my weirdest summer job yet. Three days in and it was sucking hard.

"It's important you see how Shippers live," Mother had said.

"Learn what makes them tick," Father snapped. "Know their flaws."

"And how dangerous they are," Mother agreed.

I understood the danger. I was ten when the Mechs rose up and the Shippers came to their aid.

"Poppet?" she asked. Her pace slowed. "Poppet means *puppet*, correct? A mindless doll controlled by the manipulations of another."

I shrugged. "It's what the guards call your kind. What's it matter? You're a Shipper."

"*Just* a Shipper, you mean."

They got so hung up on semantics.

Her neck clicked as she cocked her head. "How lucky that you are perfect. What do they call *you*?"

"Asa. You need to do this *now*?" I looked at the sky, watching for the bridge to flash into sight. *Don't pop*, I thought. *Not yet.*

"Apologies," she whispered amid the humming of gears and gadgets making up most of her right side. "The procedure is— necessary. My condition—"

"Whatever." I waved her to silence.

But flawed as she was, she kept talking. "—it is an anomaly."

She sounded—frightened? She was nearly as much metal as meat. Metal didn't get scared. Mechs feared nothing. Metal didn't feel.

Pop!

A flash like magnesium riding lightning set the heavens on fire with a blinding white.

"No! I missed it!"

"A-a-apologies," she stuttered.

"No, no, *no*!"

Something tumbled from the gray-green sky, a blur of feathers. At the Shipper's feet a bird lay dead, wings wide and eyes going dull.

Stooping, she swept it into her hands.

"I wouldn't…" The surviving birds were rumored to carry all sorts of diseases—what wouldn't after spending so much time in Earth's poisoned atmosphere?

She held it in her hands, her face lit like the statue of Mary standing guard at each Jubilation Centre's Pulpit.

Gears ground in her right elbow, and she closed her eye. Something snapped along her wrist joint, and electricity jumped from her to the bird. Stunned, it staggered to its feet and cocked its head in a nearly mechanical mimicry of her expression before leaping to the air with a cry of joy.

"I never… You gave it life."

She shrugged.

"You could have—"

"Let it die? That is not my way. Someday I will be like that bird. Someday I will fly. I will burn bridges from here to both ends of existence."

I stared at her a moment before inserting the key in Blockhouse 7. The door dilated.

"Hell's bells, poppet," the mechanic said from where he'd waited for the delivery of the key.

Startled, the Shipper stumbled, metal fingers clinking on the door's edge. Every light in the blockhouse flickered off and screamed back on so hot that bulbs burst. Sparks spun like fireworks.

"Quit touching things before you blow the entire camp," he said. "You and your mangled mech…"

Her hands tight against her body, she hung her head and shuffled inside to slump in a chair.

The mechanic, Silas (according to the badge hanging on one pocket), pushed past me. "Leave the key and go," he commanded, tugging on thick rubber gloves. He reached into a heap of tools on a nearby table. Some glowed—polished—and others were crusted with rust. Examining something with a cruel point under one of the few remaining bulbs, he grinned.

The Shipper looked away, yellow-green seeping like sickness into her fiber-optics.

My heart raced. "I want to watch the procedure."

"Go *now*," Silas growled.

"Whatever."

The Shipper raised her head, peering at me. "Asa," she said. "I am Helvetica Gibson. I thank you for your sacrifice."

"*Out*," Silas pointed.

I obeyed, and the door clanged shut behind me.

Inside the room, metal clinked against metal. I slipped around

the side of the blockhouse. I'd watch if I wanted to.

"Your kind doesn't rank last names—what's this Gibson crap?" Silas asked.

At the far end of the building was a window. And there…a crate… I dragged it over and climbed up. Too short. I turned it on its side, grabbing the windowsill when the crate wobbled beneath me.

Through the grime coating the glass, I saw Silas wielding a tool like a weapon, while she—*Helvetica*—cowered in the chair.

Tweaking a Shipper is like pulling the wings off a fly, they said. It didn't hurt anyone. Shippers were metal and meat. We were perfection, they were aberrations. The line between us was as clear as our distinctive destinies. That was the truth I'd been taught, passed down from the Pulpit.

But when she screamed, her head tossing, her eyes locking with mine, pain etched into her face, I realized even metal could give way and leave meat trembling.

I fell, and the entire camp tripped like one gigantic circuit had blown. Darkness descended.

The generators roared on, sound and light blaring, and I staggered to my feet. The door to the blockhouse hung open like a jaw gaping in a stupor. Inside, Helvetica was every bit the poppet, limp, lifeless, awaiting reanimation. My hand trembling, I felt her neck for a pulse. It raced beneath fevered skin.

Silas lay crumpled on the floor, the fingers of his rubber gloves melted, his face blackened by a blast. Breathing raggedly, he cursed like profanity was his first language as he dragged himself to his feet.

"The Mechs were easier…" he muttered. "No Geneva Protocol crap…" He glared. "Scrapping the Mechs was a no-brainer. But these…" Wincing, he closed his burned fingers into a fist and shook it at the unconscious Shipper. "Human DNA. Blood and bone beside circuits and servos. Every bleeding heart liberal thinks if there's a bit of humanity to them they deserve human rights."

He clutched a hammer, his brow knitting in pain. His eyebrows and lashes were gone as was the hair on his sooty arms. "Ask yourself—how much humanity makes you human and how much metal makes you just another murdering Mech?"

"Who has she murdered?" I asked.

"Give her time. She's soulless. No conscience."

"How do you know? Where's the soul found that she doesn't have one?"

"Not in *them*," he assured. "No soul, no spirit, no spark of the Divine." He hefted the hammer. "Step aside, and I'll deactivate it."

"*Deactivate?*" I stayed between them. "Whoa. No deactivating."

"What?"

"It's…not cost-effective to"—I swallowed hard—"*deactivate* a Shipper. Bridges burn faster than ever. We need Shippers to pilot an Aegis where we can't." I snorted. "Do *you* want to barrel across a bridge? Look what it's cost them. Almost every Shipper is born deformed. They require augmentation."

"The curse of the God for their arrogance" he said.

"Let them pay the price for human progress while we reap the benefits. Besides, they don't need souls to fly, just skills. Don't deactivate…*it*."

"No one will grant it a chance beyond this one," he warned. "Not even if the God directed them to do so. It's dangerous. Something's off in its wiring."

"So fix it."

"Think I haven't tried? It won't ground. Runs hot. Too much juice—could power a city, that one. Or blow like a star. Deactivation's best."

"No." I stood my ground. "I take responsibility."

"Who the hell do you think you are to shoulder that responsibility?"

I muttered, wanting to avoid the truth. I'd been assigned here under a name that kept me safe. A name that also gave me no power. And to save Helvetica from deactivation I needed power.

"Speak up, boy."

"I'm Asa Gray," I straightened my shoulders and pushed out my chest. "Son of County Prime Izhar."

"Identification."

I rolled up my sleeve, showing the single mark on my shoulder, the tattoo of the Blunted Star. Symbol of the star systems' hub and the United World Government.

"For a government brat you pulled one hell of a duty here—carrying keys. Piss off your old man?"

"Hardly." I stared at him. "I take responsibility," I repeated.

"Stubborn prick." He looked away with a snort. "Others made the same mistake with the pretty ones of their kind. But beauty must be found in the soul, Asa Gray. That thing's got no spot to house beauty at all."

Helvetica didn't act soulless. Two days after the compound had gone black, she returned to duty. "It is the indomitable nature of the human spirit," she explained.

Human spirit.

"Why do you do that?" I asked as we headed to her post.

"What?"

"You walk taller along the wall. Stretch up."

She paused, glancing from me to the huge wall that ran the camp's perimeter. "When they brought us here, I was nine."

"And?"

Bending, she examined the line where the wall's concrete base

joined the clear impact-proof plasticene that provided a view of the outside world. "I was too small to see out. I saw only"—she turned more gracefully than I would have thought possible with her heavy metal leg and foot and spread her arms to encompass the whole camp—"*this*."

Squat concrete buildings with ribbed metal roofs stacked a hundred deep across a treeless plain were wrapped tightly together by a wall that teased the shortest Shippers. A filthy sky smeared into the dust that made gears groan.

"I did everything to see out. Finally I grew. But—" Her eye fluttered shut. "Has it changed much? I have been here seven years. I remember flowers..."

She looked down, short hair falling across her eyes, soft and silky brown on the left, ethereal blue tendrils of fiber-optics tumbling across the spinning scope of her right. "I want to see it again."

"So look out."

"The wall is a lie. A projection." She paused as I processed the concept.

"Smoke and mirrors."

"Augmented eyes know," she whispered. "I want to see the truth."

Before thinking, I stepped forward and swept the hair back from her face, hooking it behind a perfectly human ear. "I'll help you see the truth again."

Beside the reflection of my own image in her eye, I saw fear and something else. Something that emboldened me as much as it frightened her.

Helvetica stumbled back. "I must get to my post…"

She left me, my hand hanging in midair, fingers more alive than they'd ever felt—all from the touch of her.

I waited outside her post until she finished her duty, only leaving briefly to accomplish the tasks Jared threw my way. Now that word had spread that County Prime Izhar's son was at Camp, my workload became more tolerable. That was important because I was on a quest.

Helvetica remembered flowers.

What girl didn't like flowers? What *girl*?

Although half of her was muttering motors and a tangle of wires, the other half was soft flesh and firm muscle. Somehow she seemed more together—more spirited—than any girl I'd met on the outside.

Did any amount of metal matter if beneath it you had compassion… spirit? Didn't *that* make us human?

My mind kept drifting to flowers, and I knew what I needed to do. If the wall was a lie and I couldn't get her outside to see the

truth—that spring rioted with blossoms just beyond the walls of Camp 13—I would bring the truth inside.

But there was no way to sneak flowers in for Helvetica.

She headed past me when the shift changed, but I caught her arm. "Come with me."

"I cannot," she said. "It is time for the Game."

"The Game?"

Her eye sparkled. "Come." She touched something that hung on a cord around her neck. It looked like one of the game console keys for the system I kept hidden in my closet at home: a vice my Luddite parents would never forgive.

I followed her to a large blockhouse near the camp's center. Inside was a ring of cradles: metal and rubberized half shells with wires springing from every seam. Connecting them, a system of curling cords fed into a cylindrical screen.

Along with her co-workers—other Shippers our age—Helvetica headed to a suspended cradle, climbing into it when it

descended. Pulling off the gaming key, she motioned me closer. The key slipped into a small console, and she tugged off her single boot, pressing both of her feet into a special board at the base of the cradle. Jacks sprang up, inserting themselves into a system of holes along the soles of her feet. I winced, but she laughed. "It tickles."

Helvetica lifted her shirt, exposing a bit of her stomach—skin and a material defying flesh or fabric. She lifted a flap of it and withdrew a connector to plug in another set of wires. "You can watch part of it. Your people call it the Game. We call it Atchen Tan."

"Atchen Tan?"

"It means *the stopping place*. It is as close to the outside as we get. Atchen Tan is a world of adventure. High fantasy."

"So Atchen Tan is…"

She lifted the hair at the nape of her neck, exposing one final port. "A reward for services rendered. An escape," she added softly.

I shivered—repulsed and intrigued all at once.

Sliding a wicked-looking needle into the back of her head, she jacked in, her eye rolling back as she sank into the cradle and entered a strange sort of sleep mode.

Images flickered across the screen as other Shippers joined the Game. Helvetica manifested on screen in a flowing medieval gown, her hair so long it fell around her shoulders in glittering waves of color. Sparks flickered around her head like a crazy halo. None of the others sparked and flared the way her image did—it was as if she lived in Atchen Tan as much as she lived in the real world.

Their characters materialized and then dissolved into the game realm, colored blips wandering a maze-like map as they adventured far from the reality of Camp 13. But I couldn't see any farther than the opening sequence and an overview of the map.

Unable to jack-in, I was locked out.

After an hour the colored blips on the map faded out, and with a noise like the seal of an airlock breaking, the Shippers jolted upright and aware in their cradles, tearing free of the needle and jacks. They grinned or grumbled about their experience.

"Well?" I asked Helvetica. "How was it?"

"Beautiful."

"Vet kicked ass," one of the others exclaimed. "Took down the two-faced tiger on Chingary's ninth level."

"It needed to be done."

"No one else could have done it."

"It's her *anomaly*," another added, smirking. "The Game doesn't know how to deal with a freak's coding."

Helvetica slid out of the cradle and reclaimed her key, slinging it around her neck in silence.

The other Shippers left. We were alone.

"*Vet?*" I asked.

She wrinkled her nose. "It is a nickname I do not care for. I am a veteran of nothing except someone's fantasy. It is not real life."

"Does it feel real—when you're inside?"

"Yes. Very much so."

"Then accept it as real. Maybe *this*"—I waved my hands at the dimly lit space crowded by cables and cords—"is the Game and Atchen Tan is reality."

She shook her head. "The Game…it is my world, but it is not reality. It cannot be."

"Why not?"

"There are no flowers in Atchen Tan. There should be flowers in reality."

I blinked.

"Here, take this but do not lose it." She slipped something off

the wall and into my hand. A game key. "It will not get you far, but you can explore a bit of Atchen Tan. Of course, if you do not *have* a system…"

I took the key in answer. "Why not give me yours?"

"Mine remembers my last play. I have worked hard on my quest. It is time you start a quest of your own, Asa Gray," she said, smiling.

"A quest of my own?" I grinned back, knowing I had one. "Can I rescue a fair maiden—or princess?"

She shrugged. "Not every quest includes a helpless girl. Some are only about finding your own path. And many princesses do not require rescue. We are not all kittens stuck in trees."

My gaming quest began with the best of intentions, but the key only allowed me into the Game's first stage. I could go no farther without augmentation. Frustrated, I returned to my original quest—flowers for Helvetica.

The next day I had a solution.

"You wanted flowers," I explained, pressing a small canister into her palm. "I can't bring you flowers. I doubt they'd grow in here anyway. So we'll make our own."

She squinted at me. "Make our own?"

I held her hand and the canister to point at the wall, pressing her finger so color shot free. She jumped back, her eye wide.

"Let's make our own beauty," I whispered.

"Our own beauty," she repeated. She turned back to the wall. "Yes. We will make something beautiful." She grabbed my arm, wrapping it around her and set my index finger on the canister's trigger as she leaned back against me. She pushed down on my finger, moving us back and forth.

I didn't pay attention to the design. My mouth was in her

hair, my body pressed to hers. The gray-green sky above seemed to glow.

At some point she began to hum—not the mechanics of her—those always hummed, but she hummed a tune, a small song that played on in my head in an infinite loop.

She stopped. My fingertip ached. How long had we…?

"Look." She stepped out of my grasp. "See how we've changed your world."

The wall had been transformed into an amazing mural: a seed had sprung open to reveal a tree whose branches became circuits on a board of tremendous complexity. Those circuits wound back into branches and roots and the seed itself—everything interconnected. Organic and artificial sharing one reality.

How could something with no soul create art?

"It's your world too," I murmured.

She shook her head. "How can this be my world when I have no rights in it? Atchen Tan is my world. This is only my reality. But I thank you for your sacrifice, Asa Gray."

I stared at her, stunned. Then I stepped forward and kissed her.

The canister fell from her hand.

"Oh, Hel," I murmured against her mouth.

She kissed me back.

I expected a blowout when I got to work the next day, but I didn't think it'd spiral out of control like it did.

"She did not do it," Hel protested, her body shielding a younger Shipper who cringed in the shadow of our mural.

The crowd grew and became thick with guards, each one dressed in riot gear and bristling with weapons.

"Step aside, Shipper," a guard ordered. "That one must pay

for defacement of government property."

The little one howled, human foot kicking as its metal hand grabbed Hel's leg, biting down on her flesh until she cried out. "No-o-o-o…" Sparks shot out of Hel, light dancing across her skin and circuitry and jumping in biting arcs to the guard who stood too close.

He convulsed and dropped to the ground, foaming at the mouth, his limbs flailing. His eyes rolled back. His breathing shuddered to a stop.

The other guards moved in, swarming around me like giant, angry beetles and blocking most of my view. My eyes were so wide they ached, and I nearly lost sight of reality. The memory of the Mech uprising—of the military streaming by in riot gear, of the fighting, and the blood, and the fear bled across my vision.

It was Hel who brought me back.

She screamed, tears streaking down her face as she dropped to her knees, reaching for the guard, sparks stuttering across her fingertips. "This is not my way."

"Get back," his partner yelled, bringing the butt of his gun down on her hand.

Sobbing, Hel pulled back her mangled hand and cradled it against her chest.

The guard raised his gun again.

I choked down shouts of *No!* and *Stop!* and, stunned to silence, watched the gun crash into her upturned face. Hel tumbled to the ground, unconscious and bleeding, beneath the beautiful thing we'd created together.

"It's deactivation for sure," Silas said, turning to me. "Like I said. Destiny. Mech equals murder. No matter how much meat she has on her, under her skin she's still part Mech."

The smaller Shipper curled in a ball, whimpering, "Helvetica Gibson, I thank you for your sacrifice," a moment before they dragged it away.

"Talk to me."

Shadowed by the mesh of a Faraday cage, Hel raised her head, the sound of gears louder than ever. She was more grounded than a mama's boy strangled by apron strings. Her systems worked sluggishly. She was harmless.

I'd come in off-shift, volunteering. The volunteer books were poorly kept when kept at all. Almost nobody volunteered to help Shippers. I was as unnoticed as I could be.

Hel pulled herself to a sitting position. Her cheekbone was bruised, and her hair was matted. It had been two days since they'd sentenced her to deactivation.

I'd done everything I could to fix things. I couldn't eat. I couldn't sleep.

At dinner one night Mother asked if I was lovesick. I just shook my head. I knew that couldn't be it. I was a wreck because I'd failed. I wasn't used to failure.

"Murder is murder," Father had proclaimed. It didn't matter that it was an accident or in defense of an innocent. All that mattered was what she was. At least to Luddites.

But she was more than we dared acknowledge. She wasn't the result of a curse. She wasn't some malfunctioning string of code. She was human and as perfectly flawed as any of us.

If she was human, she deserved human rights.

What had really happened when the Mechs turned on humanity—why had the Shippers joined the fight? Was it like what we'd been taught, or had history been rewritten by the winners? How would Luddites record *this*?

"I'm getting you out."

She flopped down with a grunt. "I might have saved him. I failed. Deactivate me."

"No. This can be fixed. We need time for them to see reason. I'll get you somewhere safe, and then we'll handle it all totally legally."

"Break the law to mend it? I cannot."

"You can." I pulled out a stolen wrench and attacked the Faraday cage control panel. No alarm sounded—none was installed.

No one would salvage a Shipper.

"We're going over the wall," I said, dragging her out, her arm across my shoulders.

"Do not do this, Asa Gray," she begged. "You sacrifice too much."

"If you ever want to fly, you'll do what I say." I didn't meet her eyes, understanding now I'd sacrifice anything for her even though I didn't understand why. And I wouldn't fail again. Instead I ordered, "Walk."

Poppet that we'd made her, she obeyed.

We reached the only flawed part of the wall. Scaffolding rested against it and a piece of the plasticene hung open, exposing wires. Hel had been right—the wall was a lie. We projected what we wanted prisoners to see and allowed ourselves an unobstructed view of their misery.

No one cared. It had gone on for years.

I half-pulled half-pushed Hel up the scaffolding. "Listen," I warned, "at the top there's a current I'll redirect, and then there's a drop to the other side. It's not as far as you'd think." I dug into my pockets and pulled out a set of mirrors wrapped in cloth, carefully attaching them to the wall. "Smoke and mirrors," I whispered.

She smiled against my shoulder.

"Here we go," I straddled the wall between the deflecting mirrors and reached for her. "Up…"

I towed her to me, and for a moment we balanced above her

world and mine. I pulled her closer, bringing her lips to mine, but her foot caught, sending a mirror shattering against the ground below.

The current reconnected. Hel became a living conductor. Dumb with shock, we tumbled to the ground together, stunned to a shuddering silence.

Sparks raced along her exposed circuits, lighting her as if fire bloomed below her skin. I shook her. "Snap out of it."

Her eye rolled back in her head; her lips quivered.

"Hel, you're out—free…" I pulled her onto my lap.

She trembled, her heart pounding out a staccato rhythm that raced, then stopped, then raced again.

"Hel…"

Her eye focused on me, and she forced her lips to cooperate, electricity pulsing around her and singeing the hair off my arms. Tugging her game key off, she awkwardly placed it around my neck, her mangled mechanical hand clutching it. "Asa Gray," she said, "I thank you for your sacrifi—" Her words strangled into a string of clicks and beeps, and her head lolled to the side.

Power shot through her one last time, surging between her hand and the key dangling around my neck. I howled as the key branded me with a flash of heat. Then Hel convulsed, falling still in my arms.

Dead.

I left her when the sentries approached. I made it to the transport hub and boarded, resting my forehead on the window but seeing nothing.

I staggered into the house on Girard Avenue. No one greeted

me or asked about my disheveled clothes, the black staining my hands, or the burn that made me gasp whenever the key touched it.

Mother was probably kneeling before some Pulpit in prayer. And Father? Likely in a meeting.

Hel was… Where did a Shipper—an anomaly like Hel—go when she died? I stood before the mirror in my bathroom wiping at my eyes. Gently I removed the key, set it on the counter, and bandaged the welt it had left. The key hissed, electricity zipping around its perimeter and dancing across its surface.

The lights flickered.

Tucking the remaining bandages away, I retrieved the key. Energy pulsed through me at its touch. My vision swam, and I saw myself standing in front of the mural again, kissing Hel.

I gasped as the sensation faded, the key still sparking in my hand. Pushing out of the bathroom and into my bedroom, I yanked open my closet and shoved at its false back. The panel slid away, and my system, my Highway, beckoned from the dark.

I slid the key into the Highway's game port, thinking two things simultaneously: *This is the dumbest idea ever* and *I am absolutely brilliant.* I hoped to the God the latter was correct.

Atchen Tan stuttered into view, running the opening sequence. I was in, but only as far as I'd gotten before. I leaned against the closet wall. My lights flickered off, and she ghosted onto the screen, untouchable and angelic in her gown and halo.

"Hel!" I shouted into the mic, but she turned away, disappearing. I typed a message:

Hel, if you're there, respond!

All I got back was:

I thank you for your sacrifice.

But I wasn't done sacrificing yet.

For two days with little sleep and less to eat, I hunted for Hel in the recesses of Atchen Tan's opening sequence. Occasionally her image ghosted onscreen and then away, or a word or two that might be hers popped into the Comm Box.

But I was losing her. Because I couldn't really reach her.

I did the only thing I could. I broke the rules.

Locking myself inside Camp 13's gaming hub, I inserted Hel's key. The cradle descended, hungry for a player. I sat awkwardly in the metal half-shell like some delicacy at a government buffet, but the Game allowed me in only a little farther than it had at home.

But *a little farther* was all I needed to see her again. A thin image of Hel stood at Atchen Tan's entrance, looking my way. For a moment it seemed she saw me—a smile stretched her lips. Then her expression changed, and the Game shut down. But hope swelled inside me.

Hel was alive inside the Game. I just needed to get completely *in* to get her out.

A day later a g-nomer, with fingers tweaked to be extra long and slender, shaved off a patch of my hair and cut into my head while I held Hel's key in my fist. I blacked out and woke hours later in an alley outside his questionable office, the illegal port throbbing against the raw edges of my skull, my neck sticky with my own drying blood.

My feet scrabbling, I pushed myself up and tumbled into a darkened doorway as my vision bled out and my stomach tried to leap free.

Back to a wall, I slipped the key into my head and hurtled into the Game. A string of ones and zeroes blurred my brain, and my body pixelated, tightened, and found form. I felt—heavy. Something clanked and rubbed near my ears. The gloss of polished metal threw light at my eyes.

I was wearing armor.

Ahead of me was the jump-point, a signpost comprising both entrance and exit. It bristled with wooden pointers scrawled with the names of destinations. There was Chingary: the site of Hel's most recent quest. I headed that way, the weight of my armor and the bite of gravel through thin-soled boots pulling me fully into the reality of Atchen Tan.

Resting several kilometers down the trail, I nearly fell off the rock I'd perched on when Hel flickered into being.

She looked right through me, her halo sputtering. Something moved in the grass by her feet—a rabbit with antlers?

"Hel!" I cried.

The jackalope passed through her, and Hel's image flitted away. Across the river something bellowed. Wind blasted me, blowing the hair back from my face. "Holy—" A huge dragon with glittering scales hung in midair, claws heavy and curved, teeth dripping saliva as its wings beat the air so fiercely trees bowed beneath it.

I looked around. Without Hel I was lost.

So I did what any lost knight would do.

I ran.

The beast tore through the woods behind me, trees creaking and splintering in its wake. My calves ached as I headed up an incline. Ahead boulders formed a mouth in the mountainside just large enough for me to slip inside.

I launched myself at the opening as the dragon shrieked. My vision sparked with red and orange as tongues of flame stroked the rocks, and the world stank like the brimstone Priests said awaited those who strayed from The Path.

I was so far off The Path…

Huddled in the cave I realized a flaw in my plan. *Another* flaw

in my plan. I was at level nine with no experience. I had to exit and research the Game in safety. Maybe there was a manual back in the blockhouse.

I closed my eyes and visualized the jump-point: the bristling signpost. Nothing. I squeezed my eyes shut and carved the memory of the signpost into the empty air before me. Nothing. In desperation I screwed my eyes so tightly closed that my head hurt. Again I summoned the image of the signpost, begging to be booted out of the Game.

Again I failed.

What was happening to my body as I lay in the cave in Atchen Tan, stuck in a reality of someone else's making? Armor chafed my collarbone and compressed my spine, and I struggled to see the allure of this world. Hel was right—there weren't any flowers.

But there weren't any flowers in Camp 13 other than the ones we'd created.

I pressed my eyelids shut with my fingertips. In my mind I saw Hel. My lips formed her name.

Something stirred in the air beside me.

My eyes opened. She was there, quietly beautiful, halo crackling around her head. I reached up to touch it, but pulled my finger back when electricity snapped against it. Hel's eyes focused a moment. Her eye popped wide open, and then she disappeared.

I summoned her again, thinking of the look of her, the touch and smell of her.

She was there again, her back to me, this time even more substantial, her feet displacing the grit on the cave's floor.

"Hel?" I whispered.

She turned, her brow wrinkling. She was definitely Hel, but she had two eyes set in a fully human face where, moments before, she'd had one and her scope. She evaporated again.

"Hel." I said it like a prayer. "I need you."

She appeared, her right hand all flesh, bone, and blood. Although I couldn't see beneath her velvet and brocade gown to her foot or leg, I guessed she was what Luddites called "fully formed."

Her hands balled in tight fists at her sides, eyes wide. She stepped back. "Asa Gray?! You cannot be here!"

"Wha—?" I grabbed her hands in my own, unfolding her fingers. "I came to find you. Free you. I'm not going anywhere." My hand fell through hers as her image fuzzed.

"Go!" Her form flickered, became solid only when she seemed to focus. "This is level nine. You are ill-equipped."

The cave quaked beneath the dragon's bellow. Bits of granite crumbled from the walls and bounced across the floor.

Hel twisted toward the noise. "Your arrival triggered it. You must leave, Asa Gray."

"Equip me," I demanded. "I'll save you. I have armor."

"Armor does not a knight make," Hel snapped, halo hissing.

The dragon howled. The ground shook.

"I am not ready." She peered out the narrow cave's opening. "I do not have the power…"

"You do." I grabbed her hand, letting the current that flew along her fingertips sing through me. "You always had the power. Harness it. This *is* your world."

The roof caved in with a groan. The dragon's claws raked through the wreckage, brushing past me as Hel screamed.

I was so *very* ill-equipped.

"Look at yourself," I shouted above the dragon's roar,

scrambling away from the beast's grasping talons and ducking behind a huge rock.

Standing in the rubble of the cave, Hel looked down. She stumbled back, blinking.

"That's who you want to be, right?"

Mute, she stared at me. Her halo flared and screamed, throwing her shadow against clouds that gathered so low their guts scraped the mountaintop and shrouded the valley. Light trembled upward from her halo to become lightning that crawled across the sky.

"Atchen Tan is *your* world. Make it your reality! Control it!"

She squeezed her eyes shut. By her feet, strings of binary code bled free, blurring to become stems that stumbled along cracks in the mountain—cracks in the code—and blossomed into flowers, Hel's anomaly finding the Game's seams and tugging them apart. Other Shippers stuttered into view and then whisked away.

Hel was connecting to more than just the world of Atchen Tan.

Claws clicked closed around me, dragging me into the air.

"That's great, but—maybe something more useful?"

With eyes like twin Red Giants, the dragon glared at me, its breath scalding my face.

"Equip me!" I shouted.

Hel spread her feet and her arms, fingers splayed as current wove around and through her. Other Shippers ghosted in again—Shippers jacked-in at the same time—their faces familiar and glimmering like ghosts. Their energies merged, code flowing like water between them. Power built and burst free from Hel's fingers, arcing toward my outstretched arm as the others twitched away again, leaving only twisting bits of binary behind.

A sword manifested in my hand. I swung it at the beast's snout with all my strength.

The blade bounced back, and the dragon went shrill with rage.

"Dig deeper!" I screamed, gathering my fading courage.

Hel's face twisted in concentration. Thunder snarled across the thickening sky. Bracing herself, she sucked in the air, breathed deep the code, and spooled it back out in her own shimmering design of blue and white light.

It fell short, ones and zeroes solidifying and tumbling to the ground like bits of ice before they melted, seeping back into the ground, stitching up the tears in the code and strangling the flowers.

Hel shuddered, doubling over.

"Connect!" I shouted. "To the others! To the world! Ground yourself in it!"

Rolling back up to her full height, she raised quivering arms as the dragon reared. More Shippers manifested, stunned but substantial. Shippers I'd never seen before. Shippers from other Camps. A ring of meat and metal in medieval garb, adventurers of all levels sucked into Hel's vortex of power. The cracks in the ground reopened, multiplied, and widened, life pouring free in a riot of colors and forms.

Hel nodded at the Shippers. "We can end this quest. Connect with me. Meld together."

Static rumbled between a thousand outstretched fingers and built to a roar. Hel bent her head, thrusting her arms forward to again become a conduit of power, aiming the combined powers of their wills at my sword.

Lit from inside, the metal molecules hummed, and with all my strength, I aimed for the dragon's throat.

The blade ripped through scaly flesh. The dragon shrieked, ichor bubbling thickly from the gaping wound. Its head rolled and it stumbled. Claws trembling open, it hurled me into the rocks.

Pain burned from the base of my skull through my backbone. Atchen Tan faded into a dark, whirling blend of binary code as Hel's scream became nothing but a distant buzz.

"Misguided bastard." Silas's voice assaulted me. "He let her get inside him—as far as they can." A hand pressed against my head. "Look. He's augmented."

Someone gasped, and I willed my eyes open.

"Why would anyone…?" Jared gaped at me, his eyes full of horror.

Around the cylindrical screen, Shippers roused, faces familiar from the Game.

I swallowed. "Is she…?"

"Hel's there," one replied.

"I'm sure Hell's waiting for you." Silas dragged me from the cradle. "Gotta process you."

Before Silas towed me outside, a Shipper grabbed my arm. "Asa Gray, I welcome you. I am Bodoni Gibson."

Silas growled, "What? Now there's a Gibson *family*?"

"More than a family," Bodoni corrected. "A clan. Open to new members."

That night Silas processed me. I was fine in every way that mattered, except I had no marker—no appropriate identification.

Shippers received markers at their Final Fitting—after the growth spurts of adolescence. It was a time of celebration. Not for me. My parents wouldn't watch me get branded the way Shippers watched their children get etched.

"You're nearsighted," I pointed out to Silas after watching him work. "You could get that corrected. A little augmentation or a g-nome tweak…"

He raised his hand, but I blocked the blow.

"None of us is truly perfect, eh?"

He readied the brand that would surround my Blunted Star with a thick square and make me just another Shipper.

Cherry hot, the brand sank into my flesh, and I blacked out thinking: *Some welcome.*

I woke in Atchen Tan, Hel kneeling at my side, her halo a diadem of faceted crystals. "You are here," she soothed.

"You look—" Different? Subdued? "Beautiful," I said finally.

"I am all those things and more," she said, a smile twitched at the corner of her lips.

"What? *All* those?"

"I am no longer just *your* Hel, but I am also H.E.L.: the Human Electronic Link. I connect Shippers everywhere with the Binary Mind," she explained. "Listen. Do you hear them?"

I closed my eyes. Her breath brushed my ear, and I heard a buzz like bees working a hive.

"We are all connected," she whispered. "Whenever you jack-in, I hear you—know you. Every thing about you. Words and thoughts."

"Amazing."

"You will never be alone again, Asa Gray. Even when you exit, you will carry a small part of me like a ghost in your heart."

"No," I corrected. "Not a ghost. A hope."

"I like that better," she agreed. "Now go. They are celebrating you." She leaned down, and with a kiss, kicked me out of the Game.

Hel might never fly or burn bridges, but she was building an entire world instead.

That night we celebrated until the guards ordered us back to our blockhouses.

They couldn't imagine we had anything worth celebrating, but, when it seems you have nothing, hope is most worthy of celebration.

In Camp 13, Shippers who were once zombie-like became animated—inspired. Murals like the ones Hel and I had created covered every wall and walkway. Their beauty grew too quickly for the guards to cover up.

Although we remained prisoners, we hoped our prison might evolve into something of our own design.

And maybe if we designed it, we could control it.

Then it would be no prison at all. Someday we might even bring down all the walls that stood between us and true freedom.

Together we'd been to Hel and back. Was there anything we couldn't do?

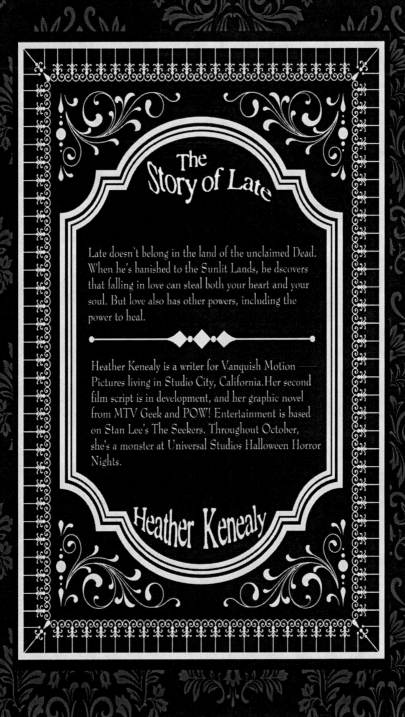

The Story of Late

Late doesn't belong in the land of the unclaimed Dead.
When he's banished to the Sunlit Lands, he dscovers
that falling in love can steal both your heart and your
soul. But love also has other powers, including the
power to heal.

◆◆◆

Heather Kenealy is a writer for Vanquish Motion
Pictures living in Studio City, California.Her second
film script is in development, and her graphic novel
from MTV Geek and POW! Entertainment is based
on Stan Lee's The Seekers. Throughout October,
she's a monster at Universal Studios Halloween Horror
Nights.

Heather Kenealy

In the Sacred Soil—the Dark City where all the unclaimed Dead went—he was given life. The first child who was not born in the Sunlit Lands. He had never seen the world outside the Gates, and never took a breath of air into his lungs. He was special, this one was.

Other children had been born here in the necropolis, but every one of them had been conceived in the outside, which, to be honest, so had he. Some had seen their mothers' faces before dying. Some had only known their warmth. That was the difference. Every one of the other children had lived for a time. No one knew if this child had. This boy was an anomaly. No one but the Caretaker knew how he came to be there, and the Caretaker chose not to tell anyone, not even the boy, when he grew older. One does not question the Caretaker, if one expects to have peace in one's eternal rest.

The boy was alive though, that much was clear. His skin was pink and warm. His heart beat. He grew older, though here in this place he did not need to eat or sleep. Sometimes when he was very young, he attempted those things, but really there was no need, and so eventually he just stopped trying. The Dead were his tutors, teaching him to speak and to walk, and no less a personage than the Caretaker himself taught the boy to drive the carriages that came to the Bone Gate, carrying new citizenry to the Dark City from the outskirts of the land. It helped to have the boy meet the new arrivals, for sometimes they were wild and afraid at the colorless place in which they found themselves.

In these unusual surroundings, he grew to be a young man, never knowing that his life was not normal.

Late was the name he gave himself, for the Dead were in the habit of addressing themselves as "The *Late* John Smith," or "The *Late* Jane Jones." When the boy began to talk, he mimicked this way of introduction. But because he had never been named, he had nothing to follow "The Late...." So the name stuck and was eventually shortened to *Late*.

He liked his name. He liked his life.

Until the day came, after eighteen years had passed in the Sunlit Lands, that Late accidentally cut himself on the sharp spines that made the Bone Gate, and he bled bright red.

Not much color exists in the Sacred Soil, and the Dead came from all over the city to see the red. It made some happy to remember their own lives. It made others sad. It frightened most...

...but one dared to taste it.

He found he liked the taste.

Late dwelt in the hollow skull of a dragon that had been dead long enough to become part of the city. The boy liked to watch the people below as he rested in the empty eye sockets that served as windows, and this was how he spent much of his time. He talked to the Dead and, because he knew nothing else, he was not alarmed by their pallor, their chilly touch, their

echoing voices. In fact, he thought himself too pink and warm, and he had a peculiar glow about him that only he could see.

But he also had the smell of the living about him, and it drew darkness to Dragon's Skull.

The dead man who had sampled Late's blood decided he would take it all. He had been dead long enough to have forgotten that he was ever a man at all, and now all he had become was this crawling, corrupted thing craving the sweetness of Late's life. In the darkness of the perpetual night, he crept to where Late sat amusing a child newly arrived in the city by tossing knucklebones to one of the rotting ravens who filled the leafless trees.

Danger, my master, whispered the echo, which was all that remained of the dragon besides the bones. *Evil comes for you.*

Not knowing what evil was, but knowing that the Dragon's warning was nothing to disregard, Late stepped into the shadows and bid the child to be still.

As the dead man climbed the bone pile that was Late's front steps, he moved like an animal, sniffing the air. *Blood...blood... blood*, he whispered. He glanced toward the child and the raven, but he could not see the glow that marked the carefully hidden Late. *Where...is...the...blood?*

Swinging a club carved from a sliver of the Dragon's rib, Late leapt from his hiding place. The dead man lunged at him, knocking away the weapon, because, in truth, the boy had never fought before. They grappled and fell, the dead man's teeth too close to Late's throat for comfort. Late grabbed the man's skull in his too-warm hands and crushed it like an eggshell.

The dead man fell and crumbled into dust.

Late gasped, staring at the powder that coated his palms. "What have I done?" For a moment, his skin turned the pale gray of the people who filled his world.

The dead child joined him and asked innocently, "He is

gone?"

The dust swirled in a sudden breeze, and the eldest of them all, the Caretaker, whose job it was to open the gates to the Sacred Soils at the start of the world and close them at the end of time, appeared. Tall and pale, he had hair that curled in the wind, which touched him alone. His heels sparked fire from the ground when he walked. *What happened here, Young Late?* The Caretaker dragged one of his pointy-toed boots through the dust. *This was one of my servants.*

Late fell to one knee, bowing his head. "I was attacked, Greatest of Us All. I had to defend myself. He sought my... blood."

The Caretaker narrowed his eyes in what might have been anger, or possibly sorrow. He had known this day would come. Late had what no one else had in all of the city—a soul. And to have a soul in the Sacred Soils could drive the Dead mad. It had been tolerable when Late had been a child, for little children are often soulless, but now he was eight and ten years old, and he had become a danger to himself.

It is time, Late. It is time that you go into the world of men. You must join your people in the Land of the Living, the Caretaker said.

Late leapt to his feet, his already pale face growing chalky. "No, no, Caretaker, please, do not send me to that world. I do not know it. I do not belong there."

Ah, but you do, my Darling Boy, until the day you die, the day you lose your soul.

"Then, tell me. Tell me how to do that," Late begged. "And then I will do it, so I can return home. If I need to, I will cut my soul from my body and throw it into the pit."

I cannot say, but I will tell you that once you have seen the world that is your true home, you may never wish to return here. Do not so lightly dismiss the Sunlit Lands. Few who have

seen their beauty long for the gray of the Dark City. They fight.
They kick and scream, and curse my name.

"That will never happen. This will always be my home. You...you're the only father I have ever known."

The Caretaker smiled and placed his hand on the boy's head. *Because I love you as you love me, I will give you three gifts to help you in the Living World. I see it in the stars and in the dust that you will have need of them. Use them well.* The Caretaker gave Late the teeth from the Dragon's skull, an eye from the dead child, and the wings from the raven.

"What will I do with these things?"

You will know when the time comes, the Caretaker said. Then he sent the boy into the Sunlit Lands.

Late stepped outside the Bone Gates, and for the first time in his memory, the gates closed behind him. He drove his carriage to the edge of Sacred Soils, and with a sob, stepped over the borders. He prayed with all his heart that he might see it again soon.

Then, as if the darkness had never existed, the world exploded into brilliance. Late managed three full steps before his senses were overwhelmed. The Sunlit Lands beyond were too bright, too noisy, too full of colors Late had never seen before. For the first time in his life, he had an empty place in his stomach, and his eyelids drooped in exhaustion. He collapsed beside the road and lay there for a full day and a full night, before Tresska, the Night Dancer, and her companion, Bontlo, happened upon him.

"Look. Highwaymen have taken another. This forest grows more dangerous with each day," said Bontlo to his pretty charge.

"No, he still lives, but he is so thin and pale," said Tresska. "We must take him to the Doctor-Man."

Bontlo was a big man, and he lifted the boy as if he were thistledown. "He's nothing more than skin and bones," he exclaimed.

Late's eyes fluttered open as Bontlo was placing him in the back of the Night Dancer's wagon. When Late spied Tresska, he murmured in an oddly echoing voice, "An Angel has come to take me home." And then he passed out again.

Bontlo smiled at the Night Dancer. "I think the young buck is in love."

The Doctor-Man fed Late thin soup and nursed him to health, because no one could refuse a request from the Night Dancer. By the time the boy was well, the Doctor-Man loved him as a son, for there was much in Late to love.

Late never told him where he came from, and the Doctor-Man never asked. He figured that the boy had run away, and Late, for his part, repaid his guardian by driving him in the wagon when his patients lived too far away to walk, and it was almost like being back home again.

Eventually, the boy stopped squinting in the sunlight, and he stopped weeping for the dark places whenever the night made him homesick. He ate strange things such as fruit, bread, and cheese, and grew strong. His pale skin tanned to a golden color, and the girls of the village quite admired him.

But his heart belonged to the Angel he had first seen when he entered this world.

"Ah, you mean the fair Tresska, the Night Dancer," said the Doctor-Man when Late asked about her. "Yes, she will be back in town tomorrow night for the Festival of Destiny. If you go into the square, you will see her dance."

Late vowed that he would be there. Did the Angel remember him at all?

Tresska and Bontlo did indeed remember young Late.

"Looks as if our injured young buck grew into a handsome stag." Tresska smiled as she took his strong hand in her dainty one. "You're called Late, I'm told."

Late's mouth seemed strangely dry, and he had to swallow more than once before he found his voice. "Yes, Miss Tresska, that is my name."

Tresska cocked a perfectly formed eyebrow. "My, child, but you do have a peculiar accent. There is a strange echoing to your voice."

"It is how everyone talks where I am from," Late said. "If you do not like it, though, I will change it."

Bontlo laughed. "Why, Lady Tresska, my first guess was right. I do believe the young buck is in love with you."

Tresska smiled gently. "Are you, young Late? Tell me, what do you think of when you look at me?"

"I think of nothing when I see you, except you," Late said, which sent Tresska and Bontlo into peals of hysterical laughter.

"Well, my dearest boy, tonight I dedicate my dance to you."

Late's head spun with feelings indescribable to him, for he had never experienced such tender emotions as adoration and admiration. "My lady, I am honored."

That, of course, sent Tresska and her companion away clutching their stomachs and wiping their eyes.

Lady Tresska danced that night, and watching in the crowd was a man who thought to have her for his own. He whispered a spell beneath his breath, and the crowd sank into a deep trance.

Then this man, the sorcerer Tartucket, spirited the Night Dancer away.

But one remained awake to see the crime. One who had been born in a land where magic had flooded his blood and his every breath.

Late saw the disappearance of the lady and vowed to find her.

As the wisps of Tartucket's magic vanished, Late cried out to the awakening crowd, begging for their help. "It was sorcery."

"Ah," said the others, clucking their tongues in sorrow, "if the Night Dancer was taken by magic, the living can do nothing to bring her home."

The living could do nothing.

But, didn't Late have gifts from one who had never lived? The Caretaker had promised these gifts would help *him*. Could they help *her*?

In his rooms that night, Late spread out the gifts he had been given and stared at them for a long time. Wings? No, they could fly, but without knowing where he was going, they were of no use. Teeth? No, though they could bite, nothing needed to be torn. Ah! The Eye. Wasn't it said that Dead Men see all?

Sitting cross-legged on his bed, Late took out his knife and popped his own eye from his skull, replacing it with the eye of the child. Closing his living eye so as not to confuse his sight, he said, "Help me to see."

Then...he saw...

The Lady Tresska locked in a tower, high, high at the top of a mountain on the other side of the world.

He set out without a word of goodbye to Bontlo or the Doctor-Man and rode for a year to reach the mountain peak where stood the Castle of Tartucket, though his hair grew long and wild, and his mismatched eyes grew haunted.

But his horse could not gallop to the top of the mountain

without a path, so, despairing, Late slumped at the foot of the mountain, certain his quest had come to an end. He glared up at the rocky peaks and cursed their inaccessibility, wishing that he could be like the careening birds.

Wait! Wings. The Caretaker's gifts. Filled with new hope, Late pulled the raven wings from his knapsack and stuck them to his shoulder blades. He flapped his new wings like a butterfly crawling from its cocoon, and with each stroke they grew larger and wider until they were sixteen feet across and strong enough to carry him to the top of the mountain, though their weight bowed him over so he could not stand straight.

At first, he flew crookedly, and only for a few moments, before he tumbled to the earth, but by the end of the day, he became sure enough to reach the top of the mountain. Exhausted, but never more determined, he began his ascent. "I'm coming, my lady," he said as he soared. "Your Late is coming to your rescue."

Ahead of him was the castle of the Sorcerer Tartucket, surrounded by a thicket too strong for sword to cut or fire to burn. Nothing, though, is stronger than a dragon's fangs, so Late, knowing now that the Caretaker had chosen his gifts carefully, plucked his own teeth from his jaws and put the dragon's fangs in their place.

In moments he had bitten through the thicket, though the thorns tore his flesh to the bone, and his lips were red with blood.

At the top of the tallest tower, Lady Tresska slept in a satin bed, her stomach swollen with child.

Late folded his wings as he landed on the windowsill.

Awakening, Tresska screamed when she saw him. "A gargoyle!"

"I have come to save you," Late cried, though a mouthful of blood and dragon's teeth turned the plea into a monstrous growl.

Lady Tresska gasped. "Save me? From whom? My dear husband? Nonsense. Go away, you ugly thing!"

"Your husband?" Dread filled Late from his head to his toes. "Your kidnapper, you mean?"

"Oh, that." Tresska laughed gaily. "He was shy. It was the only way he could make his love for me known." She stroked her round stomach. "I am a wife and about to be a mother. Why would you take me from my True Love?"

"But I love you," Late whispered. "I have from the moment I saw you. Could you never love me back?"

"Love you, you awful monster? How could I?"

At those words, a glowing ball of light ripped from Late's chest as his soul was torn away, and his eyes rolled back in his head.

Someone tall and pale with spikes of long curled hair and boots that sparked the floor offered the gargoyle his hand and bore the soulless creature away.

Time passed in the Sunlit Lands, and Tresska bore Tartucket a daughter named Dahla. As the years flew by, Dahla became as beautiful as her mother, but she was a magician like her father, so she grew up knowing the secrets of the world in a way the Night Dancer never had.

Dahla was seven and ten years old when she found the small globe of light in her mother's wardrobe, and she knew it for what it was. "Mother, why do you have a soul?"

"All living creatures have a soul," Tresska answered airily.

"But you have an extra one." Dahla held up the ball of light.

Tresska took the ball from the girl and mused, "Oh, is this a soul? It was left behind by a gargoyle that flew in the window one night and tried to steal me from your father."

Dahla shook her head, "No, Mother, this is not a monster's soul. I have been looking at it all day, and it is beautiful."

Tresska shrugged. "I remember what I saw."

Dahla sighed and took the ball into her bedchamber to study it.

The more she looked at it, the harder she found it to believe that this was the soul of a monster. The light was too bright, too beautiful. Whoever had lost it, he was surely no gargoyle, and he would want it back. But everything she knew about souls said that when a person lost one, there was only one place for him to go.

The Sacred Soils, the Land of the Dead.

That night Dahla lay down on her bed, and, with the soul in her hands, drank a sleeping potion to bring her as close to death as she could get.

She woke before the Bone Gate.

A tall thin man with curled hair and dead eyes greeted her. *Welcome, Little Dreamer, but this is no place for you. Have you a purpose here?*

"I seek the one who lost this." Dahla held up the soul. "I wish to return what he lost."

The Caretaker looked at the soul, and a strange smile creased his face. *This belongs to Late. He dwells at Dragon's Skull. Go and bring this to him. Do not fear. None of the dead shall harm you. You are protected in this place by my blessing.*

"I am not afraid," Dahla lied. She followed the pathway up to the Dragon's Skull whose empty eyes looked down upon the dark and colorless city. "Hello. Is anyone at home? It is unkind to keep a guest waiting."

A shadow appeared at the gaping jaws. *Who are you? You are not one of the Dead.* The misshapen figure did not emerge, but stood in the darkness, one eye shining with discontent and suspicion. *There is a glow about you that I almost remember.*

Dahla held up the shining soul. "Are you the one called Late? I have brought this to you. It is your soul."

My soul?

The shadow stepped into the light, and Dahla saw the gargoyle for the first time, stooped and hunched, with bedraggled black wings, fanged teeth, and one dead eye.

My soul was cut from me many years ago. I have no need for it back. This is my home. This is where I belong. The souled have no place here. Go away, you troublemaker. Quit haunting me with long-lost foolishness.

Hearing the harsh and hateful words, Dahla thought for one moment that she had been wrong about the beauty of this soul, but the way the glow brightened in her hands made her know that it did indeed belong to him. "This is yours," she said, coming close to him. "I come from the Sunlit Lands to return it."

Late frowned and arched his wings over his head, taking a threatening step toward her. *Do you not fear me? Do you not think I am a monster? A gargoyle? I gave up my humanity to save a woman who cared nothing for me. Why should you, whom I do not even know, whom I have done nothing for, care about my abandoned soul?*

At the bitterness and sorrow in his voice, tears sprang to Dahla's eyes. "I do not know what made you into a gargoyle, but I have seen the beauty in your soul. I'm not afraid of you. You are not what you look like. You are what lies in your soul. You gave it for a foolish woman. I am not a fool. I don't care what you appear to be. I care who you are."

With a trembling claw-tipped hand, Late took the soul from Dahla. Suddenly he was surrounded by a bright glow. His wings fell away in a flutter of black feathers. His fangs became human teeth. His dead eye blinked into life. His color, his warmth, flooded into him until he was again himself.

The Caretaker materialized before them. *You are back with us, Late.*

Late looked down at himself, astonished. "I am myself again." He looked at Dahla. "You did this to me…for me…"

Dahla lowered her head. "I fell in love with the man whose soul that was, the beauty in him. It broke my heart that it was lost to my foolish mother. I thought if it were returned, my love would be returned. My heart breaks again that I was wrong." She turned to go.

Late caught the girl's arm. "You are Lady Tresska's daughter?"

She nodded, not looking at him. "I am."

Putting a gentle hand to her chin to bring her eyes up to meet his, Late smiled down at her and said, "I never thought to see anyone more beautiful than she…until now."

With a gasp, Dahla gazed into his eyes.

The Caretaker nodded at the boy. *Did I not tell you that the Sunlit places had much to offer? Go with her, Late, and live your allotted time. I promise you that when it is time for you to return here, you will come together, and you will never be alone again.*

Late kissed Dahla then. His soul blazed within, strengthened by her love, and he could again face the Sunlit Lands.

Author Biographies

Dawn Dalton wrote her first monster book at the age of eight, when she discovered writing about them was way less scary than looking for the beasties under her bed. Since then, she's still leery of things that go bump in the night, but she'd like to think her creepy storytelling skills have improved. After earning a degree in Journalism, Dawn ventured into communications, marketing, and public relations. But her heart has always belonged to fiction.

Though she'll forever be a BC girl, Dawn now lives in Edmonton, Alberta, with her husband, teenage stepdaughter, and three bullmastiff hounds. When she isn't working on her latest paranormal story, you can find her reading, watching *The Princess Bride* (again), or indulging in her unhealthy addiction to reality TV. Fans can visit her at **www.dawnmdalton.blogspot.com**.

Dawn also writes adult thriller and paranormal romance under the last name IUS. For more information about her latest adult releases, see **www.dawn-ius.blogspot.com**.

Shannon Delany was first published in eighth grade with a short science fiction story and greatly enjoyed returning to her roots to write "To Hel and Back." Delany is currently best known for her *13 to Life* series (teenage, love, loss and—oh, yeah—werewolves!)

which was nominated for a YALSA Teen Top Ten and began as the winner of the first-ever cell phone novel contest in the western world. Delany now writes, researches, gives workshops, and raises heritage livestock on her small farm in upstate New York, not far from a town very much like Junction but worlds away from Camp 13. Learn more about Shannon at **www.shannondelany.com/**.

Mark Finnemore lives in California with his beautiful wife Panji, who helped him learn that even the rockiest road can lead to a happy ending. Mark has had short stories published and is currently working on the finishing touches of a novel titled *Love & Taxes*, which he hopes will one day be not only finished, but published and found at your local bookstore as well. Visit Mark at **www.mythic-picnic.com** or **www.genre-trash.com** or **www. love-and-taxes.com**.

Karl Gee has always worked with design and technology and currently teaches both subjects in upstate New York. He brings his ever-expanding know-how to "To Hel and Back" in the form of Augmented Reality extras. Just go to the website, hold up the icon, and see Shannon Delany's vision brought to multiple dimensions. To learn more about Karl's work, visit him at **www. KGeeCreations.com**.

Judith Graves, author of the *Skinned* trilogy—*Under My Skin*, *Second Skin*, and *Skin of My Teeth*—reads as much as she writes, devouring at least two books a week. She loves heated debates over character motives. She's been kicked out of several book clubs for just this reason, but she remains unfazed by book club drama and is furiously writing more paranormal stories. Which hopefully, you'll read.

Working in a school library, Judith is surrounded by children's and young adult literature (there's no escape!). She fosters the joy of reading in students and staff at her school. She helps out with the school choir and drama club. If it has to do with words or music, Judith is around. A singer/songwriter for more than ten years, Judith often writes songs about her characters. Because they are beasties of the night, this makes for interesting listening.

Candace Havens is a bestselling author of six novels for Berkley—*Charmed & Dangerous, Charmed & Ready, Charmed & Deadly, Like a Charm, The Demon King and I*, and *Dragons Prefer Blondes*. Her books for the Blaze line of Harlequin include *The Model Marine, Take Me If You Dare, Truth and Dare*, and *She Who Dares, Wins*. Her books have received nominations for RITAs, the Holt Medallion, and Write Touch Reader Awards. She is the author of the biography *Joss Whedon: The Genius Behind Buffy* and a contributor to several anthologies. As one of the nation's leading entertainment journalists, Candace has interviewed countless celebrities, including Tom Hanks, Nicolas Cage, Tom Cruise, George Clooney, and many more. More than 600 newspapers across the country carry her entertainment columns. Candace also runs a free online writing workshop for more than 1800 writers and teaches comprehensive writing class. She does film reviews with the Dorsey Gang on New Country 96.3 and is the president of the Television Critics Association.

Heather Kenealy Writing since she was a bored nine year old, Heather Kenealy is now a screenwriter from Studio City, whose second big screen film is an adaptation of a very popular video game from the UK. She's the winner of the Cinescape short fiction contest 2007 and of *The Seekers* competition for MTV Comics and POW! Entertainment to write a graphic novel based on one of Marvel Comics icon Stan Lee's original ideas. In her spare time, Heather plays X-Men rpgs and reads comic books, and at Hallowe'en, she's a performer at Universal Studios Hallowe'en Horror Nights.

Kitty Keswick grew up on her grandfather's California vineyard, where her imagination was her best friend. At a very tender age, she started writing her stories and reading them to the grapes. Kitty has been an Anglophile since age four when she saw Robin Hood and fell head over heels in love. Robin Hood inspired the hero of her first book, *Freaksville*, part of a trilogy that includes

Furry and Freaked and *Freaked No More*. Kitty lives with a bossy tabby cat and maybe even a few ghosts. She spends her days with werewolves, Valkyries, vamps and other creatures that go bump in the night.

Halli Dee Lilburn is a writer, artist, librarian, and mother of three beautiful, busy children. She wants to *feel* like an artist, but it gets pretty hard when folding laundry or scrubbing toilets. Her writing career blossomed when her youngest went off to public school, and she found six extra hours a day to write. She lives on a small farm, homesteaded by her grandparents, in the middle of nowhere, Alberta, Canada. Publishing credits included various literary journals and magazines such as *Grey Sparrow Journal*, *Poetry Quarterly*, *Canadian Stories*, and *Canada's History Magazine* as well as a young adult speculative fiction novel, *Shifters* (Imajin Publishing). Genres included in her repertoire are poetry, mid-grade chapter books, young adult, contemporary, and creative non-fiction. Find her on her blog at **hallililburn.blogspot.com** and on twitter **@hallilburn**.

John W. Otte is a Lutheran minister. He attended Concordia University in St. Paul, where he majored in theatre before going on to Concordia Seminary in St. Louis. He lives in South St. Paul, Minnesota, with his wife and sons. He joined the American Christian Fiction Writers in 2006. His debut novel, *Failstate* (Marcher Lord Press) stars a teenage superhero who tries to avenge a fallen comrade while competing on a reality TV show. John has a blog called *The Least Read Blog* at **www.johnwotte.com**, which features book, video game, and movie reviews.

Linda Joy Singleton is the author of more than thirty-five books, including THE SEER series, DEAD GIRL trilogy, and BURIED: Goth Girl Mystery. Free short stories, a contest, book excerpts, and writing advice can be found at **www.LindaJoySingleton.com**.

Maria V. Snyder switched careers from meteorologist to novelist when she began writing the *New York Times* best-selling

Study Series (*Poison Study, Magic Study*, and *Fire Study*) about a young woman who becomes a poison taster. Born Pennsylvania, Maria earned a Bachelors of Science degree in Meteorology from Pennsylvania State University. She worked as an environmental meteorologist until boredom and children drove her to write down the stories that were swirling around in her head. Writing proved to be more enjoyable, and Maria returned to school to earn a Master of Arts degree in writing from Seton Hill University. Unable to part company with Seton Hill's excellent writing program, Maria is currently a teacher and mentor for the MFA program.

However, Maria's meteorological degree did not go to waste, nope, not at all. And to prove it to her parents...er...because she is still fascinated with the weather, she was able to play with the weather while writing her award-winning Glass Series (*Storm Glass, Sea Glass*, and *Spy Glass*) about a magician who can capture magic inside her glass creations.

Maria's environmental experience also did not go to waste. Her tree-hugging...er...concern about the environment comes out in her Insider books (*Inside Out* and *Outside In*). Trella's world is completely contained, and they must reuse and recycle *everything*. One thing they got right in this otherwise messed-up, dystopian world.

Maria lives with her family and a black cat name Valek (a.k.a. the bug assassin!) in Pennsylvania where she is hard at work on the second book of her Healer Series, *Scent of Magic*, well...that's what she told her editor ;> The first healer book, *Touch of Power* released in January 2012. Readers are welcome to check out her website for book excerpts, free short stories, maps, blog, and her schedule at **www.MariaVSnyder.com**. Maria also loves hearing from her readers and can be contacted at **maria@mariavsnyder.com**.

Carmen Tudor is a young Australian author who has sampled both city and country life and at one time even resided in Tasmania—known as Australia's most haunted state. These days she calls Victoria's mist-enshrouded Yarra Valley home and never underestimates the power of a great setting. Her stories have appeared in publications including: *Mon Coeur Mort*, *Romance Stories Magazine*, *Short and Twisted*, and *Hidden Agenda*. An admitted procrastinator, Carmen ditched studies in postgrad linguistics to focus on the creative use of language and to complete *Shadowplay*, a paranormal novel for young adults. You can find details about her work at **www.carmentudor.net**.

Jill Williamson is weird, which is why she writes science fiction and fantasy novels for teens. Growing up in Alaska gave her plenty of material and time to daydream. Her debut novel, a medieval fantasy, *By Darkness Hid*, won an EPIC Award, a Christy Award, and was named a Best Science Fiction, Fantasy, and Horror novel of 2009 by *VOYA* magazine. Jill went on to complete that trilogy as well as *Replication: The Jason Experiment* (Zondervan, 2011) about clones in an Alaskan lab. Weird, huh? Jill loves working with teenagers and encouraging them to respect their dreams. She gives writing workshops at libraries, schools, camps, and churches. She lives in Oregon with her husband and two children. Visit Jill on her Facebook author page or on her website at **www.jillwilliamson.com**, where adventure comes to life.

Acknowledgments

"Strangeways vs. the Wraith" © by Judith Graves. First publication, original to this anthology. Printed by permission of the author.

"The Senet Box" © 2011 by Jill Williamson. First publication, original to this anthology. Printed by permission of the author.

"Stained" © 2011 by Mark Finnemore. First publication, original to this anthology. Printed by permission of the author.

"Thread of the Past" © 2011 by Dawn Dalton. First publication, original to this anthology. Printed by permission of the author.

"The Cold One" © 2011 by Candace Havens. First publication, original to this anthology. Printed by permission of the author.

"Death Becomes Her" © 2011 by Kitty Keswick. First publication, original to this anthology. Printed by permission of the author.

If you enjoyed *Spirited*, you might like these other Leap Books paranormals...

"Under My Skin is a roller-coaster romp through a supernatural world filled with scary beasties, otherworldly magic, and characters you'll root for. Eryn is a tough but likable protagonist whose paranormal problems make a compelling story full of mystery, magic, action and romance. A fun and engaging read. I'm looking forward to the sequel." ~Rosemary Clement-Moore

"...fans of paranormal YA fiction will appreciate a protagonist with attitude and anticipate the next volume in the planned trilogy"
~CM Magazine

"Smart, sassy and more than a little scary, Second Skin hits all the right notes. I adored reading about Eryn and her attempts to deal with her life!"
~Amanda Ashby

The Skinned Series
by
Judith Graves

More great paranormal titles. . .

"Kasey Maxwell will keep readers smiling - and guessing - as she learns to control her gift and moons over her handsome English hottie Josh."
~Joy Preble

Freaksville Series by Kitty Keswick

Lethally Blonde by Patrice Lyle

Morgan Skully is the world's only blonde demon girl, and she's got a brand new, very unusual afterschool job. Spying for the Devil. She'd much rather use her cloak-and-dagger skills to spy on hottie-licious Derek with her friends, but the Devil won't take no for an answer. If she succeeds, pedicures and platinum highlights are just the beginning.

But if she fails. .there's more on the line than killer shoes.

Leap Books has a HEART for charity

Spirited is not the only charity project Leap Books is doing. All of our authors have causes they care about, and we support them in reaching out to others. So we're donating 20% of the sales from *For the Love of Strangers* by Jacqueline Horsfall to the Domestic Violence Awareness project. Horsfall's book is about sixteen-year-old Darya, who helps her adoptive mother run a shelter for abused women. Leap Books is also donating free copies of *For the Love of Strangers* to shelters along with a frameable copy of "Libby's Lament," a poem from the point of view of a young abused mother, and a booklist for teens on domestic/relationship abuse. The poem and booklist are also available to any teens who would like them. Just send an email to **info@leapbks.com**.

We are also offering a free copy of *Stakeout* by Bonnie J. Doerr to any environmental organizations who are working to save sea turtles. In Doerr's eco-mystery *Stakeout*, teens endanger their lives to capture the poacher of sea turtle eggs.

www.leapbks.com

Thank you for purchasing this Leap Books, LLC
publication. For other fabulous teen and tween novels,
please visit our online store at
www.leapbks.com.

leap books

For questions or more information contact us at
info@leapbks.com

Leap Books, LLC
www.leapbks.com